D0008150

Jordon's Showdown

Also by Frank C. Strunk

Jordon's Wager

Jordon's Showdown

Frank C. Strunk

Walker and Company
New York

First published in the United States of America in 1993 by Walker Publishing Company, Inc.

Published simultaneously in Canada by Thomas Allen & Son Canada, Limited, Markham, Ontario

Library of Congress Cataloging-in-Publication Data
Strunk, Frank C.
Jordon's showdown / Frank C. Strunk.
        p.   cm.
     ISBN 0-8027-3222-4
          I. Title.
   PS3569.T743J65   1993
   813'.54—dc20   92-37671
                              CIP

Printed in the United States of America
2 4 6 8 10 9 7 5 3 1

Acknowledgments

Writing a novel, for me at least, is neither simple nor easy. Any number of big or small things can help or hinder. Thanks to all those who, in one way or another, through word or thought or deed, helped. I cannot name them all, but they include Al, Ann, Barbara, Betty, Bill, Carl, Carol, Charleen, Connie, Dianne, Dolly, Ed, Elenora, Ellen, Erma, Ernie, Gail, Garry, George, Glenda, Hap, Herbie, Lydia, Norman, Tracey, Wilma, and others I'm sure.

Special thanks to Phil Griffith for valuable talk about guns and ammunition; to my aunts Vinnie and Flonnie and Mildred and Babe—er, Lucille—who lived through the "good old bad old days" recalled in this book and its predecessor, *Jordon's Wager*, and who have shared their marvelous memories with me since I was no bigger than a tadpole; to my aunt Ruth for being so good to me—boy and man—in so many ways; to my agent, Matt Bialer, at William Morris, my editor Michael Seidman at Walker, and my friend Gary Provost (I can only guess at where he is), for guidance and encouragement; to Peter Rubie and Robin Hardy, who saw something they liked in *Jordon's Wager*; and to Janet Hutchings, who read and bought and edited *Jordon's Wager* while she was an editor at Walker and I was struggling to get a novel published. Without Janet, who knows?

Finally, to all those who read and liked *Jordon's Wager*, and told me they hated to see it end, thank you. Here's another one for you. I hope it doesn't disappoint. All things being equal, there may be more.

Jordon's Showdown

$\triangledown$

Prologue

Travis County, West Virginia
May 1934

THE PROFESSIONAL HUNKERED DOWN for a moment, then seated himself on the thick layer of pine needles that carpeted the ground. His movements were precise, deliberate, catlike.

He was tall, thin, very blond, and not yet forty. There was a natural fluid grace about him.

He leaned back against one of the cluster of massive gray rocks in the grove of yellow pines he had selected. From here he had a clear line of vision through the sparse undergrowth in front of him.

He could see everything that might happen along the row of small frame coal miner's houses in the hollow nearly three hundred yards below.

Anyone looking up from the houses, though, could not see him. It was the kind of vantage he always looked for. And generally found.

A robin perched on the peak of one of the rock outcroppings nearby and began to sing.

The professional turned to smile at it. "You're right, of course, my fine feathered friend. It is a good morning to be alive." After a moment he added, "Not a bad morning to die, either, for that matter."

He removed the round, wire-frame spectacles from his face and placed them on the ground near the trunk of a tree, being careful not to touch the plain-glass lenses.

He took out his pocket watch. Seven-fifteen. He still had time to spare.

He picked up the smooth leather gun case beside him and undid the ties. He took out the 1903 Model Springfield .30-06 rifle and ran his hand along its unblemished barrel to the front sight and back.

He caressed the checkering on the shortened forearm of the flawless walnut stock, sliding his hand down to stroke the sweet curve of the butt, admiring every detail along the way, inhaling the pungent aroma of the thin coat of gun oil that covered the entire weapon.

Out of a small leather satchel he took the six-power Mauser telescope Griffin and Howe had fitted for the gun when they customized it for him three years ago. The star-gauged barrel had been specially selected, and the trigger had been reworked to give it a crisp four-pound pull.

With astonishing accuracy at a range of up to a thousand yards, the Springfield was the perfect rifle for the Rocky Mountain sheep he had told the New York gunsmiths he wanted to hunt.

It was also perfect for the quarry he stalked in the Appalachians.

But that was his business, not theirs.

He didn't really need the scope at this range, but he took pleasure from observing the results of his efforts. He never spent a lot of time afterwards watching, just a few seconds, long enough to appreciate his art.

For that was how he had long since come to think of it—as an art.

With the scope attached, locked in on zero, he took his firing position, sitting with the rifle cradled in his left hand, which he rested on the rock in front of him. He trained the scope on the front door of one of the houses below.

The little front porch was empty except for a mongrel dog napping at one end.

A wisp of blue smoke escaped from the chimney and

danced a moment in the freedom of the world outside before disappearing.

Using his right hand, the professional swept a strand of fine, almost white hair back from his high, unlined forehead.

He fingered the thin pink scar that angled from the edge of his left eye down across his clean-shaven cheek to a point near the jawbone, recalling how he had received it and smiling at the memory of what he had done to the man who had inflicted it.

After waiting motionless here in the early-morning light for upwards of twenty minutes, his mind wandered to the plug of Bloodhound in his pocket. The thought of the dark sweet tobacco caused him to salivate a little, but he would forgo the pleasure of a chew for the moment.

The subject below could step through the door now at any moment. And when he did, everything must be carried out with perfect precision and attention to timing.

Suddenly, as if by some prearranged signal, the subject appeared at the front door of the house, hesitated a moment, then came out onto the front porch.

The professional knew it was him, had watched him in town over the past several days, knew when he arose in the morning, knew his daily comings and goings.

The subject took a final pull on a cigarette, inhaled, and flicked the butt into the bare hard-packed dirt yard. He rubbed the stubble of black beard on his thin leathery face. He stretched his arms over his head, yawned, spit off the edge of the porch, then thrust his hands into the back pockets of his bib overalls.

The professional watched him through the scope, waited until his movements had stopped and he stood still there on the porch, basking in the warmth of the early-morning sun.

The professional moved the cross hairs to the center of the subject's face, took a deep breath, and exhaled part of it.

At that moment, a slender young woman appeared at the door and came out onto the porch. She wore a simple flowered dress that might have been made from a feed sack, and she was dark-haired and pretty.

She smiled at the subject, stretched up to brush a quick kiss against his lips, then leaned against him as he put his arm around her shoulders.

The two of them stood very still, gazing across the railroad toward a little stand of spruce just beyond the creek.

The professional did not hesitate. Experience had taught him never to allow a perfect opportunity to slip away.

Again he set the cross hairs on the middle of the subject's face, took another deep breath, exhaled, then squeezed the trigger with a slow, even pressure.

When he felt the solid jolt of the rifle, he grasped the bolt, pulled it back, and ejected the empty cartridge, then thrust the bolt forward again, chambering another round, all this in one smooth, fluent movement that took no more than a second.

On the front porch of the house below, the subject's skull exploded. Fragments of bone and brains and hair splattered against the screen door and wall as his body jerked, spasmed into an arch, then withered and collapsed.

The professional watched through the scope as the woman recoiled in wonder, saw her facial expression turn from surprise to shock, then to disbelief and horror.

She threw herself on the twisted body of her man, then lifted her head like a wild animal caught in a trap and screamed.

The professional listened as her high, keening wail reached him from across the distance, echoing up and down the hollow's early-morning silence.

For a moment, but only a moment, he considered shooting her, too, maybe in the leg. He imagined her scuttling across the porch in pain and terror. Then he chided himself for the aberrant thought. She was not part of the deal.

It would be satisfying, he thought, to linger and watch for a little bit longer, but he knew he must not.

With practiced speed and skill he flipped the cam locks on the scope mount, replaced it and the rifle in their cases, picked up his plain-lens glasses, and put them on his face.

He retrieved the spent cartridge and pocketed it, then scuffed up the area where he had been, scattering pine needles over his tracks.

He scanned the entire area and, satisfied, turned and strode off through the woods, his tall lithe body covering the ground swiftly.

As he walked, he began to whistle a song remembered from his boyhood days sitting in church in the little mountain community where he was born on the Tug Fork of the Big Sandy here in West Virginia, listening to his white-maned father hoarsely shout his passionate sermons and watching his hands hover above the pulpit like a wrathful Jehovah pouring vials of righteous vengeance on a deserving world.

That was long before the two of them, father and son, had ultimately confronted one another in their final bloody scene.

Across all the years since then, the professional had enjoyed the haunting strains of the melody of "Amazing Grace," though he had never understood what people found pleasing about the words.

He could not imagine what it would be like to go through life thinking of yourself as a sinful wretch.

Now he stopped for a moment and reached into his jacket pocket for the Bloodhound. He took out his Russell barlow pocketknife, precisely carved a small neat wedge from the plug, and placed it in his mouth, chewing on it two or three times and savoring its rich sweet tang before using his tongue to tuck it into a comfortable place in his right cheek.

Resuming his walk, he allowed himself to begin thinking about breakfast. By the time he had hidden his instruments and reached town by way of his roundabout trail, he would be starved. He decided he'd have three—no, four—eggs, over light with ham. And a couple of big cathead biscuits and some red-eye gravy. Maybe a little sorghum molasses or blackberry jam.

He felt entitled to enjoy a hearty breakfast. It had been a fine morning's work.

And after breakfast, there was Pearl.

$\triangledown$

1

B ERKLEY JORDON CAME WITHIN an ace of losing control of his Model A Ford coupe as he swerved to miss a big blacksnake stretched out halfway across the narrow ribbon of mountain highway.

Jordon was just rounding the last sharp curve before the town of Buxton when he saw the snake. It had crawled out onto the blacktop after having swallowed some kind of small varmint, maybe a ground squirrel or rabbit, making a big bulge in its body about a foot back from its head.

Some folks would automatically kill every snake they came across, regardless of whether it might be poisonous. But not Jordon. A blacksnake was harmless, beneficial even. Unless this particular one moved on across the road, however, its future was about to be past.

After straightening out his car, Jordon drove on up the road a piece, pulled off to the side, and stopped. He was on his way to the railroad depot to pick up a package, but there was no great hurry.

He had ordered a green-baize crap table layout from a supply house in Chicago. Not that the game he ran at the Little Casino required a fancy professional table layout, but Della wanted it, "just for looks," and Jordon went along. It really made no difference to him.

Jordon got out of the car, grasped the small of his back

with both hands, and stretched, arching his spine backwards, listening to his vertebrae pop.

Standing just a shade under six feet and carrying about 160 pounds, he was thinner than he had been in years. It wasn't anything deliberate on his part. He just didn't seem to have much appetite lately. Since his unsuccessful campaign for high sheriff of Stanton County last fall, and considering what had happened to him since then, with Cassie and all, he hardly ever felt like eating.

If it weren't for peanuts and an apple once in a while, he'd probably look a lot thinner, not that he cared much, one way or the other. The way his life was going, and the fact that he wouldn't be seeing fifty again, hell, nothing these days generated a lot of enthusiasm in him.

Jordon pulled a handkerchief from his pocket and wiped the sweat from his face, then smoothed his full dark mustache and took out his watch. Nearly an hour and a half before midday, and already it was hotter than a fiddler's bitch, even out here in the woods.

Jordon got back in the car and drove casually on into Buxton, watching the heat waves shimmer up from the surface of the road as he approached a little open rise.

It was in the midst of dog days, that lethargic time of the year when Sirius, the Dog Star, rises with the sun, and the combined heat of the two produces sultry nights and pestilential days.

This was the time of year when people said dogs were more likely to go mad, cows were apt to give bloody milk, and water became polluted.

Children were warned not to walk in the weeds barefooted in the morning dew or go swimming in the millpond or the creek because if they got a cut, or even a scratch, it would surely become infected and might even set up blood poisoning and kill them.

It was the time of the year when snakes went blind and couldn't tell where they were and so might slither up anywhere and inflict a mortal bite.

It was a time to take care, great care, even in places where normally you would not expect danger.

It had come as no big surprise to anybody when, a few days previous, Jordon's buddy Willis Dobbs had discovered a five-foot timber rattler coiled up in the high weeds near the edge of the little garden plot behind his house near Buxton.

Willis shot the snake in the head with a .22 rifle and took it in to Kings Mill, the county seat, and showed it to the men and boys lolling around on the courthouse lawn.

The snake had thirteen rattles and a button. Old Lady Price brought her Kodak out and took a picture of it to put in the paper. Folks said, Oh, yeah, this one might be dead, but where there was one, there were bound to be others, and being blind, well, hellfire, they'd crawl right up and strike you without so much as a kiss-my-ass or go-to-hell.

Just talking about it was enough to send chill bumps running up your back. Everybody seemed to enjoy doing it.

Arriving in Buxton, Jordon went directly to the depot and picked up his package. He decided to stop at the Buxton Drugstore for a cup of coffee and a copy of the Louisville *Courier-Journal*, which came in on the Greyhound bus every day.

Lately, his restlessness had made him more than ordinarily interested in what was happening away from Buxton and Stanton County and the Middle Fork of the Cumberland River. Some days he thought maybe he would pick up and leave the mountains again, even though in the past he had never been able to stay away for good.

In the drugstore, Jordon took a seat at a little table near the big plate-glass front window. Half a dozen others, including two plump, well-dressed middle-aged women he took to be wives of Buxton Corporation executives, were in the place. The two women sipped Cokes and chattered in low voices, their talk punctuated from time to time by laughter.

Jordon could look out on the main street of Buxton, watch the occasional car or horse-drawn wagon crawl up the street, see the idle coal miners strolling by or huddled in little groups talking. The mines, HR Buxton's as well as those of the other operators in the county, had only been running a day or two a week, and the men had a lot of time on their hands.

In spite of the things President Roosevelt was supposed to be doing in Washington to try to get business rolling again, the depression hung on like a bloodsucking tick. There was little market for coal, little work for miners, and little hope for change anytime soon.

"You low-down egg-sucking sonofabitch!" It was not quite a yell, but it was loud enough to cut through the heavy summer air and be heard clearly by Jordon through the screen door of the drugstore from the street outside.

Jordon looked up from his paper and saw a lanky, nearly bald man in overalls heading across the street toward the drugstore.

"Goat, goat, goat," Jordon heard a man's voice chanting someplace outside. Then someone else picked it up. "Goat, goat!"

A shorter, thicker man detached himself from one of the little groups and angled across the street to intercept the tall bald man, catching up with him just outside the door of the drugstore.

The thick man took the tall one by the arm, turned him around, and said something to him. The tall man jerked his arm loose, swung a fist, and missed. The thick man gave the tall one two fast left jabs in the face, followed by a powerful right hook that connected with a *thunk* like a melon makes when you drop it.

This fellow moves like a boxer, Jordon thought.

The tall man slumped to the sidewalk, and the thick one stood over him. "Goddamn Judas," the boxer said, and spit on his fallen opponent, who made no effort to get up.

Jordon saw Ike Sewell, Buxton's chief of security, walking so fast it was almost a trot toward the site of the fracas. Ike had his coat pulled back to expose his nickel-plated pearl-handled .44 Smith & Wesson special, which everyone knew he would use without hesitation when the occasion called for it.

"What's going on?" Ike said, his strong voice carrying all the authority delegated to him by HR Buxton to do whatever was necessary to keep order on Buxton property. Ike was built like an ox, lots of muscle and bone to go with his voice and his badge and his gun.

"A personal matter, Ike," the boxer said. "Nothing for you to be concerned about."

"I'm concerned about everything that happens on Buxton property," Ike said. He looked at the man on the ground, who was sitting up now and wiping his bloody nose on the back of his hand. Then Ike turned back to the boxer and said, "I'm going to have to take you in."

"What for?"

"How about disturbing the peace? That suit you?" Ike took the man by the arm.

At that moment, Jordon saw a miner he knew vaguely, a man named Turner Lott, approaching Ike and the fighters. Lott was a medium-sized man somewhere in his forties who had already lost most of his dark hair. He moved with ease and power. Jordon knew him from playing poker with him sometimes.

Turner smiled at Ike. "It was just a personal thing, Ike," he said. "Why don't you let the boys go on and forget about it?"

Ike glared at Turner. "You'd best be minding your own business."

Turner stood his ground, still smiling. "This is my business."

Ike continued to look a hole through Turner. "I'm warning you, Turner, stay out of it."

Turner said, "You got it backwards. It's me warning you. Let it be." Turner glanced around, nodding his head toward the dozen or so men who had begun to move in closer on the little group. Most of the men wore bib overalls and blue work shirts, many were unshaven, and nearly all of them had their right hands in their pockets.

Ike said nothing, glancing from face to face as he sized things up.

Jordon could almost smell the tension in the air. He had seen this kind of situation too often in the mountains not to recognize where it was headed. Unless both sides could walk away without anybody seeming to back down, some of them would be carried away.

Jordon stood up and stepped outside, letting the screen door slam behind him. He took a position not quite between Ike and Turner, one where they could both see his face.

"Ike, I do believe this is a personal matter between these fellows," Jordon said.

Ike gave Jordon a look that Jordon figured was hatred, or close to it. The two of them had never got along, even though Jordon had had to work with him a few times in the past when he was a deputy.

But however Ike felt about him, Jordon knew he was not a fool. Ike had to realize that he'd be taken away from here today feet first if he went up against this group. Still, Jordon knew enough about Ike to be sure he would not be the only one to fall.

Ike's expertise with his .44 Smith, plus the bulletproof vest that he wore year-round regardless of how hot it might be, would guarantee that he would not die alone.

"What do you know about it?" Ike asked Jordon.

"I was having a cup of coffee," Jordon replied, nodding toward the window where he had been sitting. "Saw what happened. I'd say it's a personal thing between these fellows."

Jordon saw what he took to be a glimmer of understanding flicker in Ike's eyes.

Ike glanced down at the man sitting on the sidewalk, then at the one who had hit him, as though thinking it over. "All right. I'll take Jordon's word for it," Ike said. Then to the rest of the crowd, "Let's break it up now." He looked at the two fighters and said, "Keep your personal disputes off of Buxton property. I won't be so agreeable next time."

As the crowd started to disperse, Ike caught Turner Lott's eye and said, "Another time."

"Any time, any place. Now or later." Turner's look didn't waver. "I'm always around."

"Nobody's always around," Ike said, with the little twitch of his mouth that passed for a smile. "Nobody."

Jordon went back inside and picked up his newspaper, then stepped out on the street again. He glanced up at the Buxton Building, toward the big window in the office of Harrison Randolph Buxton, "HR," "the old man," owner of the Buxton Corporation and all its holdings—the town, its streets and houses, its stores, its mines, its mills, its thousands of acres of timber and coal land, and, some even said, the hundreds of men, women, and children who survived by virtue of jobs in his enterprises.

Someone, Jordon was sure it must be HR Buxton himself, stood there gazing out the window onto the scene below.

As he got into his car and headed back out of town, Jordon asked himself why he had stuck his nose into this fracas.

He was no longer a lawman. Keeping the peace wasn't his job anymore.

And there damn sure was no love lost between him and Ike Sewell. For that matter, he could say the same for Turner Lott. The man might be a cousin of Willis's, but he had an abrasive way about him. Along with a sharp tongue and poor judgment about when to use it.

Jordon sighed and reached into his pocket for a handful of roasted-in-the-shell peanuts. He cracked one expertly with one hand, dropping the shells on the seat next to him and popping the kernels into his mouth.

Hell, maybe he had stepped in just because he didn't want a lot of stray bullets flying around while he was trying to have a cup of coffee.

Or maybe he wasn't up to the smell of burnt gunpowder and fresh blood on such a blistering day.

Or maybe it was because the climate wasn't the only thing that was becoming unbearably hot around the coalfields these days.

Jordon had a dark uneasy feeling, shared by a lot of other folks, that the right spark at the right time could ignite a firestorm in the mountains of Stanton County that would consume the lives of many and scorch the lives of all the rest who lived there before it finally burned itself out.

What came close to happening today could have been that spark.

2

H R BUXTON GESTURED TOWARD one of the heavy leather chairs in front of his massive walnut desk, and Jordon sat down.

"I'm pleased you didn't let our past differences prevent you from coming today," HR said. His voice was warm and friendly, and while he had lived in the mountains for many years, his accent still was tinged with the flavor of someplace else.

There was no warmth in Jordon's reply. "Our differences aren't past." He sat with his back straight, hands on his knees, unwilling to relax and be comfortable here. "You said it was urgent."

HR gave a little wave of his hand and smiled. "Maybe urgent's not the best word for it. Perhaps I should have said critical."

Jordon shrugged. He ran a hand through his thick, gray-flecked black hair. "Whichever suits you. What is it you want?"

HR studied him a moment and shook his head a little. "One of the few things I like about you is that you cut right through to the heart of any situation. Like a game rooster going after a kernel of corn in a horse turd." He smiled as he said it.

Jordon eyed him coldly. "I don't pick shit with the chickens. You of all people ought to know that."

HR held up his hand in a conciliatory gesture. "That's not the way I meant it," he said. "It was a thoughtless comparison."

Hardly thoughtless, Jordon said to himself. Anyone who had ever had dealings with HR Buxton was aware of the old man's richly deserved reputation for never saying or doing anything without thinking it through and planning it down to the last detail. He could be cruel, callous, indifferent, at times even generous. But never thoughtless. "What's this about, Mr. Buxton?"

HR sighed. "All right, I'll tell you. It's about you helping me try to prevent a bloodbath here in Stanton County. You think you might be able to forget what's between us long enough to do that?"

"What's between us is something neither of us is ever going to forget, so why don't you come to the point?"

"Would you care for some coffee?" HR stood and moved toward a small table near the big plate-glass window, where a silver coffee service gleamed in the morning sunlight.

Jordon started to refuse, then thought it would be boorish to do so. He nodded. "Black will be fine."

Jordon glanced around the office at the walnut bookcases filled with matching leatherbound volumes. The room was just as he remembered it from last fall, the first time he had ever been inside it. A shaft of sunlight pierced the big, spotlessly clean window, which looked out over the town square and reflected off the waxed hardwood floors.

Jordon sat in silence as HR finished serving the two of them, then watched as the old man eased himself into his high-backed leather swivel chair and took a deep breath.

HR Buxton was a short man, somewhere near seventy, with a slight build and a full head of sandy gray hair that was carefully trimmed and combed with a neat part on the left side. His gold-rimmed glasses glinted as he moved his head. Dressed in a lightweight navy blue suit, a flawless white shirt, and a dark red tie, he was the picture of a successful executive. Which by anybody's definition he was.

He owned—lock, stock and barrel, as far as anybody knew—the Buxton Corporation and all its holdings. HR Buxton had been called the "uncrowned king of Stanton

County," a title that, to Berkley Jordon, did not seem inappropriate.

HR sipped his coffee. "We're in for some bad times here in the coalfields. I don't know how much you've been following the politics coming out of Washington, but that man in the White House is bound and determined to turn this whole country upside down and hand it over to the great unwashed that put him in office."

Jordon's expression did not change. "National politics has got nothing to do with me."

HR shook his head. "You're wrong. It's got something to do with all of us. Every last one."

HR got up and went to the big window. He gazed out on his town. After a moment, he turned his attention back to Jordon. "You're an intelligent man, Jordon. It's a mystery to me why you've never used your brain to advance yourself in life more than you have." He paused for a moment. "But as you yourself told me not too long ago, you don't know much about politics. How the game is played. Without insulting you, which I don't want to do, I have to point out that you're a political neophyte." HR hesitated. "An amateur."

Jordon's voice was cool. "I know the word neophyte."

"Forgive me. Of course you do. What I'm trying to say is there are complex issues involved in the politics of today that are rooted far beneath the surface."

Jordon was beginning to feel like a schoolboy in civics class. He was not in the market for HR Buxton's political ideas. "I don't think I'm interested in whatever it is that you seem so intent on dancing around." He set his cup on the edge of the desk and started to stand. "Thanks for the coffee."

HR turned from the window and spoke in a calm, placating tone. "Please. Sit back down and hear me out. I'm not avoiding the issue, I'm just trying to put things into context. Give me a few more minutes, then make up your mind."

Jordon sat back down. This time he relaxed a little, stretching his legs out in front of him and crossing his feet. He wore a black coat with white shirt and a slim black tie.

His trousers were gray and wrinkled, and his shoes were dusty. He had been meaning to take some things to the dry cleaner and get his shoes shined, but it was not high on his list of priorities.

HR looked directly into Jordon's eyes. His voice sounded strained, but earnest. "I'm doing my best to avoid bloodshed here in Buxton. But I'm not sure I can do it without some help. I'm asking you to help me keep the lid on things."

Jordon's voice was flat. "Keep the lid on?"

HR nodded. "Yes. I think you'd be good at it."

"Why?"

"You've got the respect of a lot of people around here."

"Not enough, evidently, to get elected sheriff."

"Oh, hell. Your defeat wasn't due to any lack of respect for you."

"No?"

"At the risk of seeming immodest, it was mostly my doing. Surely you must understand that. Regardless of how . . . strong-willed you may be, you've got to know that a man has to make some compromises to get through this life. You're too intelligent not to see that."

Jordon said nothing, but he gave a little wave of his hand, as if brushing the whole discussion away.

HR sighed. "I mentioned Roosevelt trying to give the country to the workers? Well, there are other men, just as determined, who are trying to see that he doesn't succeed."

"You and your powerful friends who want to stop Roosevelt will have to do it without me."

"They're by no means all friends of mine. And some of them have methods that are definitely not to my liking."

Jordon said, "So exactly what is it you want from me?"

"The United Mine Workers is on the march in the coalfields. John L. Lewis has the blessing of the president to try to organize every miner in the country if he can. They're already here in Stanton County, working in secret, trying to get all my men to join their union. And I know they're making some headway."

"You want me to help you stop the union, is that it?"

HR shook his head slowly. "The union can't be stopped. I've already made up my mind about that. Labor is about to rise to power in this country. It is an idea whose time has come. Roosevelt's behind it. And the public is behind Roosevelt. No, they won't be stopped this time. And I'm not going to be found trampled into the ground when the battle is over."

"You're trying to tell me you're not going to resist the union?"

HR sounded impatient. "I didn't say that. I'm going to negotiate with them as hard as I know how. I'm not giving away anything. I'm prepared to shut down my mines and sit it out with them for as long as they want. But . . . I'm not about to watch Stanton County become 'Bloody Stanton' if I can help it, the way it's being done in other places in the coalfields. Or worse yet, 'Bloody Buxton'. Not if I can stop it."

"So what do you want me for?"

"To help me keep our people's feelings under control. Keep folks from getting so caught up in the heat of this thing that they lose every shred of their common sense. Try to get them to see the wisdom of coming to a peaceful settlement. After all, not all the hotheads are on this side of the fence. You saw what happened out there in the square yesterday. That could have become very ugly. Could have set off a whole chain of bloody events."

"It didn't."

"Thanks to you, from what I understand."

Jordon gave a little wave of his hand.

"What about it?" HR asked. "Will you help me?"

"Let me see if I understand you. You want me to use my personal friendships to make it easier for you to come to terms with the union. To get yourself a better contract with them without the risk of dirtying up your name in a bloody confrontation. Is that about it?"

HR's voice sounded tight, as if he were struggling to keep his emotions under control. "You make that sound bad, somehow. A better contract for me could be a by-product of my efforts. But my primary goal is to avoid needless bloodshed. And surely you would like that as much as I."

Here is a man, Jordon thought, who would bottle polecat juice and try to pass it off for French perfume if he thought he could find a buyer. "Mr. Buxton, whatever you aim to do in dealing with your miners, you'll have to do it without me. Even if I was willing to do what you say, which I'm not, any influence I might have with my friends would disappear like a fart in a windstorm once it was known I was working for you."

"We could keep it in confidence. And your efforts could mean the difference between good people being killed and not. Doesn't that mean anything to you?"

"Why don't you use the people whose strings you're already pulling?"

"Who do you mean?"

"Ike Sewell. John Bill Trumble."

The noise HR made sounded like a snort. "They don't have your influence. A lot of folks like you, respect you. And Ike Sewell is a blunt instrument, with emphasis on the word *blunt*. When I hired him as my chief of security a long time ago I didn't realize just how blunt he was. He has no finesse, no sense of proportion. And what respect he gets is based purely on fear."

"Why do you keep him on?"

"He gets the job done. When it comes down to brute force, as it often does around here, I can count on him. But he's no good for anything else. You know that."

"How about John Bill? He was your choice for high sheriff. Now that he's been elected, why don't you use him?"

"I do use him when I can. But I can't trust him any further than I can see him. This is probably his last time to hold public office in this county, considering his age. So he's out for all the money he can make during this term."

"Then pay him enough to make it worth his while."

"I do, I do, believe me. But that won't keep him from

taking money from whoever else offers to pay him. And I have good reason to think there are people ready to pay him well to deputize an army of gun thugs to meet our local miners head-on."

Jordon said, "What people? You run this county."

HR shook his head. "Goddammit, nobody runs this county. I have some influence, yes. But as I said earlier, there are larger forces at work in this thing. Other coal operators in this county, as well as other counties, and money from anti-union forces outside. They all want to break the back of the UMW here and now. They are prepared to fight to the last ditch, and leave dead bodies piled as high as necessary in order to avoid giving in to John L. Lewis. I can't stop them by myself."

Jordon smiled. "Why are you being so reasonable? What's got into you all of a sudden?"

HR leaned back and spread his hands, palms up. "It's not all of a sudden. You're like a lot of other people who think they know me, Jordon. And none of you do. I came here to the mountains as an investor. I saw it as an opportunity to make my fortune by organizing men and money and machinery and management into an enterprise that would make me wealthy. And I have been successful at that. But I am not simply a greedy monster. I am not indifferent to human suffering. And I am not a cold-blooded killer. I have come to love this county, and I love my company and the way it functions. I don't want to see it destroyed by the union, and I don't want to see this county become a battleground between miners and those who are willing to kill them to stop them."

"It all sounds very decent and humane, the way you tell it. But like I told you, it's not my fight. I've got no horse in this race."

"At least think about it," HR said. "Will you do that much? As I said, a lot of folks around here respect you."

"And you want to buy that."

"I'd expect to pay you, of course. And well."

"I'm not for sale."

"I'm not trying to buy you," the old man said, sounding sincere.

"You just want to rent me for a while."

"I just want you to use your influence. For a good purpose."

"It's not for sale or rent, either."

"You could prevent a lot of grief for a lot of innocent people."

"Stop sounding so compassionate. It fits you like a tight collar."

"Okay, say I'm selfish. I've never denied that. I'm selfish in not wanting my county and my town and my company ripped apart."

"And your property. And your reputation, and your bank account."

"Of course. But you can't deny that together we could save lives and prevent bloodshed. If you'd work with me."

"Why do I get the feeling there's more to all this than meets the eye?"

"God only knows."

"Well, since he's not telling me, I'm afraid you'll have to keep looking. I'm not your man."

"At least keep an open mind. Maybe we can talk later."

Jordon shook his head and stood up to leave.

HR stood too. His voice took on an edge of contempt. "Running that little jackleg poker game down at Della's can't bring you a fraction of what I'd be willing to pay you."

Jordon grinned a little. "Yeah, but I like the action at the table. You know so much about me, you know I'm a gambler at heart."

"I hope you're not betting on the wrong side in this thing that's shaping up. The stakes are a little too high to take lightly."

"I'm not betting on either side. I told you, I've got no horse in this race."

"We'll see," HR said. "As things start to heat up, I hope you'll change your mind. You've got friends around here who are going to be putting their lives on the line. You could help make things a lot less risky for them."

"It takes half of my time minding my own business and the other half leaving everybody else's alone. I like it this way."

"If you change your mind—"

Jordon cut him off. "Not likely."

3

IN THE LATE AFTERNOON when Jordon swung his Model A Ford coupe off the blacktop and along the gravel road through the little stretch of tall pines into Della's compound, he could not get the discussion with HR Buxton off his mind.

This fight between the union and the coal operators was not his, and he wanted no part of it. "Damn it all to hell," he said aloud, "why can't they leave me out of their squabbles?"

Jordon steered his car along the gravel lane around the right end of Della's Place, the long, low, frame building painted battleship gray that housed the restaurant and dance hall and Della's office. It was the centerpiece of Della's enterprise.

In back of the main building were the other structures that had been built during the past couple of years, the most recent less than a year ago.

The small, tidy house Della lived in huddled near the edge of the clearing, and alongside stood a garage for her two cars, a nearly new Buick Eight and a Plymouth coupe.

On the other side were a couple of compact storage buildings, and near the center of the back area, directly behind the restaurant, stood the most recent addition, the pool hall and gambling room that Jordon called "Little Casino." It was where he and Willis Dobbs worked, and where Jordon slept in a tiny bedroom attached to the back.

All the buildings were of simple, neat, wood-frame construction, and all were painted matching gray.

In the span of a little more than three years, Della had

returned to the mountains from wherever up North she had been, bringing with her a financial stake sufficient to buy a fifteen-acre parcel of wooded land near Buxton, build her restaurant, hire Tiny Bob Dinwiddie to keep order and other people to do the rest, make friends and/or peace with the local political powers, and establish herself as one of the principal purveyors of food, liquor, and entertainment in Stanton County.

Della was a beautiful, warm-blooded, calculating young woman in her early thirties who had been born in the backwoods of Stanton County, had run away from the mountains with a traveling lumber buyer when she was still in her teens, and some fifteen years later had returned to the area and started her business.

Nobody seemed to know much about where she had been or how she got the money she brought back or who had taught her what she knew about business and politics.

But it was clear to everyone that she knew what she wanted, knew how to get it, and was a tough-minded lady who didn't take a lot of stuff from anyone.

Neither Prohibition, until its recent repeal, nor the depression, nor state or local laws, nor serious competition from hardened men had prevented her from establishing and overseeing her profitable business operation.

"Other folks have got their lives to live, and I've got mine," she had told Jordon once. "The history of the human race teaches me that people are going to have certain things come hell or high water. I decided that my life's work is going to be seeing that some of these things, like food and booze and satisfying entertainment, are available for those who are willing and able to pay for them."

When Della had offered Jordon and Willis a deal following Jordon's election fiasco last fall, Jordon had put her off until he checked out a couple of possible deputy jobs in other counties in the coalfields.

After declining the offers he received, offers to hire on as a gun thug for politically minded sheriffs, he came back to

Stanton County and talked things over with Willis. Neither of them had had much difficulty in making a decision to take Della up on her offer.

Within weeks, the Little Casino building had been erected, equipment shipped in on the train, and the new enterprise was underway.

Willis ran the pool hall and Jordon the gambling "casino" in the back room, and they helped each other as the need arose. Actually, the gambling operation consisted entirely of a poker game, sometimes alternated with blackjack, and a crap table.

Jordon was dealer, croupier, manager, and bouncer when the occasion arose, as it sometimes did. Some nights nobody showed up to play, but on weekends, both the poolroom and the gambling tables were often busy, an extra dealer might be hired, and the money that crossed the tables was sufficient to make the house's take more than just worthwhile.

Jordon found it easy to work with Della, and he knew Willis felt the same. Jordon was glad to be offered a setup like this where he could practice his only marketable skill other than that of being a lawman—gambling.

Jordon swung his car around to the rear of the pool hall, parked it, and entered the building through the back door. He found Willis diligently brushing chalk and talcum off one of the three pool tables. A lone player was practicing bank shots at the table at the end of the room.

Willis looked up and grinned when he saw Jordon. "So how did it go with HR Buxton?"

Jordon gave him a sour look. "The old bastard is pulling strings, as usual. And he tried to haul me into his boat."

Willis laughed, hoisted himself on his crutches, and moved to the other end of the pool table, where he leaned against it and stood on his one leg as he continued his brushing. A wiry man with bright blue eyes and an open, friendly face topped by short-cropped cinnamon-colored hair, Willis looked a little like an oversized leprechaun. And he was probably, no absolutely, the closest friend Jordon had ever had.

They kept few secrets from each other. "What did Buxton want you to do?" Willis asked.

Jordon eased himself onto one of the high stools that stood along the wall near the rack of cue sticks, drew his legs up, and hooked his feet on one of the rungs. "He asked me to come to work for him."

Willis stopped brushing and looked at him. "Doing what?"

Jordon ran his hand through his hair. "I'm not exactly sure, but he said he thought I could help him hold down trouble with the union here in Stanton County."

"He wanted to hire you as a gun thug?"

"No. At least that's what he kept insisting. He said he wanted me to use my influence to help him keep the peace around here, help keep this place from becoming 'Bloody Stanton' or 'Bloody Buxton.' Something like that."

Willis brushed the green-baize cushion slowly and methodically. "Just how did he figure you would be able to do that?"

Jordon shook his head. "That's the part he wasn't real clear about. I got the impression he maybe wanted me to be a spy for him. Or be a mouthpiece for his views. Or maybe both."

Willis interrupted his brushing and gave Jordon a serious look. "What did you tell him?"

"That I'm not his man. That when it comes to the fight between the union and the company, deal me out." Jordon stared at Willis. "Wait a minute. What the hell did you think I'd tell him?"

Willis grinned. "Just about what you said. I didn't figure you'd turn into a Buxton man this late in life."

"Not likely." After a moment, Jordon scowled at Willis. "And what's this 'late in life' bullshit? I'm not that old. Some days I feel like a two-year-old stallion, just let out of the stable."

"How many days?"

Jordon sighed. "Lately, not that many, I reckon, when you get right down to it. Maybe I need a change."

"Times like these, a man's got a half-decent way of making a living, he'd best hold on to it." A moment later he added, "That's why the miners have got to have a union. For a little more money and a little bit of protection."

Jordon stared out the window for a while, then nodded. "It's hard not to sympathize with them when you think about it."

"I've been trying to tell you that for months. You mean you're finally about to get involved?"

"No, I'm not finally about to get involved. Like I've said enough times."

"You won't sign on as a gun thug under some sheriff's badge, and you won't help HR Buxton, yet you won't lift a hand to help the union. I still can't understand it."

Jordon's voice was tight, almost angry. He felt the frustration rising from his gut and coloring his voice. "You just won't recognize my right to stay out of it, will you, Willis? Well, by God that's what I aim to do. The miners can organize their union and strike without my help. According to what Buxton says, they've got Roosevelt behind them. They seem to be doing just fine without me. Same goes for HR Buxton. I've got no stake in helping him hang on to his millions and make a few more. Or keep his precious reputation shined up."

Jordon swung one foot off the rung of the stool and down onto the floor. He felt the anger rising in him, could hear it in his voice. "Goddammit, I'm a gambler. I run a poker game, and a crap game, and sometimes a blackjack game. That's what I do, and that's all I do. Why can't you and HR Buxton and the rest of the people around here accept that? Seems to me we've had a conversation like this before, anyhow."

Willis's voice was quiet. "You know enough about what it's like in the mines and what it's like trying to raise a family on a couple of dollars a day, a couple of days a week. You oughtn't to have to ask the question why. Maybe it's time you picked a horse and got interested in the outcome of the race."

"I'm riding my own horse. It's called 'Little Casino.' "
Jordon waved his arm toward the back room. "And it's sta-
bled right here."

Willis finished cleaning the pool table, then slipped his
crutches under his arms and propelled himself to the high
counter in the corner of the room and took his seat on the
stool behind the brass filigreed cash register.

Jordon slid off his seat and followed Willis. He leaned his
arm on the counter and scanned the large glass jars contain-
ing pickled bologna sausage, pickled boiled eggs, and large
cucumber dills. He considered a boiled egg, but decided
against it. It would give him heartburn for sure.

Willis still carried the brush he had been using. He laid it
on a shelf behind him. "So what are you going to do?"

Jordon glared at him, and his voice was sharp. "Mind my
own goddamn business! Like somebody else I know ought
to be doing." The instant he heard himself, what he'd said
and how he'd said it, he would have given a million dollars
if he could have taken it back. Willis Dobbs had saved Jordon's life. Not once, twice.

In the Argonne Forest during the war, Willis had spotted
a German sniper and killed him when, had he not done so,
the rifleman surely would have killed Jordon. Willis had tried
to make light of it, pretend it was nothing, that maybe somebody else had done it. But Jordon knew better.

Then, last fall, when Jordon's trap for Milton Graham
slipped a cog and Graham shot Jordon in the arm, had it not
been for Willis being there, it could have been all over once
again. Hard looks and sharp answers were not what a man
used on someone like Willis Dobbs.

Willis said nothing. He busied himself with a piece of
paper on the counter.

Jordon's voice was quieter when he spoke again. "Hey,
look. I'm sorry. I'm wound up a little tight. Forget what I
said, okay?"

Willis scraped a kitchen match on the underside of the
counter, waited until the sulphur flash had burned down,

and touched it to a Camel. He took a long pull and inhaled deeply, then looked at Jordon and grinned. "What were you saying?"

After a moment Jordon spoke, his voice slow and deliberate. "What I'm saying is, I'd do anything in the world for you. Except let you decide which causes I ought to support. I guess I have to reserve that right to myself. And my cause these days is me."

"Sure," Willis said. "We all have the right to do what we think is best for ourselves." After a moment, he added, "By the way, Della walked over here a while ago. Said she'd like to talk with you when you get a few minutes. Also, if you're not running a game tonight, you think you could take care of the tables in here so I can leave early? I got a couple of things I need to do."

Jordon nodded. "Let me know when you get ready to leave." Jordon took his gold Waltham out of his pocket and looked at it. "Quarter after five. Maybe I'll try to catch Della now. I'll be back in a little while. Okay?" He reached for Willis's shoulder and squeezed it as he turned to go. "Maybe somebody will come by and we can get a little action going."

Willis grinned and nodded. "A little action never hurt anybody."

Jordon wagged an index finger at him. "Hey, buddy, it's not our job to see that nobody gets hurt. We're just supposed to make sure it's not us."

$\triangledown$

4

DELLA GLANCED OUT THE window of her office, which was attached to one side of her restaurant, and watched as Jordon came walking across the gravel lot.

She liked the way he carried himself, the sense of assurance he always seemed to have. It wasn't a swagger or a strut, just a sort of determined gait that seemed to say that whatever he was moving toward, he would know a way or find a way to deal with it.

She felt a little surge of excitement the way she did every time she saw him, starting with the very first time nearly a year and a half ago.

When she heard his knock on the door, she fluffed at her stylishly cut, short black hair and licked her lips. She had just applied fresh lipstick to her generous mouth and dabbed perfume behind her ears and on her throat not more than half an hour before, right after she had seen him drive into the compound.

Again she opened her compact and gave her face a once-over, though it was not as if she needed to. Since she had been thirteen or fourteen, now some twenty years ago, she had been acutely aware of how attractive men found her to be. She knew the effect she had on them.

And she knew enough about Jordon to know he could not be entirely immune to her. Yet he had never made a pass at her. It was something she wondered about more often than she liked to admit.

Making her voice husky, she said, "Come in."

He opened the office door and stood framed in the doorway. "You wanted to see me?"

"Come on in. Close the door and sit down." She waved toward a chair near her desk. "I've been wanting to talk to you about several things, but I stay so busy I never seem to get caught up. You know how that is?"

"It's not so bad for me these days. Just mostly trying to keep the tables going. Make a little money for us." He grinned.

"Last year when you were running for sheriff and trying to figure out who killed Bitsy Trotter, you reminded me of a monkey with two—well, you were a busy man."

He laughed. "I'm not so busy now. Sadder and wiser, too, as the feller said."

She studied him for a moment. "Seen much of Cassie lately?"

He shook his head. "We travel in different circles these days."

"She still working for her cousin in the county court clerk's office?"

He nodded. "I expect it keeps her pretty busy."

Della shook her head a little and sat musing. "She was the best worker I've ever seen. I wish she had stayed with me. I'd come to depend on her. Too much maybe. It always seems to lead to trouble when we start depending on somebody too much. You think so?"

He was looking at her carefully. "What are we talking about?"

"Cassie and me. What else?"

He shrugged. "You're leading the conversation."

"So I am." She noticed that her voice was coming out with a little more edge to it than she meant it to. With an effort, she softened it. "I just wondered how you two were getting along. How she was doing."

"For the record," he said, "we don't see one another at all."

"I'm sorry to hear that."

"Look, it's nothing to be sorry for. She thinks my way of life is too uncertain for her to deal with. Causes her too much pain and worry. And who can argue with that? It's not exactly a new problem between us."

Della studied him as he stared out the window. His words said one thing, but she detected something else. She figured his feelings for Cassie must run pretty deep, considering the effort he seemed to be making to sound casual about it.

Men. They were little boys in big bodies, most of them, despite their huffing and puffing. So many of them had trouble keeping sex and romance apart. They were supposed to be the uninvolved ones, taking their pleasure with a woman and leaving her to cry.

But in practice, it was just as apt to be the other way around. When they found a woman they were really at home with sexually, they thought it was love, or something. She knew about that. And when they fell, it was a dreadful thing to behold.

From the tone of Jordon's voice and the way he controlled his words about Cassie, it sounded like he might have it worse than he was letting on. Or maybe, God forbid, worse than even he suspected.

Della decided to console him with a smile. Perhaps at some point she'd give the poor soul something more substantial if it looked like he really needed it. And could handle it. "I didn't mean to pry," she said. "And it's not just nosiness makes me ask. I have a reason for wanting to know."

He seemed surprised. "What reason?"

She arose from the desk and walked to the window looking out on her little domain. "Things are beginning to get kind of touchy around here. And I find myself involved in . . . things . . . meetings, stuff like that. There are times when I'd feel better if there was a man with me. A man I could depend on if need be."

Jordon leaned back in his chair and stretched his legs. "What about Tiny Bob?"

Della shook her head. Tiny Bob Dinwiddie was the huge young man who had been appointed deputy constable at her request. He did a good job of keeping order when the music and moonshine stirred her customers' blood a little too much. Or when some roughneck decided to see how far he could go. But that was the extent of Tiny's usefulness to her. "Tiny's work here keeps him busy most of the time," she said. "Other times, I'd prefer someone else. For reasons of my own."

Jordon nodded. He seemed to be thinking about it.

His hesitation irritated her. "If you'd rather not do it . . ." She heard the edge creeping back into her voice.

Jordon shook his head. "It's not that. I was just thinking of my own hours. I'd be happy to go with you anytime I'm not tied up running a game."

Della picked up a silver ruler from her desk and ran her finger back and forth along the edge. She was pleased with Jordon's answer. More than she should have been, she thought. After all, who was he but an out-of-work deputy sheriff, running a little backroom gambling operation for her, and nursing a big-time case of the blues? He was on the other side of fifty from her, and there were some who'd say he was over the hill—or at least rapidly approaching that point. Especially since he'd lost the election last fall.

Yet, there was something about him, some quality that had always appealed to her. And still did. He was not exactly handsome. But his dark, gray-flecked hair and mustache, his lean strong body, even the hard lines in his face, all held a tingling fascination for her.

Most important, Jordon seemed to have some inner sense of himself, to know what kind of man he really was, and to like this person he knew. It was a quality she rarely saw, in men or women.

Maybe she was reading too much into this one, but she wanted to know more about him. In the interest of peace, harmony, and business, she had deliberately stayed away from him during the time Cassie had worked here and while he and Cassie were involved.

But none of that applied now. Yes, she wanted to know him better.

At the same time, she was determined that she would continue to protect her independence against all comers. For many years, now, she had done so with the fierceness of a momma bobcat. Her involvements with men she kept on the surface. She had physical needs that she took care of without hesitation or shame or regret, and she almost always had one particular man in her life. Right now, though, she had just recently disconnected from one.

None of the men she became involved with had ever got to her down deep in her innards where she lived, except for the very first. And she had given that sonofabitch, freely and without reservation, clear title to her body and heart and life, the whole goddamn works. And he didn't have the brains or the feelings to realize what kind of woman she was. At one time she would have died—or killed—for him.

When she had walked away from him seventeen years ago, after three years of increasingly shabby treatment, she vowed that no man would ever mean that much to her again. And no man had.

She tapped her desk lightly with the ruler, then laid it down, placing it precisely parallel to the side of the leather-edged blotter. "So," she said, keeping her voice carefully neutral, "I can figure on having you go along with me when I need you."

Jordon smiled and nodded. "Sure."

"Good. Just so we understand one another, this is strictly business. I don't want to intrude on your social life. Or your gambling."

"My social life these days makes very few demands on me, to put it politely. And most evenings early in the week are pretty quiet over there in the back room. Most days, too." He paused a moment, then added, "Let me know if I can be of service to you."

Della wondered if he used the word "service" deliberately, but then decided, So what if he did? It could come to that.

When she said nothing else, Jordon asked, "Is there anything more you need me for now?"

She nodded. "I wanted to talk with you a little bit about this union organizing business that's got everybody on edge lately. Are you and Willis having any trouble with arguments or overheated discussions in the poolroom or at the tables?"

Jordon shook his head. "We have a policy that religion and politics, and now union talk, are all off limits. If they want to talk about stuff like that, they take it off the premises."

Della nodded again. "I agree. Try to keep their minds on gambling and things will be a lot more peaceable."

Again she was silent. Finally Jordon asked, "Was there something else?"

He seemed anxious to leave, and it bothered Della. And the fact that it bothered her, bothered her more. "You in a hurry?"

He shook his head, relaxed, and grinned, eyeing her directly. "Not really, if there's something else you want to talk about."

Sometimes, she thought, his self-assured manner, whether it's real or feigned, becomes a little tiresome. "I just wanted to say, if things should get out of hand over there, and if you need help, send somebody to get Tiny Bob." She hesitated, then added, "With the two of you and Willis, it shouldn't be too hard to keep things under control."

Jordon nodded. "I'm making a point of staying out of this union controversy," he said. "I'll be glad when it's finally settled."

When she spoke, she could hear the frustration that had crept into her own voice. "It doesn't look like that's going to be anytime soon. And I'm afraid staying out of it's not going to be that easy." She felt like sharing the weight of some of her problems with him, but quickly dismissed the idea. She shook her head and sighed. "Sometimes we get pushed into things we'd be a lot better off to stay out of."

"Not me," he said, "if I can help it. I aim to mind my own business and let other folks do the same."

Walking back across the lot to the poolroom, Jordon tried to figure out exactly what Della had been driving at. She'd asked him if he would go with her to some kind of meetings from time to time. That would have taken her about ten seconds to find out.

She wanted to know about Cassie and him, how they were getting along, which really didn't have much to do with the other question, in spite of what Della had said.

The truth was, there was a picture of Cassie in his mind everywhere he went. She was never far from the surface of his thoughts. But he would be damned if he'd carry on about it to anybody.

Let Cassie live her life any way she wanted. So would he.

But going back to Della, if her interest in him was "strictly business," as she'd said, what difference could it make how he and Cassie were getting along?

And Della had wanted to know if union discussions were causing any trouble in the poolroom or at the gambling tables. Willis could easily have answered that when she was talking to him.

He smiled a little. Della was a fascinating young woman, young enough, in fact, to be his daughter. Why she might find him interesting was beyond his imagining. Yet that sure seemed like what it was. Well, she was a pretty thing, no question about that.

From painful experience accumulated over a lifetime, however, Jordon had learned to try to keep his work and his private life as far apart as possible. For years, he'd made it a matter of personal discipline to do so.

Opening the doors between the compartments in your life could bring you lots of grief, he knew. But he couldn't help wondering if he was going to stick to this policy now.

Or if, maybe this once, despite what experience had taught him, he should bend it a little.

As he listened to his silent soliloquy, and heard his line of thought, he suddenly shook his head and laughed out loud.

Jordon, he said to himself, you are some piece of work.

5

HR Buxton opened the lid on the cedar humidor and extended it to Fenwick Gruber, who everybody in the county called "Pennyrile" because as a boy he had spent as much time as possible in the woods and had picked pennyroyal and rubbed the fragrant plant on his body to ward off ticks and chiggers.

Pennyrile took a cigar and passed the box along.

"Cuban," HR said. "Nothing finer in the world when it comes to a smoke."

"Some of our silver-spoon boys in the Bluegrass would argue with you about that," Pennyrile said. "They keep their nests feathered right well by convincing folks their light burley is the top of the line."

HR waved his hand. "What do they know? Besides, they're prejudiced."

Pennyrile grinned. "Who ain't?"

Asher Jennings looked the cigars over carefully before finally selecting one, even though there appeared to be no difference in any of them. He said nothing as he offered the small box to Myra Chastayne.

"I'm partial to Camels, myself," she said, "but, what the hell. Haven't had a good Havana seegar in a month of Sundays. Probably need a dose of that Cuban spit." She grinned at HR. "That is the way they make 'em, isn't it? Roll 'em up with spit and let 'em dry?"

HR smiled back at her. "It's your story, Myra. I wouldn't dream of pretending to know more about it than you."

She handed the humidor back to HR and the four of them lit up, filling the room with a haze of fragrant smoke.

HR leaned back in his leather swivel chair and regarded his three guests. A motley gathering, he thought. Or maybe no more varied than any four people you would take at random off a street anywhere. He quickly discarded this last thought. Each one of this group was an individual, unlike anybody else you'd routinely run into. That's why tonight's meeting was going to be a little tricky. Their common interest in money and self-advancement would be the glue that would hold them together, if anything would.

Pennyrile Gruber made a show of taking a beautiful engraved gold watch out of his vest pocket, opening the case, and giving it a quick glance before lifting his eyes to meet HR's. "Not to rush you, or anything, but could we get started?" He winked and gave HR a lascivious grin. "I've got another engagement, as they say, in just about an hour."

Pennyrile's watch, while not small, seemed lost in his hand, a hand made for work—big, strong, yet moving with grace and sureness. It was like Pennyrile himself. For all his bulk and rough look, there was a curious kind of smoothness about him. Except for his talk, which he used with delight to shock those who allowed it. He had to be close to sixty, but he moved and acted like a man half his age.

Myra took a hard pull at her cigar and shot a stream of smoke at Pennyrile. "The stuff you've got an engagement with won't spoil. Matter of fact, if memory serves, the longer you wait, the better it gets." Her voice was hoarse and low-pitched, like a man's. She sat in a wheelchair she'd been using for several weeks since returning from the hospital, where she'd undergone some kind of surgery.

HR smiled at her, sitting straight and alert, tall, thin, her reddish gray hair perfectly done, wearing a little makeup. She must be nearing seventy, and she looked like an aging queen in her severe dark dress with its high lacy collar.

Pennyrile tossed his almost bald head back and laughed, showing a mouthful of big solid yellow teeth. "It only gets better if you don't wait too long, darlin'. And it's not my practice to wait a long time for anything. Willingly, that is."

HR spoke up. "You're both right. Some things are better if you wait for them. And we do need to get on with our business."

Asher Jennings spoke for the first time. "Which is, I presume, this wretched union business."

Jennings adjusted his round silver-framed glasses, which made his bulging eyes, which he blinked almost constantly, look even bigger. He peered at them through his thick lenses. He was a thin, medium-tall man with a weak chin and lips that barely covered his large teeth. His brown hair lay neatly against his scalp, and the color of it matched his carefully trimmed mustache perfectly.

HR nodded. "Exactly. I called this meeting so we could talk a little about how we are going to deal with this thing. I thought it would be better if we got together in the evening, just us, and not the whole Stanton County Coal Operators Association. Not that there's anything wrong about our meeting, but I figured the fewer people know we're getting our heads together on this, the better it will be."

"Agreed," Jennings said. "We need some sort of plan, or approach or something. And we don't need a lot of official discussion or attention."

"I'm not so sure," Pennyrile said. "Maybe attention is exactly what we do need. Take an open stand. Let some of these bastards know we don't aim to lay down and let 'em screw us without a whimper." He glanced at Myra. "Excuse me, honey, but you know how my talk goes. Can't seem to help it. Don't mean to offend a lady."

Myra pointed her cigar directly at Pennyrile. "Forget the lady crap, Pennyrile. I'm here because I intend to look out for my interests in Stanton County, okay? So don't let the fact that I have plumbing that's different from yours give you any ideas about what I will or won't do when it comes right down to it. All of you should know this about me by now, but I reckon you have to be reminded every once in a while."

HR smiled at her. "We all know you can take care of your-self and protect your interests, Myra. You never did fit the role of a helpless little widow woman." He quickly added, "But that doesn't mean we don't have the highest regard for you as a lady."

Myra rolled her eyes at the ceiling and took a puff of her cigar. "If I may add my voice to that of the romantic Mr. Gruber, can we get on with it? For all any of you know, I may have an engagement of my own after this little gathering."

As usual, Asher Jennings watched and listened. HR knew, however, that when the time was ready, Jennings would weigh in wherever he believed his own best interests lay, without regard to anybody else's. He was as cold and efficient as a well-tuned machine. HR addressed them all. "Let's see if I can state our problem in a nutshell. First, almost every-body in the country is stampeding off after this man Roose-velt, evidently willing to go wherever he wants to lead them."

The others nodded.

"And," HR said, blowing a cloud of smoke over their heads, "one of the things he's decided to do is throw the weight of the federal government behind the unions. My sources in Washington tell me he's got new legislation being drafted that will nail us to the cross. And there's not enough backbone left in the entire Congress to stand up to him. Even under existing law, he's pushing, telling the union bosses to charge full steam ahead. I understand they've got people driving through Harlan and Bell and other counties in the coalfields already with loudspeakers blaring, telling folks that the pres-ident of the United States wants them to join the union."

"That's true," Pennyrile said. "But what can you expect from a goddamn Democrat?" This time, he didn't bother to even glance at Myra, who nodded her agreement.

"They're moving in on us every day," HR said. "Organiz-ers, secret agitators, who knows what all, stirring up as much trouble as they can, signing up our workers and threatening to strike our mines if we don't knuckle under to them."

"I say we hire our own people," Pennyrile said. "Outsiders

we can depend on, men who'll do what they have to, what they're told to do, have them deputized and show these bastards who's in charge here."

HR studied him for a moment before he spoke. "And earn the name 'Bloody Stanton'—or worse, 'Bloody Buxton'? I personally intend to do everything I can to avoid that. You want to see it get so bad here that we have to ask Governor Lafoon to send in the National Guard to preserve order, like he's already done other places? I can't believe you do."

Pennyrile made a noise that sounded like a hog snorting. "With apologies beforehand, Myra, screw the unions, and their organizers, and screw Lafoon and the National Guard, too. I can take care of my own affairs, and I've got the balls and the money to do it."

HR's voice had a soothing quality to it. "Nobody doubts your courage for an instant, Pennyrile. Nor your resources. But do you really think that a direct confrontation is the best way to deal with this thing?"

Pennyrile studied HR for a long moment before he replied. "We're different, you and me, HR. We come from different seeds planted in different ground and grown in a different climate. You're from someplace up north, some city where you went to high school and college and associated with refined types who hold their teacups with their little fingers sticking out while they nibble on delicate little cookies and sandwiches with the crust trimmed off. And you inherited money from your daddy and brought it here to the mountains to turn it into even more money." He paused for a moment. "Is that about right?"

HR nodded. "More or less." His voice and expression were cool.

Pennyrile went on. "Me, I started with nothing. Not a pot to piss in. Born in a log cabin with a dirt floor not fifty miles from here. My daddy scratched around on a little old rocky hillside farm all his life for what we had to eat. And he had me and my brothers and sisters and our mother out there scratching right alongside him, day after day, just barely making it. I had one pair of britches with patches on patches when I was going to school."

For the first time, Asher Jennings spoke up. "What's your point?"

Pennyrile Gruber waved his cigar like a baton between HR and Jennings. "I'm going to make my point. Just a minute more, and I'll shut up. When I was thirteen, I left the home place and took a job in a coal mine. Worked in it for two years. Saw what it was like, and was determined that I wouldn't stay in it all my life. I also saw how mine operators were making money, started to understand how their system worked. So I stayed in the mines four more years, stayed away from liquor and women and saved every nickel other than what it took me to barely survive—I was good at that— and one day I took the train out and I went north to . . . well it makes no difference where, but I worked and scrimped and saved and did a few other things I won't mention to get enough money to come back here and get myself a start in the coal business."

HR cleared his throat and took a long pull at his cigar.

Pennyrile continued. "I picked me up some mineral rights for a decent price, and I opened a little mine, and . . . well, you all know most of the rest. And I think you know this, too: What I've got, and it's by God enough and then some, I've made it myself. I work like hell ever goddamn day. Always have. Always will, I guess." Here Pennyrile Gruber paused and gave each of the others a hard straight look. "And there ain't no friggin' president or governor or union boss or bunch of ragged-ass miners going to take what I've got. Not unless they kill me first. And that, my friends, will take some doing." Again he paused. "That's all I've got to say about the matter." He looked at his watch again.

HR Buxton waited awhile before he spoke. "Pennyrile, nobody expects you to give up what you've worked for. Certainly none of us here does. We're all going to do whatever is possible to hold on to what is rightfully ours. This is still a free country, and I intend to run my own business the way

I want to for as long I am able to. But the question comes down to means, not ends. *How* we meet this threat is the question, not *whether*."

Asher Jennings nodded, and Myra Chastayne said, "I agree. We ought to be judicious about whatever action we take. But I also agree with Pennyrile. We oughtn't to lay down and let them screw us without making a whimper."

HR looked at his cigar. It had gone out. He placed it in one of the ashtrays. "Can we all agree on this much? I'll try to formulate a plan that we can all live with. Each one of us will have the maximum freedom to do what he feels like he has to do in his own interests, and we'll work in concert on whatever we can, maybe like getting some better information on what the other side is up to. But we'll all agree not to take any precipitate action, not do anything that would ignite a firestorm. At least not without talking to one another about it? Can we agree on this?"

Myra nodded.

Jennings said, "That's a good start. When shall we talk again?"

"A week from tonight?" HR asked. "All agreed?"

Pennyrile said nothing as he consulted his watch once again and stood to go.

"Let us hope," HR said, "that our little group will be up to its task in the weeks and months ahead."

"Which is . . . ?" Pennyrile sounded skeptical.

"First and foremost, to keep the peace around here, if there's any possible way to do that," HR said.

"My first order of business," Pennyrile said slowly and deliberately, "is to keep what's mine. Whatever it takes to do *that*."

As they prepared to go, Myra Chastayne, Asher Jennings, and HR Buxton glanced at one another, and HR said, "Well, then, we are adjourned until next time."

"Enjoy yourself, Pennyrile," Myra Chastayne said with a grin.

"My constant purpose," he replied. His sly smile left no doubt that he expected tonight to be no exception.

$\triangledown$

6

W HEN PEARL STARTED TO whine, Moody McCain glanced up from the Louisville *Courier-Journal* he was reading. Though a small wave of irritation rippled through him, he kept his face free of expression.

"Moooody," Pearl said, "I can't do stuff like this. I really can't." She cocked her head to one side and formed her lips into a pout. "And you oughtn't to make me."

Without saying anything, McCain laid the paper aside and stared at her. At twenty-four she was prime for his needs. She stood there in the spare little kitchen, legs spraddled, wearing pink silk panties, nothing else, and he could see the dark triangle of her pubic mound through the sheerness of the fabric, even see little tufts of hair peeking out around the edges of the elastic. He could also see the network of pale blue veins just underneath the surface of the milky white skin of her full firm breasts. Her body was beautifully proportioned. Small waist, flaring hips, arched back, rounded buttocks.

Something, however, had gone wrong with her face. It was not just one thing, either, he had decided the first time he saw her almost six months ago. It was a combination of things. Her nose was a little too long, her eyes a little too far apart, her lips a little too full, and her chin a little too pointed. Any one of these flaws would have been enough to keep her from being a real beauty, but all together, in some strange way, they made her almost pretty. Not quite, but almost.

It was her body, though, that Moody McCain was most interested in. Not her face, and certainly not her mind. Her body, which was beyond criticism.

As McCain studied her, he idly rubbed a finger up and down the thin pink scar that ran across his left cheek from the corner of his eye down to the edge of his jawbone.

"Mooooody," she said, "are you listening to me?"

He hoisted his spare, loose frame with ease and grace from the chair and walked over to where Pearl stood by the black cast-iron cookstove.

Thin wisps of smoke drifted up from the holes on top where she had removed the lids. He looked at the stove and then at her. "I told you," he said quietly, "first you put in the wadded-up newspaper, then the rich pine kindling, then the little lumps of coal. You don't have to pour coal oil on it, but you can if you want to, just to make it start a little faster."

As he talked, he was pulling the mess out of the stove. Pearl had put the kindling on the bottom and the papers next, as if fire burned down instead of up. He rearranged the materials in the manner he had described. When he had finished, he took a wooden match from the large box on the shelf near the stove, struck it, and touched the flame to the paper. The fire began to take hold at once.

He turned to Pearl and said, "See how easy it is? See how it works when you do it the way you are supposed to, the way I showed you?" He replaced the lids on the holes and sighed.

"Honey, I don't know about this stuff. I can't do it right." Her facial expression was somewhere in the range of bored or confused, and her voice was a singsong, with a distinctly northern city accent to it. "When we got together, you didn't tell me I'd have to learn to do stuff like this. Why can't we go out somewhere and eat? I don't like it here."

McCain said, "Fix supper."

Pearl tugged at a strand of her short wavy platinum blond hair. "Just look at this. I need to go someplace where I can get it done right. The roots are coming in dark again. See?"

McCain reached for her, grasped her forearm, and squeezed. As he applied more pressure, she let go of the large spoon she had been holding, and it fell to the bare wood floor with a clatter.

McCain clamped down harder on her arm.

"Oh, God, Moody. Please don't. That hurts. Please." The whine in her voice was real now, and her face was twisted as her eyes began to glisten with tears. "I'm sorry, honey. I'll learn. I will. Just let me go."

McCain continued to squeeze, harder and harder. His facial expression and voice never changed. "Where were you, Pearly, when I picked you up? Have you forgot?"

She shook her head vigorously and began to sob.

"Where?" he asked.

"Working in a restaurant in Pittsburgh."

"A restaurant? You mean a goddamn greasy-spoon ptomaine palace, don't you? Where you were waiting tables and hustling tips, and when you were lucky enough to spot some salesman with a couple of extra bucks you were taking him home after work and fucking him so you'd have enough money to pay the rent on your grimy little cockroach heaven? Right?" It had all come out in one breath, and he had never changed the tone of his voice.

She sobbed, then nodded.

"Right." he said. "Say it."

"Right."

."Again."

She whimpered and tried to pull loose from him. "Right. That's right, Moody." Tears streamed down her cheeks. "Please let my arm go. It hurts."

McCain gave her arm a last hard squeeze and she cried out sharply. Then he turned her loose, giving her a rough shove away from him. "Now," he said quietly, "put a skillet on the stove, put some grease in it, and fry some eggs. Four for me. You know how I like them. And make a pot of coffee. You can do that, can't you? Without my help? Or will you need another lesson?"

"No," she said quickly. "I can do it. You go sit back down and read the paper. I can do it."

What a disgusting cunt, McCain thought, like so many he had known. If it weren't for his sexual needs, he'd never have anything to do with any of them. He went back to his chair and leaned back and crossed his long limber legs. He picked the paper up and started to read again.

Pearl set a skillet over the now blistering stove top. She cracked an egg and dropped it into the skillet, then two more, then another. She stared at them with a sad expression. There was a quaver in her voice when she said, "Moody, will scrambled be okay this time instead of over light?"

He hesitated, then sighed and said, "Okay." After a moment he added, "You know I'm not hard to please."

They ate without speaking, and afterward they sat at the little rickety table and waited for the coffee to finish boiling. The rich aroma of it pleased Moody. It was called Mammy's Favorite, and it had chicory in it, something Moody had learned to like the first time he was in New Orleans years ago.

As they sipped their coffee, Pearl stared at his face, as if trying to assess how he was feeling before she spoke. "Were your eggs all right, honey? I'm sorry about breaking the yellows, but I'll do better the next time. I'm getting better, ain't I? Don't you think I am?"

He studied her for a moment, then nodded. "You're getting better."

"Good. I want to be better. And I don't want to make you unhappy. Or mad." She rushed on. "Not that you're mad very much, I didn't mean that. And you're entitled to be mad at me sometimes, the way I mess things up. But I want to do right for you. I truly do."

"Relax, Pearl. I'm fine. And you don't have to worry. I'm not mad."

"Good. You take good care of me, honey. I know you do." She smiled, hesitated, then added, "And don't I take good care of you, too? Don't I?"

He considered smiling at her. What he did instead was give a little nod.

Leaning forward in her chair, she said, "You want me to take care of you now? Would you like that?"

At first he gave no sign. Then, ever so slightly, he nodded again.

She was watching him closely. When he nodded, she got up at once and scooted the little table aside and came to stand in front of his chair. She moved close to him. Even with the odors of hot grease and coffee that hung in the room, he could smell the woman scent of her. At once he felt the tightness begin in his lower belly. When he made no move to touch her, however, she sat down on the floor in front of him and said, "Like this? You want it like this?"

Once more he nodded.

Later when she had finished, he touched her for the first time, pushing her away.

"Was it good, honey?" she asked. "Was it?"

He didn't answer, but she smiled anyway. "It was. I know it was. I can always tell."

Moody sat in a straight-back cane-bottom chair tilted against the wall on the front porch with his feet hooked on one of the rungs, slowly and methodically working on a chew of tobacco in his jaw. Pearl rocked gently in the swing.

It was just at the edge of darkness, now, and the men had only a little while ago trudged home from the mine. Up and down the row of little frame camp houses lights were being turned on. Radios would soon be tuned in to "Lum and Abner" or "Amos and Andy" or one of the other shows that provided most of the week-night entertainment in the camp. Early bedtime was a necessity for men who had to rise at four-thirty in the morning to eat and get to the driftmouth of the mine in time to catch the early mantrip inside.

From somewhere down the narrow dirt street that was black as death with ashes and fragments of coal and slate, someone was picking a guitar and singing a slow mournful blues. Something about a greenback dollar, a watch and chain, an aching heart.

"Moody, can we talk?" Pearl asked in a meek little voice. "Do you feel like it? I sure hope you do."

It was a moment before he spoke. "What about?"

"Mostly about when we might be leaving this place. We've been here more than two weeks." She added quickly, "I'm not complaining. I know you don't like that. I'm just asking. How soon do you think it might be?"

Moody shifted the cud of tobacco in his cheek, then leaned over toward the edge of the porch and squirted a stream of juice into the yard. "When my work here is finished."

"Do you have any idea when that might be?"

"Not exactly. But it won't be too long, I reckon."

"Will we be able to go out anywhere while we're here, to dance or listen to music or anything like that? I could wear the red dress you bought me in Knoxville. You know, the one you like with the low-cut front? I could wear it for you."

McCain sighed and shook his head in the darkness. "First of all, there's no place to go. And second, you know I have to be careful around here. Not draw attention to myself."

"I don't see why union work has to be so secret."

"You don't, but I do. And the rest of us do. There's people who'd do anything to stop us from organizing the union."

"Anything?"

"That's right."

"Even kill you?"

Moody spit again. "Even kill us."

She was quiet for a while before she spoke again. "I'm proud to be with you for what you're doing, Moody. Helping working people get together and make things better for themselves. In spite of the danger. It's a real brave thing you're doing. My daddy worked in a steel mill in Pittsburgh, and I know how hard he worked and all. I just think it's real fine what you're doing."

"Somebody's got to do it. And those of us who do, have to be mighty careful that we don't get killed for it. That's why we have to be so secret about everything." He made his voice sound as urgent as he could. "You musn't ever be out there talking over the back fence with these other women, or with anybody else, about me and what I do, you understand? You never know who might be a fink. There are company spies all over the place who'd as soon turn me in as look at me. You see what I'm saying?"

McCain wished sometimes he'd never brought her along. But he knew having a woman with him made him stand out less. Also, and much more important, he needed the touch of a woman, needed sex, and he needed it often. Times when he had to do without it, even briefly, he began to get tight, wound-up, and he started to have headaches, and his temper became short and violent. He had learned long ago that his need for sexual release was greater by many times than that of the ordinary man.

But then he was no ordinary man, never had been, and never would be. So he considered sex for himself the way he considered gasoline to be fuel for a car, or coal to be fuel for a train. He had to have it before his system operated efficiently. At times when he thought about it much, it made him despise women, all women, hate them for the way he depended on them. But he knew it was impossible to exist in the world without what you took from others. And he was too smart to ignore his needs.

Pearl's voice broke the silence. "Honey, you know what I'd like to do when we leave here?"

"What?"

"Go someplace nice, like when we went to Cleveland. And Chicago. I liked it when we went there. The hotels and the restaurants. And the dancing. I like to dance with you."

McCain said nothing.

"You know what I'd really, really like? I'd like to go to Hollywood. You know, California. I'd just truly love to do that."

Moody shook his head in disgust. Jesus Christ. "You don't know anything about Hollywood. You don't know whether you'd like it or not."

"I do know something about it. I've read about it in magazines. And I've seen the newsreels. I know I'd love it."

He made no effort to conceal his contempt. "What would you do in Hollywood? Become a big star? Is that what you think?"

"No," she said in a small voice. "I'd just like to see it once, that's all. See all the famous people."

McCain was silent.

"Then how about Broadway?" she said. "Wouldn't you like to go there?"

"Broadway's a street," he said. "You know all about it, too?"

"Some. I know I'd like to see it."

McCain despised such prattle. But he tolerated a certain amount of it because he was a man not given to make-believe. He knew his requirements. And Pearl was as good a solution as he could have at this moment. The risk of having a woman with him who was too bright was more than he could accept. Nor could he risk traveling in the mountains alone. He knew the problems that could arise in a small community if he came in and started trying to take care of his sexual needs with a local woman or women. He could not take the chance that he'd be found out. And his need was not just a once-or-twice-a-week thing. It was more like once or twice a day. It was important that he have a woman available to him when he needed her, not just when he might be able to arrange it.

Certainly he had never had any trouble getting women. They were attracted to his tall, slim body and neat appearance. And they loved his "pretty blond hair" and his "beautiful face." Even the scar didn't bother them. Lots of them thought it made him look brave and mysterious. Especially when he made up some romantic bullshit for them about how he had acquired it defending some woman's honor or something. And the plain-glass specs he wore for cover. Some said they made him look more intelligent, more interesting. But most important, beyond what he looked like, he always

had money. And during times like these that was really all
that mattered. You could look like Lon Chaney all made up
to play Frankenstein if you had money. Which he had and
would continue to have. The demand for the services of a
professional of his caliber was at an all-time high, in the
mountains as well as other places.

"What are you thinking about, honey?" Pearl was saying.
"Are you worried about what the gun thugs might do if they
find out you're with the union?"

"Yes, I am concerned. That's why you never can say anything about what I do."

"Don't worry, Moody."

Moody looked at her swinging back and forth. He could
just barely make out her form there in the darkness. A certain level of stupidity was something he sought out in looking for a woman to travel with, but this one had to run off
at the mouth all the time. He almost felt sorry for her, but
sympathy was something that had not been a part of his
range of emotions for many years.

Not since he had walked out of his dying mother's house
while his father blubbered and cursed through a face full of
blood. Moody McCain had smothered all feelings of sympathy from that day forward.

Pearl had accepted his story that he was a secret organizer for the union without any sign of doubt. It had
seemed to him the safest thing to tell her. And she had to
have some plausible story, or she might get too curious—
and dangerous.

Well, he would not have to contend with her babbling for
very long. His employer had said just one job here, most
likely. And then it would be good-bye, Stanton County. Mc-
Cain would head out for other opportunities. Unless, of
course, something further presented itself here. Which was
always a possibility.

In any event, sooner or later, he knew he would find it
convenient to get rid of Pearl. She would get too inquisitive,
or too demanding, or her chatter would become more than

he was willing to bear, or something else, as had been the case with the others. And when she did, he knew what to do with her. There had never been the slightest problem with any of them. And nobody was left behind to talk about him. He never left any tracks anyone could follow. And he never would. He was a professional.

"I have to go out for a while tonight," he said. "Union business."

"And I have to stay here," she said quietly. "I know."

A few minutes later, he stood up, stretched, and stepped from the front porch into the hard-packed dirt yard. Without saying anything or looking back, he got into his car and drove off into the night.

▽

7

JORDON LEANED AGAINST THE wall outside the front door of his Little Casino with his hands jammed down into his pockets, staring at the ground.

He lifted his head and gazed off toward the mountaintop, where the sun had disappeared only minutes before, wondering if maybe he ought to catch a train and go someplace, Louisville, or south to Knoxville, say, or farther, and find a decent game of poker and something a little more entertaining to do.

Jordon sniffed the air and caught the smell of frying fish wafting across the lot from the restaurant kitchen. Earlier, in the afternoon, he had seen a skinny young man in overalls carrying a big blue catfish in the back door. Must have been close to four feet long, weighed maybe fifty pounds or more. When he was hungry, Jordon loved catfish, and was happy the Middle Fork was full of them. But right now food did not interest him. Nothing, actually, seemed to.

Jordon wondered, as he often had, why he had never really been satisfied anywhere, no matter what his situation. Never, from the time he had first gone into the army to fight in Cuba when he was barely old enough to enlist, to his hard time in the penitentiary for killing the two men who had beaten him half to death at Stateline, to his stints as a deputy sheriff in several Eastern Kentucky counties, his soldiering in France, even when he had been married to Vera so long ago. As much as he had loved her, he had always felt a nagging discontent, as if something, some vital part, had been left out of him and he had to keep on looking for it, even if the search ruined his life and the lives of any unfortunate souls who might care for him.

He shook his head in wonder as he thought about his son Danny, settled down with a family, seemingly happy and satisfied to be working for HR Buxton in one of his stores. Danny, despite the fact that his childhood had been so uncertain, seemed to have no missing parts.

The aroma of the frying fish touched Jordon's nostrils again, and he knew he should eat, but he put it off once more.

Glancing toward Della's office, he wondered what she might be doing. It had been several days now since the two of them had had their discussion about his riding shotgun for her, if that's what it really was. He had thought of it more than once, but she had not mentioned it again.

He sighed. Maybe he was just bored. The gambling business had been slow.

But this was Friday night, and things ought to pick up some.

He took a deep breath, expelled it slowly, and went inside.

Willis and half a dozen others were gathered around a pool table where a shooter was trying to make the stripes in a game of eight ball. Willis and a few of the rest sat on the high stools against the wall.

Jordon took a seat behind the counter and reached for a deck of cards underneath and shuffled them, then riffled them, shuffled, riffled.

The men were talking, as usual, about the union. Jordon had heard most of it before, in one form or another, and knew he was going to hear it again, in spite of the efforts he had made to discourage it.

"It may not be as easy as you think," Speedy Robbins said. "HR Buxton ain't the type to lay down and let you do it to him without a fight."

Turner Lott, whose people had lived in the mountains for generations and most of whom had always been high-tempered and outspoken, said, "He ain't going to have a

choice by the time we're through with him. We'll put something in his hands he'll have to deal with. All the coal mines
in this country are going to be organized before it's over. The
hard way or the easy way, it's going to get done."

Speedy, who seemed to Jordon never to be very confident
about anything, said, "That's your opinion."

Turner said, "Not just mine. A lot of people back me up."

"For instance?"

"For instance," Lott said, "John L. Lewis and Bill Turnblazer, to name just two."

One of the others spoke up. "Turnblazer? Hell, they say
you can't get him out of his hotel room when things starts
heating up. That man's got a disappearing act that a magi-
cian would kill for."

"They's others don't mind being seen. And heard, too.
Before it's over, HR Buxton will be on his knees begging to
sign a contract." Turner stretched and rolled his shoulders
like a fighter.

Elmer Hagen grunted. "It'll be a cold day in hell when
anybody gets HR Buxton on his knees for anything. I've had
enough dealings with that old bastard to know you can't
push him around."

"We'll see how he holds up when it gets down to the
nut-cutting," Lott said.

Jordon decided to intervene. "Would it be possible to interest any of you kibitzers in a few hands of poker?"

Several of them followed Jordon to the back room, leaving
the two eight ball players to themselves, with Willis still
watching from his perch on the stool. He had said nothing
during the discussion, but Jordon knew he strongly sup-
ported his cousin Turner Lott.

Jordon dealt a few hands and got their minds on poker for
a little while, but soon the union was back as the topic of
discussion.

"Are you going to call Oscar's last bet or what?" one of the
players said. "Can we play poker instead of striking the Buxton mines?"

"What's the bet, a nickel? Call, goddammit," Turner Lott said. "Nobody mentioned anything about a strike. I'm just talking about everybody organized into a tight union." He smiled as he said it.

"But a strike's what it finally comes down to, ain't it?" Speedy said.

"It could, if other means of persuasion fail."

"My bet is that your other means, whatever they are, ain't going to be enough. Specially with a man like Buxton. A strike is where it ends up at."

Lott shrugged. "If that's what Buxton wants, then so be it. The way things are going in the coalfields these days, if they don't starve us to death they'll end up shooting us."

"What do you mean?"

"I got a letter a while back from a cousin of mine over in West Virginia. Said one of his best buddies had his brains blowed out by a sniper while he was standing on his own front porch."

"Well, it seems to me the ones of us trying to keep a roof over our families' heads on a day or two's work a week would be foolish to strike and try to do it on no work a'tall. I don't see how you can think a strike would help us."

"That's the point," Lott said. "You don't see. And a lot of other folks don't either. One or two days a week at starvation wages is not living, it's just barely existing. A man working like that ain't no more than a mule, pulling a load and getting paid off with just enough feed to keep him from starving to death."

Hagen spoke up. "Who you calling a mule?"

"Nobody. I was just making a point."

"Sounded to me like you was saying a man works for Buxton is a mule. I work for him."

"I do, too," Lott said. "But some of these operators got no feeling for nothing but money. Take Pennyrile Gruber, for instance. He puts more value on a mule than a man, that one does." He looked at Hagen and said in an even voice, "I didn't mean it the way you're trying to make it sound."

"I ain't trying to make it sound one way or the other. You're the one said it. But I ain't no mule."

Jordon laid the deck of cards on the table and took a deep breath. "Gentlemen, this is a poker game. It's being run for fun and profit. It's a house rule that political or religious discussions are left outside."

Lott said, "Who made that rule?"

Jordon said, "I did."

"Well, we ain't talking politics or religion, we're talking union."

"Not here," Jordon said.

A quietness settled over the game.

"What's the matter with you," Lott said. "Don't you care about what happens to the coal miners around here?"

Jordon eyed him coldly. "I care about what happens to my friends, and I've got friends who are coal miners. Some are for the UMW. Some for some other union. Some for no union at all. When it comes to your union business, I stay out of it. You can go up against Buxton or not, as you please."

There was a challenge in Lott's voice. "You a friend of Buxton's?"

Jordon gave him a straight-on look and said evenly, "Not that it's any of your business, Turner, but I don't think anybody who knows both of us would call HR Buxton and me friends."

"You saying you're enemies?"

"We leave each other alone."

Turner Lott showed a tight little grin. "Kind of like two rattlesnakes."

There was no smile on Jordon's face. "I'm beginning to think I don't much care for you, Turner."

Lott shrugged. "A man's going to have to make up his mind before this thing's all over. He's going to have to come down on one side or the other."

"I'm on my side," Jordon said. "And right now, that happens to be keeping this poker game moving. If you all want to play poker, fine. If you want to debate your personal causes, take them outside and I'll take a break." The way he said it didn't leave any room for argument. "It's up to you, Charley. Henry bet a nickel and Lott called."

Charley didn't hesitate. "Call. And raise a dime."

"The price of poker just went up," Jordon said. "Fifteen cents to you, Dick."

While Dick was making up his mind, Jordon glanced toward Turner Lott, who was staring back at him with his thin little smile. Jordon was not sure what it was intended to convey. It could have been arrogance. Or a challenge. If the man had not been Willis's cousin, Jordon might have made something of it, if not here, then afterwards. But Jordon was willing to let it pass.

Anyway, he was determined not to let outside conflicts interfere with his gambling operation. He needed the income. Controversy and conflict were enough of a problem in poker and crap games anyway, without letting Lott or anybody else bring their causes into the game.

Lott's comments about miners and mules, however, stuck in Jordon's mind. Being a coal miner was a hard and danger-filled way to make a living, Jordon knew. And he also knew a mine operator could lose a coal miner and replace him at no cost. Other men were waiting in line. But a good mule cost money.

After Jordon ruled against further discussion of union matters, the game settled down to poker and small talk. It had been going on for an hour or more when the door opened and a tall, slim man with light blond hair stepped inside. He was a stranger to Jordon.

Jordon looked up at him and their eyes locked for a moment. The first thing Jordon noticed was the thin scar that ran down the side of the stranger's face. Then the round wire-frame glasses he wore. In Jordon's mind, they didn't quite seem to go together for some reason.

The tall man looked them over for a moment before he spoke. "That old crippled boy out front seemed to think I'd find a poker game back here. Looks like he was right." There was something about the man's voice that sounded strange to Jordon. It was not quite halting, but the words didn't seem to run together in any natural rhythm. However, it was what he said that bothered Jordon.

Jordon's voice was cold. "Mister, first of all, that's a man out there, not a boy. His name's Willis Dobbs. And I don't think you know him well enough to be even mentioning his missing leg."

The man said the right words, but neither his look nor his tone of voice gave them support. "I'm sorry if I offended you. Or anybody else. Can a stranger sit in, after getting off to a bad start?" He gave them a cool smile.

Jordon nodded, and two of the others scooted their chairs apart so the tall man could get to the table.

Jordon said, "Nickel ante, dime on an open pair, quarter on the last card. Three raises, no check and raise. I'm the dealer, house cut's a nickel a pot, but I let some of the small ones pass me by. We're playing five-card stud, but I might change that at some point."

"I guess I can handle the stakes," the stranger said, somehow making it sound a little like he thought it was a chicken-shit game.

Nobody said anything.

The stranger turned to Speedy Robbins and stuck out his hand. "I'm Moody McCain."

As Jordon dealt the next hand and the players peeked at their hole cards, each man introduced himself to McCain.

The players, more relaxed now after McCain's entry had upset their balance, got back to stud poker.

Elmer Hagen won the first hand after McCain joined them. He took it with a pair of queens, after hitting on fifth street, and raked in a pot of maybe a dollar and a quarter. Maybe that didn't seem like much to McCain, Jordon reflected, but it was as much as a lot of men in Stanton County were making for a day's work—when they could find it.

As Jordon shuffled the cards again, Turner Lott said,

"What line of work are you in, Mr. McCain?"

"Call me Moody. Right now, I'm a timber buyer."

"You've come to the right place," Speedy said. "We got lots of trees around here."

"You buy coal, too?" Lott asked.

"I don't know anything about coal," McCain said. "Or mining, either."

After a moment, Lott said, "How about unions? Know anything about them?"

Jordon thought, why can't he let it rest for a little while?

But McCain was looking at his hole card. "Nothing at all," he said casually. "Just timber. And a little bit about poker." He smiled as he tossed a coin into the pot. "Bet a nickel," he said. "See where the power is."

Later, after everyone had left and Willis and Jordon were closing the place, Willis said, "What kind of a poker player is that new fellow?"

"Just fair. Moody McCain, he says his name is. He picked up a little change is all."

"He struck me as a kind of strange bird."

"What did he say out here when he first came in?"

"Not a lot. Just that somebody over at the restaurant told him there was a game here."

"What do you make of him?"

Willis thought about it for a moment. "Nothing much, I guess. A little strange, as I said. But then, I reckon strangers are supposed to be a little strange, right? Anyway, we get enough of them these days. There's been a half a dozen men in here shooting pool the last couple of weeks I never saw before. Who knows who they all are? Or what they may be here for."

Jordon took a deep breath and sighed. "I dread what's liable to happen before this stuff between the operators and the miners is over and done with. We could see some mighty rough times."

Willis put his hand on Jordon's shoulder. "We've seen

rough times before, you and me. And most of the rest of the folks around here, too. Our mothers have a rough time bringing us into this world, and we don't see the end of rough times till we're six feet under. But rough or easy, certain things have got to get done."

Jordon shook his head and stretched, arching his back and hearing it crack a little. "Well, let's lock up. Be careful on the way home. I'm going to bed and see if I can get a decent night's sleep."

Willis looked at his watch. "It's not yet midnight. I've still got to go somewhere and meet some of the boys."

Jordon held up his hand. "If it has to do with what I think it might, I'd just as soon not know about it."

Willis grinned. "Don't you know I'd never do anything to cause you to lose sleep, buddy?"

In his room a few minutes later Jordon lay on his back, with his little table lamp on, enjoying his firm, narrow bunk bed, the kind of bed he'd learned to love during his two hitches in the army.

Each time he lay down in this bed, he relived a little piece of those times, the Spanish-American War and the World War. In spite of the bullshit he had sometimes received from arrogant officers, and the wild, heady mix of fear and elation he felt when bullets were singing past his head, and the mud and filth and rats in the trenches, in spite of all of that, and the dying and the threat of death all around him, or maybe because of some of it, soldiering was a chapter of his past that he missed, yearned for, even ached for sometimes.

There was a closeness, an excitement, about being bound together with other men in a great and dangerous effort under his country's flag that had given him a feeling unmatched by anything else in the world.

Well, the way things were taking shape in the coalfields, it sure looked like a war could be starting here. He dreaded to see it, to see mountain men killing and being killed by one another, and by strangers who didn't know or care about anything but the pay they received for their bloody work.

He had heard enough about what was going on already in some of the other counties, and though he hoped it would not come here to Stanton County, he was afraid it would.

As much as he hated to admit it, Jordon was beginning to feel that HR Buxton sounded like a voice of reason in a pit full of passion. The problem was, Jordon didn't trust HR any farther than he could throw an ox.

Jordon rolled over and took a volume from his little shelf of books, his "library." *The Story of Philosophy* by Will Durant. Even though he only read little bits and pieces of it at a time, the ideas in it were endlessly fascinating to him.

As he turned the pages, his eyes fell on a passage from the writings of the German philosopher Arthur Schopenhauer.

> In general, the wise of all ages have always said the same things, and the fools, who at all times form the immense majority, have in their way too acted alike, and done the opposite, and so it will continue. For as Voltaire says, we shall leave the world as foolish and wicked as we found it.

Jordon put the book aside. He knew better than to read much of this kind of stuff tonight. He felt that his life was meaningless enough already. A little more pessimism now could be more than his system would tolerate. And he knew, had always known, that the cure for all his ills was no farther away than the holster of his Colt .44.

He switched off the lamp and willed his thoughts away from philosophers and toward Cassie, which was not hard for him to do. Then he cursed himself for heading down this path. He would never get to sleep if he started thinking about her and what might have happened between them. In his imagination he would replay their conversations, finding ways to express what he felt, making a real effort to respond with more concern and understanding to her own feelings and fears, and in the end, she would reach out for him, and it would all work out different than it had in reality. They

would be together, and what was in their hearts would overcome everything else.

He shifted his body, wrestled his pillow, and turned on his
side. Jesus Christ! Let it go, Jordon. Let it all go for tonight.

Had he been a praying man, this night he would have
asked for a good, solid, dreamless eight hours of sleep. At
this moment, that was his fondest desire.

What he got instead, when at last he drifted down into a
shallow stupor, was a visit from an old acquaintance, one
he'd known since he was a young man in his salad days . . .
the big white mare.

$\triangledown$

8

As HE ROUNDED THE CURVE that early morning in August, Willis Dobbs was driving faster than he should have been.

He wanted to get where he was going, get this visit with Turner Lott out of the way. He had plenty of other stuff to attend to before he was due at the poolroom this afternoon.

This day would be a hot one, he could tell that much already.

By the time he had parked in front of Turner's house, Willis was already sweating freely. He took a Camel from his pocket and lit up. He noticed his hand shaking a little. There were enough hand controls on the Model A steering column to make it fairly easy for him to drive with his one leg. But still it was a task he didn't enjoy. Never had. Maybe because he had never done enough of it to really be able to do it without having to pay close attention.

Sitting here now in the early-morning sun, he thought about this stranger, this Moody McCain, which was one of the things Turner wanted to talk about. McCain seemed different from others who had drifted in lately. It was nearly a week now since the night McCain had walked into the poolroom. But neither Willis nor Turner Lott nor anybody else had been able to learn anything much about him. Nobody knew where he was from, nor what he was in Stanton County for. They did know where he was living. In a house down in Chambers. With a young woman, very good-looking, so it was said. Curly Bunch lived next door to them, and his wife saw the woman out in the yard sometimes. Mrs. Bunch hadn't been able to get her to talk much yet, and so hadn't learned anything about them. She would keep trying, Curly said, but she didn't want to be too nosy and draw attention to her curiosity. For some reason, though, Turner was suspicious of McCain.

As Willis started to get out of the car, Turner Lott stepped through the door onto the front porch with a coffee mug in his hand. "Howdy, cuz," Turner said with a grin. "Light and look at your saddle. The old lady's bringing you a cup of java."

Willis got out of the car, set his crutches under his arms, and swung his body through the gate and onto the porch.

After Turner's wife had brought his coffee, Willis rocked his chair back against the wall next to Turner's and they talked. About Moody McCain. Then about the planned trip to Stanton County by some of the officials from the UMW office in Middlesboro, and a possible visit by some real big shots. Where they would put them up, how they would protect them and arrange for them to talk to the miners.

"We need to make believers out of the men who are still straddling the fence," Willis said. "No sense in spending all our time preaching to them that's already converted."

Turner agreed. "Speaking of fence-straddlers, how come your buddy Jordon don't come on over to our side?"

Willis shook his head. "I can't speak for him. He's not a miner and he's got his own reasons for what he does."

Turner made a noise that sounded like he was clearing his throat. "Aaahh, hell. He's afraid to stand up. Be counted. That's all. What's he got to lose? He don't owe Buxton nothing."

"True. But he's not staying out because he's scared. Maybe he's just seen enough trouble in his life, and don't want any more."

"I don't either, but what's right is right."

"Leave it alone," Willis said. "Jordon's made up his mind that he's got no stake in this thing. He's my friend. And I respect him. And he's a good man, no matter what you might think of him."

High up on the side of the mountain, wedged into a crevice in a cliff, Moody McCain waited. His Springfield was ready.

He had been in position for more than an hour, waiting for the appearance of the subject on the front porch. On mornings when the mines didn't run, the subject always came out and sat on the porch with his mug of coffee. And now, unexpectedly, a new element was in the picture.

This morning, the old one-legged boy from the poolroom had come there for some reason. Goddamn this cripple. McCain debated on whether to come back another day, when the subject was alone, or to do it now, and be finished with it. If he did it now, he could watch the shock on the cripple's face when he realized what was going on. That would be interesting to see.

McCain shifted his weight to his other leg. Damn it, he'd been waiting long enough, watching the subject for days now, since he'd seen him up close in the poker game the other night.

Through the scope on his Springfield, McCain watched the scene on the porch as the two of them took seats in cane-bottom chairs alongside one another, leaned back against the wall, and began to talk. A woman brought the cripple a cup of coffee, said something to him, then went back inside.

McCain considered his options. There might never be a better time. Things changed, folks became suspicious and altered their habits. Or the weather changed, or a hundred other things. And this goddamn cripple, obviously he had some business with the subject, probably was involved with him. What difference did it make?

McCain made up his mind.

He set the cross hairs on the subject's face, took a deep breath, exhaled some of it, squeezed, ejected, reloaded.

The subject's chair flew out from under him and his coffee mug fell to the porch and shattered when he took the bullet.

The cripple realized what was happening, McCain estimated, at about the same time he heard the shot echoing through the hollow. McCain trained the scope on the cripple, following his face as he fell to the floor alongside the subject, shaking his head as if he couldn't believe what he was seeing.

Then the cripple turned his head to face the direction the shot came from, his eyes searching the mountainside. He stopped, perhaps he had seen a glint of metal in the sun, and appeared to be looking straight at McCain. At this distance, if the cripple's eyesight was good, he might even be able to see McCain lodged there in the breach of the cliff.

The cripple's face was filled with rage, and he said something McCain couldn't hear but could read on his lips: "You dirty sonofabitch." He clenched his fist and shook it at the mountain.

McCain let a little smile work at his lips for a moment. What the hell. He lowered the cross hairs.

But only to the center of the cripple's chest. Then he squeezed.

The impact of the bullet threw the cripple's body backwards against the wall. McCain watched with satisfaction as the dark spot on the cripple's shirt spread wider and wider and the expression on his face faded from rage to the foolish emptiness of the dead.

As the subject's wife came screaming through the door, McCain climbed from his place in the cliff, cased his instruments, and made his way through the woods.

Two for one this day. Maybe he'd get a bonus.

At any rate, he knew one bonus he would receive. He paused for a moment and closed his eyes. He could see Pearl's flawless young body lying there on the bed, could smell her rich female musk, taste its mellow sweetness. He smiled as he felt the tight, familiar burning itch begin to spread through his groin. He laughed a little. Oh, Lord, make me duly grateful for the bounty of your grace and ever mindful of the needs of others. Amen.

He started to walk again now, faster. And he began to whistle. *Amazing grace, how sweet the sound, that saved a wretch like me.* He tossed back his head now and laughed out loud.

Wouldn't his Bible-thumping daddy be proud of his son if only he could see him now. Amen, amen, and amen.

▽

9

JORDON SPRINTED UP THE wide front steps of the Buxton Building.

Striding down the hall toward the desk of HR Buxton's secretary outside the old man's office, Jordon was a man in extreme distress. Had he given it any thought at the time, he would have certainly known he looked it.

HR Buxton's secretary gave him a wide-eyed stare. "Mr. Jordon. May I help you?"

Without stopping, Jordon jerked his thumb toward Buxton's door. "I want to see him." He almost choked on his own voice.

She reached for her phone. "I'll see if he can talk with you."

"Never mind," Jordon said, opening the door to HR's office.

"Just a minute, *sir*," the woman said, jumping to her feet, "I'll see—"

When HR Buxton looked up to see Jordon heading toward him, his face registered astonishment. It suddenly occurred to Jordon that nobody, not even his secretary, walked into HR's office unannounced. Until now, that is.

"What the hell is this?" the old man said, quickly regaining his composure and voice of authority.

From the doorway, the secretary said, in a frantic voice, "Shall I call someone, Mr. Buxton?"

HR studied Jordon for a moment, then said, "No. Just close the door."

The woman hesitated.

"It's all right," Buxton said again, and waved her away.

She gave Jordon a nasty look before backing out and shutting the door.

"Well, now," HR said quietly. "What is it you want?"

It was all Jordon could do to control his voice. He felt like screaming the words, but he didn't. "Who killed Willis Dobbs?" His voice croaked. His vision blurred as he felt his eyes filling. He stood there, clenching and unclenching his fists.

HR met Jordon's stare and was silent for a moment before he spoke. "As God is my witness, I don't know."

"Then how the hell do you know he's dead?"

HR looked at the telephone on his desk and nodded. "I heard it a few minutes ago. The sheriff called. I understand it's been less than an hour since it happened."

Jordon nodded, struggling for control. His mind felt like a whirlpool, sucking him down into some unknown darkness.

"Why don't you sit down," HR said, indicating a chair, the same one Jordon had sat in not more than a week ago when they had talked about what kind of times might be coming to Stanton County. But on that day, Jordon had not thought it would be this. Not Willis.

HR reached into one of the large drawers of his desk and took out a bottle of bourbon, along with two glasses. He poured generous drinks in the glasses and handed one of them to Jordon. "Ordinarily, I don't drink this early in the day," HR said. "But then this is no ordinary day."

Jordon hesitated, took the glass, glanced at it, then turned it up and drained it in a single drink.

HR reached for Jordon's glass, poured another drink as large as the first one, and handed it back to Jordon, who set it on the edge of the desk.

HR sipped at his drink, opened his cigar humidor and took one out, and offered the box to Jordon, who shook his head. "I forgot," the old man said, "you don't use them, do you?"

Jordon stared at the floor.

HR lit his cigar, inhaled, and blew a stream of smoke

toward the window. "A nasty habit, some folks say, but one of the few I still enjoy."

Jordon looked up to see HR watching him. Now that he was here, he wasn't sure what he was going to do. When the call came that Willis had been shot, along with Turner Lott, and that both were dead, Jordon went crazy for a few minutes. All he could think of was, go to HR Buxton, grab him by the throat, and choke him until life left his body.

On the way here, Jordon had pictured himself doing it, imagined how he would feel as he did it. Now, sitting here, he realized how close he had come. He also realized how little he might ever have known then about Willis's murder, how little chance he might have had to avenge it, to get to the man who had actually pulled the trigger, as well as whoever had ordered it done.

"You came here to accuse me of having your friend murdered?" HR asked.

Jordon shook his head. "I came here thinking I'd kill you."

Buxton sat quietly for a long time. "And why don't you do it?"

"If I did, I might never find out who pulled the trigger. I want him as well as the one who set it up and paid for it."

HR puffed on his cigar. "And you still think I might have done that, in spite of what I told you?"

"Men lie," Jordon said. "And the more important the question, the more reason to lie about it."

"As I told you the other day, I like the way you cut through the horseshit to get to the heart of a matter. Yes, we all lie. But I'm not lying now about your friend Willis." Buxton leaned forward across his desk. "Listen carefully to me now. This is exactly the kind of thing I told you I did not want to happen here. You recall that, don't you?"

"That could have been a smoke screen for what you really want to do."

Buxton waved his hand, looking disgusted. "You know the phrase, *cui bono?*"

Jordon stared at him.

"*Cui bono?* Who benefits?" Buxton asked. "It's the first question I always ask when I'm trying to analyze anything. Ask yourself. Who benefits from the death of Turner Lott and Willis Dobbs? How do I benefit from that? Lott has been trying to help get the union organized here, I know that, and your friend Willis was helping some, too. I've known that for weeks, maybe months. That's one reason I wanted you to help me try to head this kind of thing off. You could have talked to them. Willis, at least."

"I don't know that any of what you're saying is true."

"Who benefits?" HR repeated. "Me? How? I want peace in Stanton County, not war. I know it will eventually come to a contract between me and the union. I'm willing to fight that out across the negotiating table, to wait them out as long as I have to. But I don't want my company and my mines and my town torn apart. I've already told you that."

Jordon reached for the glass of bourbon and took another drink. He should have done this before he came here. Maybe he would have approached this situation better prepared.

"So if it wasn't you, who was it?"

"Again, ask yourself the question, who benefits?"

"Who are you saying?"

HR shook his head. "I'm sorry, I don't know."

"Who, goddamn it, who?"

HR shrugged and looked sad. "Somebody who believes he will benefit from their deaths. Maybe even somebody who had some kind of personal grudge against them. That's not unheard of around here, you know that." HR took another drink of his bourbon. "This is a job for the law."

Jordon thought about Sheriff John Bill Trumble. He gave HR a disgusted look. "Shit," he said.

HR stood up and walked over to his big window, gazed out at the town square for a while, then back at Jordon and nodded. "Shit, indeed," he said.

They were both silent for a few minutes, then HR spoke. "So what happens now? Look, I don't like you any more than you like me. But think. Except for you and me, who else around here is going to try to avert a union war in Stanton County? And get to the bottom of the murder of Turner Lott and your friend Willis?"

Jordon said nothing, just sat staring at the old man.

"Goddammit man, answer me if you can," HR said, waving his cigar in an impatient gesture. "If not you and me, then by God, who?"

Jordon glared at HR Buxton, then slowly shook his head and heaved a great sigh.

10

Jordon took a cue from the rack and broke the balls without interest. He had just come from the graveyard and let himself into the poolroom through his living quarters in the back.

Della had closed down everything for Willis's funeral. Jordon was a pallbearer, but had avoided talking with anyone other than to nod and say hello. Willis had been a Freemason since he was a young man, and the other five pallbearers were members of his lodge. Wearing white aprons and gloves, they conducted a brief ceremony of their own, formal and dignified, with a sprig of acacia, in striking contrast to the emotional, draining service by the preacher. After helping to bear the coffin to the grave, Jordon stood off at the edge of the gathering in the Maple Grove Cemetery, where last fall he'd stood while the young girl, Bitsy Trotter, was being buried. He listened absently to the preacher's final words, and watched Willis's body being lowered into the earth. He left then without saying anything to anybody.

As Willis was being buried in the cemetery at Buxton, Turner Lott's funeral was taking place in the old Lott family cemetery across Little Horse Creek.

Now, less than an hour later, Jordon aimed at a ball—it didn't matter which one—stroked his cue, and shot. The ball fell in a corner pocket, making a loud clunk in the silence of the empty room.

Yesterday evening, Jordon had gone by Willis's home to pay his respects. Lying there in the front room in a plain pine box and his blue serge suit, a serene expression on his face, Willis did not look like himself. He was always so brimming with life, how could he be expected to look natural as an empty corpse? But then, to Jordon, the dead never looked like the people they were supposed to be.

Turning away from the coffin, feeling only numbness mixed with hatred for whoever had murdered his buddy, Jordon approached Willis's wife, Etta, hoping in some way to comfort and reassure her. She sat, dry-eyed and passive, off to one side of the room. Jordon glanced around, didn't see Willis's two young daughters anywhere.

"He ought to be alive," Etta said, as if talking to herself. "This fight wasn't his, I told him that, more than once. He hadn't worked in the mines for years. But he never could forget that that's where he lost his leg, down there in the dark with the damp and the rats and the filth and the bad air. And the men wondering who'd be the next to go, never really believing it might be them. Willis always said it was a lot worse than it had to be. If the operators would loosen up a little bit more, they could keep it from being as bad as it is. And let a man make a decent living for his family. That's what Willis always said. He believed the companies would have to pay more attention to the men if they got the union."

Jordon had known Etta for years, but now he didn't know how to speak to her. Finally he said, "He was my friend, Etta. I owed him my life. I'll always be here, whenever you need me." His own voice sounded stilted and odd to him. Feeling helpless and clumsy, he put his arm around her and hugged her, felt her stiffen, as if, by controlling the movement of her body, she also controlled her emotions.

He left her then, stepping quietly through the house filled with neighbors and friends, some of whom would stay until dawn. "Settin' up with the dead" was a custom as old as the mountains.

Going out through the little kitchen, Jordon saw the table was laden with food, just plain ordinary grub that friends and neighbors had scraped together and carried in. He saw a stoop-shouldered, gaunt old man with wispy white hair and knobby hands standing alongside a frail-looking old woman whose pallor was stunning. Her face looked dry as parchment and was covered with a network of tiny wrinkles. She looked as though her body had been drained of blood. They stood there by the table, eating green beans, green onions, boiled potatoes, and cornbread from tin plates they held in their hands. The old man looked at Jordon with a wan smile as he passed by.

Jordon stepped through the back door and made his way around the outside of the house. In the dim light from the bare bulb hanging on the front porch, three or four little clusters of men stood smoking and talking in low voices. Some of them glanced toward Jordon and nodded as he passed, but nobody spoke.

Then, when he was almost out of the yard, Jordon spotted Emerson Calhoun, one of Willis's uncles, standing off to himself, puffing on a pipe near the corner of the porch. Jordon didn't know the man well, but he knew Willis had loved and respected him. Jordon walked over to him with his hand extended. "You remember me? I'm Berk Jordon," he said. "A friend of Willis's."

Emerson was wearing a dark suit coat and a pair of clean bib overalls with a blue work shirt buttoned up to the top. He took Jordon's hand and gave it a firm shake. "I know who you are."

"You got time to talk to me a little bit?" Jordon asked.

Emerson, who was about the same size as Jordon, but older and thinner, puffed on his pipe and nodded.

Jordon took him by the arm and steered him away from where they could be heard by the others, off into the darkness.

Emerson's voice was soft, but strong, when he said, "If you're anything a'tall like what Willis thought, you ain't taking this too easy."

Jordon looked at the ground and shook his head. "You have any idea who might have done it? And why?"

Emerson sucked on his pipe, though it had gone out and

he had not relit it. It was a long time before he replied. "I may end up being sorry for this," he said, "but if you give me your word it won't go any further, I'll rely on that."

"Is it about Willis getting killed?"

Emerson nodded.

"You've got my word, if that's good enough for you."

"It was good enough for Willis. And that's good enough for me." Emerson knocked the ashes from his pipe against the sole of his shoe, then refilled it from a can of Prince Albert that he took from the bib of his overalls. "You know Willis was trying to help organize the union." It was a statement, not a question.

Jordon nodded.

"So am I. Matter of fact, it was me got Willis started in it. I knowed how he felt, and I knowed he'd help. So, one way of looking at it, I got him killed."

"I don't think you can say that."

"I know what I know," Emerson said. "Anyhow, if you're serious about finding out who killed him, and doing something about it, I might be able to point you in the right direction, and we might be able to help each other."

"I'm serious. What can you tell me?"

"Nothing tonight. I'll have to clear it with some of the others before I do anything else."

"I understand."

"I'll be in touch with you, if the others agree. If they don't, then we never had this talk. That's the end of it as far as you're concerned. All right?"

"Why wouldn't the others agree?"

Emerson gave Jordon a straight hard look. "Some don't trust you. They say you've done straddled the fence too long. Some even think you might be working for Buxton. You know Turner Lott was my nephew, too?"

"I hadn't thought about it, but I knew he and Willis were cousins. Look, I'm not working for Buxton, and Willis damn sure knew that. I'd be grateful for whatever help I can get. But whatever you decide, as far as it ever being the end of it for me, that won't be until I get ahold of whoever killed Willis."

Emerson struck a match and fired his pipe. "You and me both. I'll be in touch."

"Soon?"

"Soon."

Now, as Jordon set up another shot on the pool table, stroked, and missed, he wondered how long it would be before Emerson got in touch with him. He racked his cue and sighed. As much as he hated to wait, he knew he could not rush Emerson.

He pulled a chair to the window and sat in the semidarkness of the poolroom and stared out into the brightness of Della's compound. He tried to get a fix on some other approach to finding who killed Willis.

As HR Buxton had said, you have to start by asking, "Who benefits?"

As much as he hated to admit it, Jordon knew HR was right about trying to prevent a bloodbath in Stanton County. If not Jordon and HR, who else would even make the effort? And if things had been ready to blow sky-high before, it was a hell of a lot worse now.

Jordon tried to tell himself it didn't make much difference to him who else might get killed. With Willis dead, Jordon's only other real friend was Black Cory Holcomb, who ran a joint at Stateline. Aside from Black Cory, now the only other person Jordon felt any closeness to at all was Cassie. And she didn't want to be close to him, it seemed. Anyway, with a woman, you could only get so close, however much you might want to. And there had been times with Cassie when he had wanted that more than anything. But it seemed to him that nature had put an invisible shield between the sexes. Why it was that way, he had no idea. Unless maybe it was there to offer them a little protection. Sometimes it seemed to Jordon that the biggest thing nature had given men and women was the power to hurt one another.

Cass had called this morning to say she was sorry about

Willis. "I cared about him, too, Berk," she said, "but not like you. I know you and Willis thought the world of each other."

"I loved him," Jordon said. "As much as a man can love another man, I reckon. But I never once actually came out and said it to him." Jordon felt his voice about to break. "I can't talk about it anymore right now, Cass."

She waited a moment. "Call me if you need me. And don't worry about not telling Willis how you felt about him. I'm sure he knew," she said. After a short pause, she added, "He knew." Then she hung up.

Remembering his talk with Cassie brought it all back now. Jordon took out his handkerchief, blew his nose, and wiped his eyes.

Looking across the compound, he saw Della come around the corner of the restaurant building and head toward the poolroom. She wore the same black dress she'd had on at the funeral, and with her jet black hair, her creamy skin, and bright red lipstick, her appearance was dazzling. Alongside her, dressed in overall pants and a blue work shirt, was the lanky young fellow who played the guitar in the little string band that entertained when Della's Place packed them in on Friday and Saturday nights.

John P. Hall was his name, but everybody had taken to calling him Slim. He was one of the quiet, easygoing Halls who had lived in Stanton County for generations. Jordon remembered how he'd thought there might be something going on between young Slim and Cassie for a while last fall. As it had turned out, the "something" had evidently been between Slim and Della. And Jordon's and Cassie's problems had been of their own making, or rather his own making, at least from Cassie's point of view.

Jordon heard Della put her key in the front door lock and turn it. She opened the door and stepped inside, followed by Slim. She looked around, spotted Jordon sitting by the window, and said, "I figured I might find you here." As the two of them approached him, Jordon stood up.

"Just sitting here thinking," he said.

Della nodded. "I don't want to seem hasty or unfeeling," she said, "but you're going to be needing some help over here now that Willis is . . . gone."

Jordon was having trouble concentrating on what she was talking about.

"And," she went on, "I figured Slim could help out."

Jordon still was trying to get his thoughts focused on what she was saying.

"We all know that nobody can replace Willis," she said, her voice taking on a businesslike edge. "But you got to have somebody. And Slim is available."

Even after he understood, Jordon was at a loss for something to say. So he just looked at Della, then at Slim, then back at Della.

"Something wrong with that?" Della asked.

Jordon shrugged. "It's your business."

Her impatience showed clearly on her face now. "That's not exactly what I wanted to hear. I'd like some indication that you agree with me. Unless for some reason you don't."

Jordon spread his hands, palms up. "What do you want me to say, Della?" Jordon really didn't feel like dealing with it now. "If it's what you want, fine. I'm sure Slim will be fine. Okay?"

Della shook her head, seemed exasperated. "Sure." She looked at Slim, who had not spoken a word since he came in. "You two talk. I've got work to do in my office." She gave Jordon another stern look, turned, and left. He watched her through the window, striding across the distance to the restaurant, shoulders back, arms swinging, tossing her head like a beautiful, fractious filly.

Jordon sat down and looked at Slim. After a moment, he said, "Pull up a chair, boy."

Slim carried a chair over and placed it where he could look at Jordon.

After staring out the window some more, Jordon finally said, "How much do you know about running a poolroom?"

Slim shrugged. He scratched his shock of dark straight

hair that always looked as if it could use a little more time with a comb. His high cheekbones and olive skin made him look like he might have Indian blood in him. "What is there to know?" he asked. "You rack the balls, you collect the money. Maybe you fix somebody a hot dog or get them a pack of rubbers. Is there something else?"

Jordon slowly turned his head a couple of degrees and gave Slim a cold, sidelong glance. "You wouldn't be trying to devil me a little, would you, boy?"

Slim gave him a level look. "No sir. But you think you could call me something else besides 'boy'?"

"That bothers you?"

"It depends on the situation. If it's said like, 'that boy and girl,' or 'one of the boys' or something like that, I don't mind. But not the way you're doing it."

"You want to tell me how you think I'm doing it?"

"Well, it seems like you're using it to say maybe I'm not up to what I'm taking on, something like that."

Jordon studied him for a long while. At last he said, "That's not how I meant it, and if it sounded that way to you, I apologize. That ought to bother you. It would me, too."

"I doubt that you run into the problem."

Jordon's face loosened up a little. "You're right, I don't. Not for a while now. But tell me, seeing we're kind of on the subject, how old are you?"

Slim smiled, and when he did, showing a mouthful of straight white teeth, his eyes squinted almost shut. "Twenty-two."

"Well, I reckon I don't have to tell you it takes more than years to make a man."

"My Uncle Ben taught me that a long time ago."

"He's one who knows," Jordon said. "So you figure you can rack balls and take care of the money and sell hot dogs and rubbers. You also have to brush the tables every day, sweep the floor, cover the tables up at night, patch the cushion when some ham-handed dimwit or half-drunk show-off rips it, retip the cues, and a few other little things. Plus keep order."

Slim nodded. "I can do all that. Or learn pretty fast."

"Tell me, what have you been doing?"

"Teaching, up until April."

"Teaching? Where?"

"Fisher's Branch. A one-room school."

"How long?"

"Last term was my second."

"You going back to it in the fall?"

"It depends. I decided to try Della's offer."

Jordon nodded. So it had been Della's idea. "Okay. Looks like it's you and me, for the time being. So be it." Looking steadily at Slim, Jordon said, "I have no problem with it, son." With mock concern, he quickly added, "You have any objection to me calling you 'son' if it comes out that way once in a while?"

Slim's face around his eyes crinkled with his broad smile. "I reckon not." After a moment, he added, "Okay if I call you 'pop'?"

"You by God try it and see how far you get," Jordon said.

Slim held up his hand and laughed. "Just testing."

Suddenly, Jordon realized he was feeling a little better. "You're right. You are a fast learner." He turned to go outside.

Slim said, "You didn't mention the games in back."

Jordon turned back around. "How much do you know about craps and poker?"

"A little."

"Blackjack?"

"A little."

"You need to know a hell of a lot more than a little to be able to run those games, son."

"You could teach me the rest. Like I said, I'm—"

Jordon held up his hand. "Yeah, yeah, you're a fast learner." Jordon again turned to leave, then asked, "Why do you want to learn to gamble?"

"Everything you do in life's a gamble, they say. I'd just as soon know how to do it as well as I can."

"That's one way to look at it."

"It's the way you look at it, isn't it?"

Jordon saw the young man was watching him intently. "More or less."

Slim pressed on. "What do you say?"

"About what?"

"You going to teach me?"

Just before he stepped out the door, Jordon looked back over his shoulder and said, "Have a little patience."

Slim grinned at him. "Does that mean you will? Teach me?"

Jordon shook his head, as if he were exasperated. Actually, he was impressed with this young fellow. He didn't give up easily. "I'll do some thinking about it," Jordon said.

$\triangledown$

11

MOODY McCAIN GASPED FOR air like a fish out of water.

He had just finished with Pearl. He had mounted her from behind, doing most of the work, and the midmorning heat in the little house was fierce.

He sprawled on his back now, collected the sweat from his forehead with an index finger, and slung it off on the floor.

"How was it, honey?" Pearl asked. "Good?"

"Like the man said, Pearl, when it's good, it's great," McCain said between huge, rasping gulps of the hot humid air. "And when it's bad, it's still pretty good."

She laughed. "I'm glad I make you feel good."

They lay quietly for a while as McCain's breathing began to slow and become regular.

Pearl spoke again. "Mooooody?"

Oh, shit, McCain said to himself. "What?"

"Honey, don't get mad at me, please. But since we're going to be maybe staying on here for a while longer, could we go out somewhere, just for a little while, some night? Where there's music and people. It's awful being cooped up here by myself all the time."

"I'm here with you."

"I know it, honey," she said, rubbing her hand along his thigh. "And I love being with you, but you're away a lot. And I get so lonesome, I can't hardly stand it."

He said nothing. Now that the business with Turner Lott was finished, he would have left Stanton County, except that he now had been told that perhaps there was more work to be done. Something involving a really important subject, a job that would command a premium fee.

After he had taken care of the one-legged boy from the poolroom when he eliminated Turner Lott, McCain had thought he might get a bonus. Instead, he got what could have turned into a chastisement had McCain been willing to stand still for it. He made it clear, however, that it was done and over, that he would not be criticized for the way he did his job. That ended it.

Now, since he was going to be here until the new assignment was decided on, he had to think of how was the best way to handle Pearl. He could listen to her whine. Or he could hurt her a little, make her shut up. But that could also make her withdraw, become sullen, and perform less well sexually. Or, he could relent a little, take her out somewhere, and pacify her. He could not, quite yet, think about getting rid of her permanently. He required her services for as long as they were here, until he could get to some city and pick up a replacement.

Moody put his hand on her belly and gently rubbed it. "Pearl, I've decided. I'm going to take you out someplace."

Her voice was excited. "Where, honey? Where?"

"Lexington. I'm going to take you to supper in the best restaurant in town and then we'll stay all night in the Phoenix Hotel."

"When?"

"How about next week?"

"Will we go on the train?"

"Of course."

She snuggled up against him, rubbing her crotch against his leg. "Can I wear my red dress?"

"No," he said. "Wear the green one."

"Why not the red one? I like it. And you do too."

"Because," he said, "I want you to wear the red one somewhere else."

"Where, Moody? Tell me."

"A place called Della's."

"Della's?"

"Right here. Stanton County."

"When?"

"This Friday night."

"We can dance and have a few drinks, and have fun, right?"

"Right," he said. Then, "How do you know Della's is a dancing and drinking place? Who told you that?"

Her response was a little slow, he thought.

"Nobody told me, honey. I just thought that . . . well, if you wanted me to wear the red dress, it must be someplace like that. Am I right?"

"Yeah, Pearl. You're right."

They lay quietly for a while, then she put her hand on his leg near his knee and began playing her fingers upward, higher and higher. He could feel her hand trembling. "You want to do it again, now, Moody? I could do the work this time."

Moody didn't say anything. But a moment later, he took a handful of her hair and pulled her head to his crotch.

▽

12

As HE HAD BEEN INSTRUCTED to do, Jordon drove through the night past the long row of camp houses at Chambers and parked his car down the road a piece, near the church.

After waiting with his lights out for ten minutes, he walked back past the coal tipple, which stood out against the night sky like a giant spindly-legged praying mantis. He made his way to the fourth house from the commissary, which, like the rest of the houses in the camp, was totally dark. He paused for a moment, then stepped up on the porch and knocked gently, two long, three short, two long.

From inside the door, a man's voice whispered, "Who is it?"

Jordon whispered back. "Jordon."

"What do you want?"

Jordon spoke the words he had been told to say. "There's an old buddy I need to see."

The door opened and a short, wiry man in overalls stepped out onto the porch, closing the door behind him. He looked Jordon over for a moment, then scanned the narrow cinder-covered street both ways. Apparently satisfied, he whispered, "Come on. Be as quiet as you can. And don't say nothing."

Jordon nodded and followed the man off the porch and around to the backyard. They picked their way carefully, with no light, through the little garden plot, past the fetid outhouse and a small chicken coop, then on toward the mountain that loomed in back of the camp. The moon was behind a cloud bank, and the going was slow. Somewhere down the row of camp houses, a dog threw a few weak challenges, got no response, then gave it up.

As they made their way through the dense woods, Jordon remembered it was still dog days. Thoughts of hot dreary afternoons and bloody milk and bad water didn't much bother him right now. What kept flashing through his mind were pictures of deadly blind rattlesnakes.

Twenty minutes later, Jordon and his guide made their way, slipping and sliding and holding on to saplings and underbrush, down a steep slope and around the end of a massive rock formation. No word had been spoken by either of them since they left the porch.

Halfway down the bank, Jordon's guide stopped. Through the woods, Jordon could hear the rush of the creek below. The guide whistled like a whippoorwill. He listened for a moment, heard a hoot owl call in response, then continued the descent.

At the bottom, Jordon was led along the base of the formation to a crevice, then through it into a small open area. Here he could see somebody had built a crude shelter by walling up the front of a natural cavern under the cliff.

Cracks of light seeped out through the boards, along with the sound of muffled voices.

The guide stepped up to the cliffhouse, pecked lightly on the door, and said, "It's Miller." Without waiting for a reply, he pulled open the rough door and entered. Jordon followed.

The room was lit only by a coal oil lantern that sat on a small table. And though the wick was turned low and the light was dim, it took a few moments for Jordon's eyes to make the adjustment from the night outside.

Nothing had been done to the rock house except for the one pine-slab wall. The rest of the enclosure was made by the natural contours of the cavern, and the floor was fine, dry dusty earth, a place that neither rain nor sun had ever reached.

None of the half-dozen men who sat around on rocks or rickety chairs made any move to greet Jordon. The man who

had brought him here went to a corner and sat down without
a word.

Jordon scanned the faces of the men. All of them wore
serious, intent expressions, but Jordon saw nothing he
would interpret as fear or uncertainty. What he saw mostly
was what he would have described as determination. Some
of the men were familiar to him, a couple of them he remembered seeing during the incident outside the drugstore the
other day. But he didn't really know any of them well. All
were miners, dressed in overalls and work shirts. Some wore
their miner's caps, others shapeless felt hats. Though no
guns were visible except for the Smith & Wesson revolver, a
.44 special it looked like, lying by the lantern on the little
table, Jordon instinctively knew that each man there was
probably armed. As he himself was. Almost every man in
the mountains carried a pistol these days. Most were Smith
or Colt revolvers, .38s or .44s, a few had .45 automatics, and
a few carried cheaper guns, such as the Iver-Johnson, or
"owlhead."

Jordon ended his survey of the room when his eyes locked
on the eyes of Emerson Calhoun, who sat behind the little
table with the lantern and the gun. Jordon nodded slightly
at him and said, "Emerson."

Emerson said, "Come over here and set by me." He indi-
cated an empty, well-worn cane-bottom chair beside him. It
had been reserved just for him, Jordon figured. The hot seat.

Jordon took his chair, and Emerson said, "You all know
Jordon from when he was running for high sheriff last fall."
Most of the men nodded, but none said anything.

Emerson made no mention of who the others were. "Jordon was a buddy of Willis's," he said. "They fit in the war
together, in France." He looked at Jordon.

Jordon nodded, but said nothing.

Emerson went on. "Jordon asked me the other night if I
might be able to help him learn who it was killed Willis and
Turner. And you all agreed it was all right to bring him here."
Emerson paused, "On my say-so." He stared directly at

Jordon and said, "I vouched for him then. And I vouch for him now. Willis trusted him. And on account of that, I do too."

Emerson stopped for what seemed at first to be a pause, but then as it went on, Jordon realized the older man wasn't going to say anything further at the moment.

Nobody else said anything either.

After a long silence, Jordon spoke. "I'm much obliged to you, Emerson, for what you said about me, and for bringing me here. Mostly, I appreciate you trusting me." Jordon's eyes scanned the group. "Willis Dobbs was my friend. My best friend. He saved my life. Not once, but twice. There's never been a man walked the face of the earth that I thought more of than Willis. For whatever it's worth to you, I'd die and go straight to hell tonight before I'd do something that'd dishonor him."

Again there was silence in the room. Then one of the men cleared his throat. He was a big man, heavyset and tall. He looked to Jordon to be well over six feet. He had several days' growth of grizzled beard on his long, sad-looking face and a cud of tobacco in his jaw. Jordon had glanced at him before, as the big man would spit from time to time in a tin can at his feet.

When the big man spoke, his voice low and gravelly, he looked Jordon straight in the eye. "Some say you are a Buxton man."

Jordon sighed. Don't beat around the bush, man, he thought. Come right on out with it. He waited for a moment before answering, then met the big man's stare. "They're wrong," he said simply.

For a long time the big man studied him. "You know old man Buxton, though, do you?"

"I know him. I've known who he is for a lot of years, like everybody else around here. But I only got involved with him personally last fall when he helped get me beat in the election."

"You talk to him, do you?"

"During the election, yes. Several times."

The big man spit in his can. "Lately?" he asked without looking up.

Jordon watched him. "A couple of times."

"You mind saying what it was about?" the big man asked in his rumbling voice.

Jordon could see the others watching him intently. Hell, he decided, might as well lay it all on the line. "I reckon not. He asked me to help him try to keep things from turning into a bloodbath in Stanton County."

"And what did you tell him?"

Again, Jordon paused, then said quietly, "I told him I've got no horse in this race." When nobody said anything, Jordon added, "Which is the same thing I told Willis when he wanted me to get involved with what he was doing."

Several of the men looked at one another, some of them nodding.

A lanky man with a leathery face and bushy hair and eyebrows asked, "What was it, exactly, that HR Buxton wanted you to do?"

"I can't say, exactly," Jordon replied. "He seems to think I've got influence with some folks around here, and I guess he thought maybe I could try to talk against men taking up guns against the company. And talk in favor of coming to terms on a contract with him. Something like that is about as much as I could make out of it."

One of the men who had been silent said, "Ain't nobody with enough sense to come in out of the rain wants to get into a shootin' war with a bunch of company gun thugs. Ain't nobody wants no bloodbath. And no strike neither. We're all in favor of a contract." He waited a moment, then added, "But it's got to be fair. And if we end up going out on strike, we ain't going to let no scabs come in and work our jobs."

Several others nodded. "They won't be one lump of coal pulled out of the holler if we go on strike," one of them said. "Any scabs go into the mines they'll have to walk in over our dead bodies."

Another man said, "And we ain't going to hump up and

let Buxton or nobody else have us picked off one by one like they done to Turner and Willis. We ain't squirrels settin' in a hickory tree fixin' to be seasonin' for somebody's dumplins."

Jordon nodded. "If I could prove HR Buxton had anything to do with what happened to Willis, he wouldn't get a chance to do it to anybody else."

The big man watched Jordon for a moment. "Did HR offer to pay you for what he wanted you to do?"

Jordon nodded. "He did."

"And?"

"I said no." Jordon noticed out of the corner of his eye that Emerson was puffing on his pipe, watching and listening to everything that went on. But he showed no inclination to enter into the discussion. Or grilling, as it was turning out to be.

Once more the big man spoke. "How come you turned him down?"

Jordon waited a moment, then glanced around the room at the others before staring into the eyes of the big miner. "For one thing, I told him that if I took his money and went out and tried to talk his line for him, then any influence I might have would disappear like a fart in a windstorm."

A couple of the men grinned. But not the big miner.

Jordon went on. "And I also told him I aimed to mind my own business and stay out of this fight. And keep on running my game at Della's Place."

When nobody responded, Jordon added, "And that's exactly what I'd be doing if it wasn't for Willis being killed."

"What about Turner Lott?"

"With all due respect to Turner, he was not a friend of mine. He played poker at my table sometimes, that's about it. But, like I said, Willis was something else again. I aim to find out who killed him. And he's going to pay for it." Jordon paused a moment before adding, "You can mark my word on that."

Nobody spoke.

"I was hoping," Jordon said, "that some of you all might—"

At that moment, three rapid gunshots punctured the silence outside, then silence again.

All eyes focused on Emerson and Jordon at the table. Emerson himself stared at Jordon. Then he said, "Come on. That's Billy's signal."

Jordon said, "Billy?"

"Our lookout," Emerson said. "Somebody's coming that ain't expected."

The other men were already leaving, some of them pausing long enough to give Jordon a final hard look.

Emerson blew out the lantern and stepped outside with Jordon. "Stick close behind me," the older man whispered. "Hold onto my galluses till we get out of here."

As they groped their way through the darkness, Jordon wondered where all this business was going to take him to. It was becoming more and more likely, he felt, that he was going to be caught right in the center of the storm that was brewing over the mountains of Stanton County, regardless of what he might want personally.

Hell, maybe he ought to just quit trying to stay out of it. He knew he couldn't stop until he got Willis's murderer. And that seemed to be leading him into the middle of all the rest of it.

Holding on to the back of Emerson's overalls and trailing behind him through the darkness, Jordon stumbled and almost fell, nearly pulling Emerson down with him.

"Try to stay off of your knees," Emerson said drily. "We got a ways to go before we're out of the woods."

▽

13

WHEN THEY ARRIVED IN Corbin, Jordon pulled into the hotel parking lot, cut the motor, and looked at Della She checked her watch and said, "It's a quarter till eight. I'll be having a private supper with some people here. Take the car and get something to eat. Entertain yourself for the next three hours and meet me back here in the lobby at eleven. If I'm not here, wait for me in the coffee shop." She paused. "Okay?"

Jordon nodded. This lady gave orders like an infantry captain. But a pretty good one, he thought with a little grin. She knew what she wanted, and she knew how to get you to do it, in such a way that you didn't mind, most of the time. A considerable bundle of assets when you thought about it.

"You're smiling," she said. "Did I forget something?" She was dressed in a simple navy blue dress that clung to the contours of her body and revealed enough of it to make certain she was not going to be ignored at whatever kind of meeting she was going to. Her only accessories were a red belt and a little gold spider with ruby eyes, pinned near the open collar of her dress.

"Forget something?" he said. "Not that I know of. See you at eleven."

She got out of the car and went inside, and Jordon drove slowly up Main Street, enjoying the solid feel of the sleek black Buick Eight underneath him. Della had good taste in most things, including automobiles. And, in sharp contrast to most people these days, the lady evidently had the wherewithal to indulge herself.

On the way over here, they had talked very little, mostly about how hot it was and how edgy things were becoming around Stanton County. "I'll sure be glad when this union business is settled one way or the other," she said. Jordon replied, "Be better for a lot of miners and their families if they get a decent contract." She had looked at him with curiosity. "I thought your favorite remark was that you've got no horse in that race," she said. He sighed and answered, "Yeah," and left it at that.

Now, after driving the length of Main Street and back, just looking over the town, Jordon pulled the car in to the curb near a small restaurant. Corbin wasn't all that far from Buxton, and he'd been there many times before, but for Jordon it was always a treat to visit the small city in the foothills of the mountains. He'd seen it alive with business generated by the railroad repair shops here. In recent times, however, it was subdued, showing many of the same signs of the Depression as everyplace else—empty stores and out-of-work men, desperately broke, wandering aimlessly along the streets, or standing in little clusters, chewing tobacco, talking and whittling.

Jordon went inside the restaurant and sat down at the counter. He looked at the handwritten menu and asked the bored-looking young woman how the chicken-and-dumplings was.

"Swell," she said without enthusiasm.

"Really?"

She shrugged. "I'm supposed to say that about everything."

He ordered. When the chicken-and-dumplings came it wasn't exactly swell, but it wasn't too bad either. The only other customers in the place were an elderly couple at a table in the corner and a man in faded overalls, a battered gray hat, and about two weeks' growth of beard. He hunched silently over a coffee cup at the other end of the counter. On the radio near the cash register, a man with a lazy, rusty-sounding voice sang something about stars falling on Alabama. The girl behind the counter filed her bright red nails.

Jordon took two bites of chicken, not touching the corn-bread or green beans or sliced yellow tomato, yet knowing he needed to eat. But if he'd had no appetite before Willis was killed, he had even less now. He stood up and spoke to the girl. "How much?"

"Something wrong?"

He shook his head and put his hand on his belly. "My gut."

She said, "Twenty cents."

He paid her and left a ten-cent tip, which brought life to her face for the first time. "You from around here?" she asked.

Jordon shook his head. "Passing through."

As he was leaving, Jordon glanced down the counter at the unshaven man, who appeared not to have moved an inch. He looked as if he was probably hungry, and Jordon wished he could offer his uneaten supper to the man, but he knew better.

Outside, Jordon left the car parked and wandered up the street toward the moving-picture theater on the other side. The posters said Wallace Beery and Jackie Cooper were play-ing in *Treasure Island*. *Of Human Bondage*, with Leslie How-ard and Bette Davis, would be there next week. Jordon turned away and ambled back toward the car.

So far, since Willis's murder, Jordon had not been able to learn anything of value about who had killed him. Nobody seemed to know anything. Following the meeting with the miners under the cliff the other night, he had not been able to get with Emerson Calhoun again.

This first trip with Della to one of her meetings might have been a pleasure under other circumstances, but as it was, Jordon felt edgy, frustrated.

He drove back to the hotel, parked in the lot, and sat staring into the night. A dozen or so other cars were there, mostly Chevys and Fords, a couple of Model A's and some later models. Parked near the front of the lot, under the light from the hotel's sign, was a shiny gray Packard sedan. Next to it sat a Buick like Della's, and next to it a Cadillac.

Jordon began to feel drowsy. He slouched down in the seat and, after a few minutes, dozed off. And there, as if she'd been waiting for him, the big white mare grazed in the lush, green sunshiny field. Then, lazily, she turned and looked at him, started her slow walk in his direction. She began to trot, then picked up speed until she was galloping headlong for him.

He turned, as he had done in so many dreams before, and tried to run, but his legs moved as if they were weighted down.

He strained to run, to escape, but it was no use. She kept gaining, gaining, and when she reached him, as she always did, she reared up on her hind legs and began to strike, slashing at him with her hooves. He stood frozen in fear and shame. He knew it was a dream, knew if he could will himself awake, it would be over.

Just before she struck him, he heard himself cry out as he came awake.

He wiped the sweat from his face and looked around the parking lot to see if anyone had heard him. He was alone. This was the same dream he'd had all his life, forewarning him, it seemed, of every bad thing that ever happened to him. He'd had it before he was wounded in combat in the Philippines during the Insurrection, again before he'd killed the two men at Stateline, and when Vera died while he was in prison, and in the war in France before he has wounded there. And last year, during the business over the murder of Bitsy Trotter. Over and over, the goddamned white mare kept coming back to him in his dreams.

He was not superstitious, damn it. At least he didn't think he was. Yet this dream, with the devil's own white mare, always disturbed him, made him anxious. And almost always it was followed by some kind of trouble. After months of leaving him alone, the white mare had started coming again before Willis was killed.

Jordon took out his gold pocket watch. It was almost eleven. He'd slept longer than he thought.

He went inside the hotel and took a seat in the coffee shop

off the lobby. A lone waitress was folding napkins. He ordered coffee. He'd need it during the drive back to Buxton.

He was studying the red squares in the tablecloth, tracing them with the handle of his spoon, when Della pulled out a chair and sat down.

"Some meeting," she said with a great sigh. "But definitely worth the effort."

Jordon looked at her. Except for the hint of fatigue in her eyes, she still looked and sounded as good as she had when they'd set out for Corbin late this afternoon.

"Want some coffee?" he asked.

She glanced around the room, seemed to be thinking it over. "You know what I'd really like?"

He shook his head.

"A good, stiff, cold highball. Bourbon, with some Coke and ice."

"Didn't you have drinks at your meeting?"

"They did, but I wanted to keep a clear head with those old boys."

"I'm sure I can find some whiskey around here. But it might not be the best bourbon in the state."

She smiled. "No matter. Outside in the trunk of my car is a small leather bag. Why don't you get it and bring it up to the suite where we had our meeting. Number two twenty-four. And I'll get the girl over there to send up some ice and Cokes."

"Nothing like being prepared," he said.

When he got upstairs to the suite, she already had the ice. He scanned the big sitting room. In addition to a long gray sofa and some overstuffed easy chairs, it had been set up with a small bar and half a dozen padded armchairs that squatted around a large round table. Ashtrays were running over, dirty dishes, empty glasses, and cups were everywhere, and the unpleasant odor of stale tobacco smoke hung in the air.

Jordon's eyes traveled to the big plush round rug on the floor. It was blue, but it must have had a dozen shades in it, running all through its pattern of circles within circles, down to a blur in the center.

"Open the window and let this place air out," Della said. "I'll fix us a drink."

"Make mine straight," Jordon said.

"Like the man himself, huh?" She smiled at him when she said it.

Jordon gave her a speculative look. "What's that supposed to mean?"

"Loosen up a little, will you?" she said. "Life is short, and parts of it, at least, ought to be sweet."

Jordon sighed as he reached for the generous drink of bourbon she had poured into a glass. "I seem tight to you?"

She laughed and took a long pull on her highball. "About like a banjo string is all."

Jordon took a seat on one of the armchairs at the table, pushed an ashtray and some glasses out of the way, and set his drink down. Della crossed to the sofa where she collapsed, kicked off her high heels, and pulled her legs up underneath her.

"It's not exactly a good time for me," he said.

"I know. You need to try to relax a little more now and then."

"I've got a few things to take care of. Then I'll relax."

"I make it a point to do some relaxing as I go along. One thing I've learned about life is that you don't know how long you're going to be here. Put off doing things you'd like to do, and you may never get the chance."

He drained about half his drink. At thirty-three, she sounded like she was pushing a hundred. "Yeah," he said quietly. He looked at her and tried to smile, but it didn't come. "I've noticed that." Suddenly, for no apparent reason, he thought about Cassie, wondering what she might be doing, who she might be with. After a moment, he said, "Maybe what I need is a little more romance in my life."

She smiled and shook her head slowly. "I think that's one of your problems."

"I need romance?"

"No. Your problem is, you're a romantic."

"What's that supposed to mean?"

"You've bought into the romance game, and it keeps you from enjoying yourself."

He didn't understand, but he decided to let it pass.

Della, however, wasn't through with it. "You know what I'm talking about?"

"I guess not." He crossed to the bar and poured himself another drink. She finished the rest of hers and held out her glass. He took it and made her another.

"I think you tend to idealize everything," she said, "and that takes most of the fun out of it for you."

He didn't really feel like being picked apart tonight, but she seemed determined to see it through.

She took a long pull of her highball. "Here's an example," she said. "Take what goes on between men and women. People, mostly preachers, but others too, have always tried to tell us that we can do all kinds of things with one another and it's okay. We can eat together, and walk together, and swim and hold hands and kiss a little. But when it comes to sex, then we have to draw the line. Without true love and romance, and the blessing of the preacher, and the permission of the state, it's supposed to somehow be shallow, without meaning or purpose. It's not nice to do it just for the sake of pleasure. And so they've taken the fun out of it for folks who listen to them."

Jordon looked at her. "What's your point?"

"I think you've swallowed the whole thing, hook, line, and sinker."

He was beginning to get irritated. "How come you're such an expert on me all of a sudden?"

She smiled. "Just tell me, am I wrong?"

"Look, darlin', maybe I was just married the one time," he said. "And I don't mean to brag, but I've known a few women in my time."

She sipped her drink. "Oh, I'm sure you have. More than a few, I expect. Handsome fellow like you. With all your manly qualities and easy charm. I'm sure you have. But the problem is, you've always felt just a little tarnished by it, haven't you? Unless it's all wrapped up with true love and romance, you figure it's not quite proper. Right?"

Who the hell does she think she is, he thought. Tarnished? Not quite proper? "How'd you ever get such a crazy notion, woman?"

Della sipped her drink and held the cold glass to her cheek. "I've known men like you before. Oh, they like women well enough. Some of them even spend most of their time and money pursuing them, but down deep they still think like little boys, think they're being naughty. Maybe they still remember what their mamas told them about it being dirty to play with their pee-pee. Or maybe it's just part of nature's plan for men like you to be born romantics." She took another sip of her bourbon and Coke. "Women, on the other hand, usually are far more realistic about such things. We put on our makeup and fix our hair, and flutter our eyelids and act coy. But down deep most women see the practical side of it all. We have to. To keep the human race going. If it weren't for us, the world would be in a hell of a lot worse mess than it already is."

He snorted and shook his head. "Just what I need," he muttered. "A lecture on love."

"Not love. Life. Philosophy. Remember? You told me once we'd talk philosophy some day." She smiled at him again. "And today's the day. Or night, to be accurate."

Jordon looked out the window into the quietness of the humid August night. He could find no words for a debate with her. Hell, maybe she was right. Maybe he was a Puritan at heart. Maybe his drinking and women and rambling and gambling were all a front, hiding his true nature. Maybe underneath it all, deep inside, he really yearned to be a saint, and knew he never could be. Such bullshit, he thought, killing the rest of his drink. How'd she ever get him started down this track?

He heard her laugh, warm and easy. "Don't be so serious," she said. "I promise not to tell you any more about yourself. At least not until you've digested this."

He looked at her, sitting there on the big sofa, as beautiful a woman as he'd ever seen anywhere. Young, fresh, yet older than the mountains. Smiling her knowing smile at him. She seemed to be taunting him, and daring him to do something about it.

So he did.

He got up and took the few steps across the room to the sofa, leaned over, and stared into her eyes. She stared back, then closed her eyes. He kissed her, and her lips were soft, yielding.

He pulled away, and she moved, making a place for him beside her on the sofa. He sat down.

"You sure you're ready for me, mister?" she whispered.

He could hear his heart thudding inside his chest. "Who knows?" It suddenly occurred to him that this tough, bright, lovely young woman was just about the same age as his daughter Becky who lived with her husband in Harlan. He wished he hadn't thought about that.

Della took his hand and squeezed it, then put her fingers to his wrist. "I can feel your pulse," she said. "I think you're getting excited." She pulled his hand to her lips and kissed the tips of his fingers.

"Shouldn't I be?"

She placed his hand on her breast. "Here, feel mine."

He could feel her heart thumping. And he could feel her nipple, big and hard and alive, straining against the fabric of her dress.

He kissed her again, and she kissed him back, their tongues caressing each other. His heart pounded. He became aware that the two of them were working at their own and each other's clothing. Then they were naked, embracing, lying on the big soft, blue rug with its circles within circles. She clung to him fiercely.

He held her away from him a little so he could see her better, the satiny smooth whiteness of her body, the firm generous breasts with their taut, brown aureoles, the springy nest of dark pubic hair that he fingered lightly.

"Don't be afraid to take ahold of me, Berk," she whispered. "I'm not a china doll." She kissed him with a ferocity that surprised him, running her tongue inside his mouth and across his teeth, thrusting her pelvis into his hand.

When he pulled away from her mouth and kissed her breasts, she sucked in her breath and arched her body toward him. Then he was on top of her. Everything seemed to fade away, the mountains, the world, his troubles, and he was alone with her, lost inside her.

When at last he came, in great orgasmic spasms, he heard her cry out. Or was it him? Or the two of them? Then they collapsed, panting, sweating, spent.

When he regained his sense of who and where he was, all he could feel were dampness and limpness and awe.

Della smiled, took a deep breath, and said, "Aaahhh."

Sometime later, he had no idea how long, he opened his eyes to find himself lying on his back on the big round rug with her head nestled in the hollow of his shoulder. She clung to him in sleep, now gently rather than fiercely, as her measured rhythmic breathing made little tufts of his chest hair quiver like the trembling in his heart.

His nostrils were filled with the clean salty smell of their sweat mixed with the musky scent of their sexual secretions.

With his free hand, he lightly touched the dark curls pasted to her forehead. He wanted to brush them back, wanted to kiss away the bruised puffiness of her lips, but he was afraid he would awaken her.

So he lay there and held her, watched her clutching on to him as she slept, and he wondered where his sorry excuse for a life might be headed now.

A little before four in the morning, after he had fallen asleep with her in his arms, Della shook him awake. "We need to get up and get started back," she said. "I have things that have to be done in my office."

Driving along the narrow, winding mountain highway through the early-morning darkness, at first they were silent.

Della slept a little. Then they talked. But not about what had happened between them in the hotel room. Della wanted to talk about politics.

"I know I can trust you," she said. "But just for the record, anything that's said or done between us goes no further. That goes for you and me both."

"Of course."

After a moment, she said, "My meeting last night went well. The connections I'm making are going to be very profitable, I think."

He drove in silence. Let her talk about whatever she felt like.

"The men I met with were Democrats mostly," she said. "Does that suggest anything to you?"

He thought about it. "Can't say that it does."

She laughed. "That's right, you're no politician, are you?"

"My campaign for sheriff is still a little too fresh in my mind to be exactly funny."

"Sorry. It wasn't aimed at your political skills. You know, I think your political floundering around is another part of your romantic nature. You want people to be better than they are. And you're always disappointed when they're not. That's why you get surprised in politics, I expect."

He didn't respond, but he wished she would just stop figuring him out all the time. It made him feel like a june bug under a magnifying glass.

"Anyhow, I'm getting pretty close to some influential Democrats in the state apparatus. And that reaches all the way to Washington. *That's* where the gravy is about to start flowing from."

"Gravy?"

"Mr. Roosevelt's New Deal is stirring up a lot of gravy for a lot of folks. Some of it's going to be dripping right on down here into the mountains. Our Democrat friends in Frankfort, and their Democrat friends in Washington, will decide who gets what. And how much. And how soon. So, I decided I better get my front feet in the trough with the rest of them."

"And that's what your meeting was about?"

"Among other things."

He was silent. It always seemed to come down to power and money. Or maybe just money. With money, you had power.

"You disapprove?"

"It's none of my affair." A little bit later he said, "But I thought you were tied in with the county politicians in King's Mill."

"I am."

After a moment, he said, "But they're Republicans."

"So?" She seemed surprised.

"I guess I'm missing something."

She sighed. "I reckon you are. I don't give two hoots in hell what label any of them stick on themselves . . . or one another. As far as I'm concerned, they're all looking out for number one. That's all I'm doing, honey. Looking out for Della."

They rode along in the darkness for a while. Finally she said, "But I've got to be very careful neither side finds out I'm too close to the other. Now that could be embarrassing. Not to mention expensive."

Having apparently satisfied her urge to talk politics, she slumped back in the seat and dozed again. Jordon glanced over at her. Her face shone with a serene, innocent beauty. Had he not known her, he never would have imagined the powerful, calculating brain concealed inside her lovely head. Wherever she had learned it, this tough-minded lady knew more about how the world worked than most people he had ever met. And she made no bones about using her knowledge to benefit herself.

Jordon sighed. For a while last night, he had been able to get Willis's murder off his mind. But only for a while. He could not escape it for long. Nor did he want to. Somehow, he had to locate and get hold of the right thread to pull that would unravel the rest of it. Finding that thread was the problem. But somebody did it. And somebody ordered it done. Jordon wanted both of them.

Dawn was just beginning to break over the top of the mountain when he pulled the big Buick into Della's compound and parked it beside her house.

She got out, stretched, and yawned. "I can use some more shut-eye. See you tonight. Hope we get some business." She turned and was gone like that.

Jordon sighed and walked across the lot and around to the back of the poolroom. He opened the door and entered the little room where he slept and kept his few belongings.

He undressed and fell back on his bunk, lacing his fingers behind his head and staring at the parallel cracks in the tongue-and-groove ceiling in the early-morning light. They reminded him of railroad tracks, leading on through the wall and into infinity. He thought once more about what had happened between him and Della in the hotel room in Corbin. It was a powerful, intense experience—for him, at least. He wondered how she felt about it.

She had not mentioned it once since their great, sweaty climax. And then all she'd said was, "Aaahhh."

14

JORDON HAD SEEN SOME fancy places in his travels, big hotels and fine restaurants in some of the world's great cities. But never had he been inside a private home that looked like the one where HR Buxton lived.

It was built along the general lines of a southern plantation house, but something about the dimensions was quite distinctive, like the man who'd had it built. HR had stamped the imprint of his own unique personality on the house, just as he had done with everything else he had touched in Stanton County.

The house was located on the hill a short walk away from the Buxton office building, a position that overlooked the town.

The sun had already slipped behind the mountain, and darkness was approaching fast when Jordon arrived.

His eyes swept across the Buxton mansion. Its exterior walls were white brick, and a broad concrete porch ran all the way across the front. Tall white fluted columns and neatly trimmed evergreen shrubbery finished the picture. Jordon guessed there must be between fifteen and twenty rooms in the place. Plenty of space for guests and entertaining. And for the regular residents to stay out of one another's way.

When Jordon rang the bell, a thin mountain woman of maybe fifty, wearing a maid's uniform and a grim expression, opened the door. "Yes, sir?" she said. Her voice was flat and cool. Jordon told her he had an appointment with Mr. Buxton, and she led the way back through a huge room with a glistening crystal chandelier and fragile-looking an-

tique furniture. Several paintings, some of which were por-
traits that looked very old and vaguely familiar to Jordon,
decorated the walls.

The woman took Jordon down a hallway to a room where
she rapped lightly on the door.

"Come on in," HR's voice said. Jordon opened the door
and entered, closing the door behind him. The large room
seemed to be a combination office, library, and hideaway. It
reminded Jordon a little of HR's office in the Buxton Building, but here it was warmer, more informal. A couch and
chairs on one side of the room clustered around a low table
with a dull shine on its surface.

HR sat in one of the chairs, holding an open file folder in
his hands, looking at some papers inside. He wore a navy
blue suit and a dark tie with a subdued pattern, just as he
did in his office or on the street. Jordon wondered if the man
ever really relaxed.

"My 'sanctum sanctorum,'" HR said with a little laugh.
"Where I spend most of my time when I'm not in my office."
He did not stand to greet Jordon, nor did he offer to shake
hands. He just looked him over for a moment, then said, "I
was in a meeting all day and couldn't take time to talk to you."

"So your secretary said. I appreciate you agreeing to see
me tonight."

"You said it was important."

"It's important to me. I hope it is to you."

HR waited.

It was not easy for Jordon to say why he had come. "Since
the last time we talked, I haven't been able to get any kind
of lead on who killed Willis Dobbs. I hope you might be able
to help me."

"Why me? We went over this before."

"Not really. We just talked about it generally, about Sheriff
Trumble and Ike Sewell. But you didn't tell me anything
about what might be behind it."

"Why makes you think I can help you? I assured you I had
nothing to do with it. And I assure you of that again now."

"If I thought otherwise, we wouldn't be talking. Even so, maybe you can help steer me in the right direction. Tell me somebody to go see. Somebody that might know. I'm at a loss."

HR studied him carefully. "It's beginning to sound like you think we might be of help to each other."

Jordon nodded. "I guess you can say that."

"Why the change of heart?"

Jordon took a deep breath. "I want the man who killed Willis Dobbs. And I want the man who ordered it done. Right now I'm stumped, and I can't rest until I find them."

"And what then?"

"Leave that to me."

HR studied him. "Vengeance."

Jordon said nothing.

HR repeated it. "Vengeance."

Jordon sighed. "Call it what you will."

"What about 'Vengeance is mine, saith the Lord'? What about that?"

"The Lord has his priorities. I have mine."

"So you really don't care about trying to help me keep the peace around here. You're interested in retribution for Willis's death, and to hell with the consequences. Even if I can, why should I help you get your revenge?"

"I'm not going to try to bullshit you. I told you what I want. I know you don't like me. And I sure as hell haven't tried to hide how I feel about you. But I remember you telling me during the election last fall that you've worked with men before that you didn't like and who didn't like you. You said you had been able to find ground that was 'mutually beneficial' to stand on, or words to that effect, if I remember it rightly. Do I?"

HR nodded, but remained impassive. "I've said something like that, more than once in my life. And it reflects how I feel, more or less."

Jordon knew HR Buxton must be enjoying seeing him in the role of the supplicant. But he pressed on, determined to get whatever he could from HR that might lead him to who killed Willis. "Then, frankly, I'd think you could see how it would be in your interest for me to find this sniper and stop him. As well as the man who hired him. There sure as hell isn't going to be much peace with a professional killer wandering around Stanton County, stalking whoever suits him or his boss." Jordon paused for effect, then added, "He might just get it in his head for some reason to take aim at you, or somebody close to you."

"What makes you sure the killer is a professional?"

"I'm not. I'm just going on that basis for the time being. But I think it's a reasonable idea. Why would anyone else want to do such a thing? Everybody liked Willis."

"How about money as a motive? Or maybe a setup to make it look like I've hired a killer to try to stop the union. Galvanize opposition to me. I probably could think of other reasons."

"Well, whatever it was makes no difference to me. I want the men involved."

Jordon was still standing. HR had not invited him to sit down. Now, HR stood up, and waved Jordon to a chair. "Have a seat," HR said, and started to pace around the room.

Jordon sat and watched him. At last, HR stopped and faced him. "For once, it seems, you have put things together and they have come out right. Or almost right. For whatever it's worth, I, too, think the murders were the work of a professional."

Jordon decided not to respond to this. He had made his case. Let it rest. He thought he had the old man convinced. And once you've got a man sold on something, whatever it is, that's when you quit. Otherwise, if you keep on talking, you run the risk of unselling him. Kind of like when you're trying to buy a big pot in a poker game. You decide on your bet and you make it. But you don't try to improve your chances with bullshit.

HR paced some more, then stopped and stared at a large framed aerial photograph of the town of Buxton that hung on one wall, as if somehow he would find something there that would solve all his problems.

"I learned today," HR said quietly, "that the man who leads all these miners, the man most of them would walk through forty acres of hell for, that man is coming to Buxton."

"Who?"

"Who does that description fit?"

"You tell me," Jordon said.

"John L. Lewis. The president of the UMWA. The United Mine Workers of America. A man who ranks right next to Jesus Christ for a lot of coal miners."

"Coming here?"

HR nodded. He walked back over and took the chair facing Jordon.

"What for?" Jordon said.

"I understand they're planning a big union rally in Pineville. And John L.'s going to stop in Buxton to meet with some of his people here. Put some new fire in their bellies."

Jordon thought about this for a moment. "I'll be damned," he said.

"We all may be before this is over. You haven't heard it all."

"What else?"

"We may have a bunch of big-shot politicians here at the same time."

"Like who?"

"My sources weren't completely certain, but maybe Governor Lafoon and some of his people. Possibly even Senator Barkley. And who knows who else." HR waited for a moment, then said, "Does all this suggest anything to you?"

Jordon nodded slowly. "If our sniper took it into his head to go to work while they are here, he could have himself a good day."

"We haven't even dreamed about how bad things could get if that happened. Can you imagine what we'd be in for if John L. Lewis got himself assassinated here?"

Jordon shook his head. "What are all the politicians going to be doing?"

"The same thing they're usually doing," HR said. "Jockeying for position. There's always another election around the corner. And they're all getting afraid that John L. will turn thumbs down on them. He's still kind of an unknown quantity, with the federal government backing the unions the way it is now. But considering the votes John L. can probably deliver, the politicians would like to stay on his good side if possible, or at least not have him attack them. Without losing any of the money that secretly flows from the mine operators, of course. Personally, I don't think they can juggle it all, but you know enough about politicians to know they'll try."

"And they'll provide a perfect opportunity for the spark that would set off a war here."

HR nodded. "The bloodbath I've been afraid of."

"So what are we going to do?"

"That's the question." Suddenly HR stood up and said, "You like models?"

Jordon was confused. "Models?"

"Model trains, things like that."

Jordon wondered what this had to do with what they were talking about. "I suppose so. It's not a hobby of mine, or anything. But, sure, I guess I like them."

"I want to show you something," HR said, taking him by the arm. "Come on." HR led the way out into the hall and down a carpeted stairway into a large basement room. He flipped on a light switch, and Jordon saw a platform, table height, that covered more than half the room. It had walking space around it and cutaways into the middle part at various points.

On the table was a miniature community that Jordon recognized at once as the town of Buxton and the surrounding area.

He stood there picking out details. There was the Buxton Building, and the house they were in now, the square, Hotel Buxton, the stores, confectionery, theater, the baseball diamond, the power-generating plant, the water plant, lumberyard, dry shed, planing mill, the houses where the corporate executives lived, and the ridge lined with homes where the lesser company employees lived, miner's houses, cemetery.

There was the railroad depot and the railroad itself, complete with trains pulling gondolas filled with coal, and flatcars with tiny logs chained on them. Down the track at the other end of the table were two coal camps, complete with their rows of little gray frame miners' houses, and coal tipples, commissaries, schools, and churches.

HR stepped to a control panel and flipped a switch. The overhead lights went out, and tiny lights suddenly shone in many of the buildings. The trains began to creep along the tracks, and a phonograph record somewhere in the room began to play locomotive sounds. Even the Middle Fork of the Cumberland River and Little Horse Creek had water flowing in them, powered by a pump hidden somewhere.

Jordon was speechless. Aside from marveling at the intricacy and authenticity of it all, the only thing he could think of was how much time, effort, and money it must have cost to create this miniature world, which appeared to be complete down to the last detail.

"An old man's vice," HR Buxton said quietly. "I don't show it to many people. I've always been a model railroad enthusiast, but for the past ten years since my wife died, I've devoted God knows how many hours to this." He made a wide arc with his hand. "It would seem silly to some, I know. But somehow I thought you wouldn't see it that way."

"No," Jordon said. "I don't." Not silly, he thought. A trifle strange, maybe. But not silly.

They watched the little trains pulling their little loads, watched as they went through the mill yard and made their way back around the town and down again into the hollows where the camps were.

HR said, "Some men with money use it to indulge themselves in women, liquor." He paused. "Gambling. In my life I've had the opportunity to enjoy an evening of poker and a beautiful woman from time to time. But my activities are greatly diminished in those areas at this stage of my life. A good cigar, a drink of old bourbon or mellow straight corn moonshine, a good bowel movement, the comfort of an interesting book, and"—he swept his hand across the table—"a little time with my models, these are my simple pleasures these days." After watching for a minute more, he sighed, then flipped the switch that stopped the trains, darkened the little world where everything worked the way it was supposed to, and bathed the room once more in the bright light of reality.

Jordon stared at the tableau, still not quite knowing what to make of it.

"I thought this might help you see the kind of man I am, understand my simple pleasures," HR said. "The only thing that's truly important to me today is how I'll be remembered. I don't want my good name smeared with blood. I don't want my town torn to pieces in a union war. Whether you know it or not, I have good friends here. And not all of them are men who work in my offices. Mine foremen, engineers, and coal miners. Mill workers, others. I respect these men. And most of them respect me. You may find this hard to accept, but money is of little importance to me. I rarely think about it."

Jordon stared at him coldly. "Things lose their importance in direct proportion to how little we need them. With the kind of money you've got, you never have to think about it." He waved a hand at HR's miniature empire. "But what about the man who's sitting down there tonight in one of your houses, without two nickels to rub together, wondering how he can pay the rent, how he can buy food for his family?"

"My men have credit at my stores. Those who are loyal won't starve as long as I can feed them."

"A man doesn't want to be reduced to having you or anybody else feed him and his family. Don't you understand that? Barely surviving is all most of them are doing now. Some not even that."

"It's the depression. I can't end it."

"Well, by God, you're sliding along through it just fine. You've got people living in your houses who are using cow feed to make bread with. And men who go to work in your mines with potato peelings in their dinner buckets. Do you know that?"

HR shook his head slowly. His voice sounded tired. "Jordon, most of the wealth I have is tied up in this town. If I took all the cash I've got or could raise, and I divided it up equally among all the people who work for me, it would be gone in ninety days. And then they'd be desperate again. And I'd be broke, too, without any power to do anything. And who would be the better for it?"

"I have a hard time seeing you broke, or anywhere near it."

HR's voice took on a sharp edge. "Can't you understand what my company is up against? The supply of coal available in this country these days far exceeds the demand. And by the time we pay the railroad to ship it to the north, we can't compete with the mines in Pennsylvania. You know anything about discriminatory freight rates?"

Jordon waved his hand in a gesture of impatience. "Stop it. You're breaking my heart."

HR's face flushed with anger. "Goddamn it, man, try for once to see beyond the end of your own nose!"

"I see hungry people here in your town. I see your stores full of food. And I see you living up here on top of this hill like a king. I can see that far past the end of my nose." After a moment he added, "And I see you doing your damnedest to try to make me feel sorry for you."

As quickly as it had appeared, the visible evidence of the old man's anger vanished. He sighed and shook his head. "Let's go back upstairs."

On the way, neither of them said anything. Back in HR's study, he invited Jordon to sit down again. HR went to a small cabinet and brought out a bottle of bourbon and two glasses. He poured two hefty drinks and reached for a box of cigars. He started to offer one to Jordon, apparently remembered Jordon did not smoke, and put the box down. He lit one for himself and took a sip of his bourbon.

There was a knock at the door. "What is it?" HR said.

The door opened and Young Harry Buxton stepped in. HR's son, not yet thirty, was a large, soft man, already putting on extra poundage around his middle. He was dressed in an open-necked tan sport shirt and brown slacks, and his thinning brown hair was tousled. His mouth was red with secondhand lipstick he had apparently forgotten to wipe off. He saw Jordon and stood there glaring at him.

Jordon glanced idly at the younger man for a moment, then ignored him and took a sip of his bourbon.

"What is it, Harry?" HR said.

"What the hell is he doing here?" Young Harry said, pointing at Jordon.

"It's none of your business, but we're having a meeting," his father said. His voice was harsh, rasping. "Did you want to see me about something else?"

"It'll keep," Harry said coldly. He turned and stalked out of the room, closing the door behind him, not gently, but not quite slamming it either.

Jordon knew very well why Young Harry disliked him. He had questioned the Buxton heir at some length in the Bitsy Trotter murder last year, not being very careful to spare the young man's feelings or worry much about his dignity. Young Harry, as far as Jordon was concerned, was a spoiled prick. And Jordon had never made any effort to conceal his feelings about HR's son. "I suppose I have to resign myself to never being a popular guest in the Buxton mansion, don't I?" Jordon said.

HR Buxton did not reply. His face had gone pale and he was grimacing as if in severe pain. He had put his cigar down and seemed to be struggling for breath. He pressed his fist to the middle of his chest.

Jordon set his glass down and went to where the old man sat. "Is something wrong? Can I help you?"

HR shook his head. He reached into his pocket and took out a little round gold box, removed a pill from it, and put it into his mouth. "I'll be better in a minute," he said.

And in a short while he was, indeed, better. Or appeared to be. He stared at Jordon for a moment and said, "I have a slight gallbladder problem. Nothing serious, you understand. It acts up once in a while. Nobody but Dr. Klein and I know about it. And now you." After a moment he said, "I'd like to keep it that way."

"Of course," Jordon said.

"Thank you," the old man said.

For a while they sat without talking.

"They say a gallbladder can be painful," Jordon said.

"What? Oh, yes. Painful indeed."

Jordon started to get up and leave. "I'll go and let you get some rest."

But HR waved him back into his seat. "In a minute."

Jordon leaned back and relaxed.

HR sat with his eyes closed for a few minutes, then opened them and fixed Jordon with a hard stare. "In most ways you and I are as different as daylight and dark." The old man's voice was quiet, a little weak. "We both know that. And the two of us will never find more than a very little spot of that 'mutually beneficial' ground to stand on. But at least, let's try to do that much." He sighed.

Jordon waited in silence.

The old man's voice became stronger. "I'll do whatever I can to help you track down this goddamn sniper. For one reason only. Because it will help me, too. Maybe we can save the asses of a few politicians, and the big boss of the miner's union. And maybe out of all of it, I'll have another little measure of peace before my race is run. And maybe my company and my town won't be destroyed, along with my good name." He took a sip of his bourbon and stared at Jordon. "And you, my hard-nosed friend, you can have your killer." He paused, then added, "If you can find him. And if he doesn't have you first."

Both of them were silent for a moment.

Then HR lifted his glass. "Done?"

Jordon held up his own glass. "Done."

"But," HR said sadly, "if you don't catch him soon, it will

be too late. The big union rally in Pineville is set for Saturday. That means those high muckety-mucks will probably be here no later than Thursday night. Today is Tuesday. You've got your work cut out for you. If you don't find your sniper by then, we could find ourselves in very deep shit."

Jordon sucked in a chest full of air and expelled it slowly. "Then let's get to it. What can you tell me?"

$\triangledown$

15

Moody McCain watched the cards fall and wondered how much longer he was going to have to hang around Stanton County. Each day he became more frustrated, more irritable, in spite of Pearl's daily efforts to keep him relaxed. McCain wanted to be done with his work here. But he'd been told that maybe something very big was in the works, something that would make his staying more than worthwhile. If for some reason it did not materialize, he nevertheless would be paid well for his idle time. Win either way. He liked that.

McCain's fifth card was a six, which gave him a pair showing and one in the hole. Elmer Hagen had an ace of clubs up, and he bet a quarter. Everybody else folded, and McCain, with his lock, raised a quarter.

"Shit," Hagen said, sounding disgusted. "I stepped in it this time. I got to call." He threw in his money and flipped his hole card. It was the ace of hearts.

McCain turned his third six faceup. "Some days it don't pay to get up, does it?" he said with a little grin.

Jordon scooped up the last of the cards as McCain raked in the pot.

"We've been playing five-card for an hour," Jordon said. "I'm going to deal seven-card for a while."

"You're what?" McCain asked.

"I'm going to deal seven-card stud for a while," Jordon repeated.

"How come?" McCain asked.

Jordon shuffled the cards. "Change of pace."

"I'm doing fine at five-card," McCain said. "I say, keep on dealing it."

Jordon did not reply.

McCain glanced at the three other players at the table. None spoke. "What do you all say about it?" McCain asked.

Speedy Robbins said, "House rules are that Jordon decides which game we'll play. He's the dealer."

McCain shot Jordon a dirty look. "What makes it Jordon's place to say?"

Jordon stared back at him. "Because I run the game. And because, otherwise, there'd be a debate every time somebody wanted to play something different, and somebody else didn't. Since this is a card game and not a debating society, I decide."

McCain thought about it for a moment. "I say keep dealing five-card."

Jordon finished the shuffle and placed the deck on the table in front of Hagen, who said, "Let me give them a whorehouse cut," which he did, using both hands to separate the cards into three or four stacks and mix them up.

Jordon picked up the deck and said, "Okay, everybody, ante up and you won't have so much." Each man threw in a nickel, and Jordon began to deal, one card facedown to each player. On the second round, he also dealt the cards facedown.

"Damn it," McCain said. "I thought you were going to keep on dealing five-card."

Jordon started another round of cards, faceup this time. "As you can see, you're mistaken. If you don't want to play, fold your hand."

"I'll take my ante back," McCain said, reaching into the pot.

Jordon stopped dealing and looked at him. "I'll let you do that if you like," he said quietly. "But if you do, you're out of this game. For good."

"What do you mean?" McCain said.

"It's plain enough. Take your ante and get out. And stay out. Or play your hand. Those are your choices."

McCain swept a strand of pale blond hair back from his

eyes and stood up. His tall, supple frame towered over the table. He could feel his heart beginning to thump. He hated this smart sonofabitch Jordon. "You sure you're man enough to back up your tough talk?"

Jordon stared at him but didn't move. "Try me," he said quietly.

McCain glanced at the others, then back at Jordon, who still had not batted an eyelash. "Fuck the ante," McCain said. "I'm going to get a breath of fresh air." He turned and stalked away.

Slim Hall was leaning against the doorway leading into the poolroom. He had been standing there with his arms crossed, watching in silence, for some time. He stepped aside to let McCain through.

Outside in the evening air, McCain took a deep breath and muttered to himself, "One-way sonofabitch." This Jordon rubbed him the wrong way, had since the very first time they'd met. But McCain was not pleased with himself for losing his temper. He knew it was unprofessional to do so. The same thing with the way he dealt with Pearl. Do what you have to do, but don't let it make you mad. Just do it and go on. Like when you are on a job. You sit there and wait, you aim, you squeeze, you get up and walk away. You don't get involved in it. It was the way he tried to do everything in his life. Stay loose and coolheaded. Concentrate on the business at hand. But then something would come up that would get under his skin and fuel his anger. He knew he had to work on this, keep his temper in check. Still and all, he did not like this bastard Jordon. And sooner or later, the time would come when Jordon would pay for his insults. Before he left Stanton County for good, McCain vowed to himself, he'd settle matters with Jordon. "One-way sonofabitch," he said again.

McCain took a deep breath and looked at his watch. Eight-thirty-five. Right now, Jordon and his high-handed ways would have to wait.

McCain had a meeting with a certain big-money man at

his home high on the mountain overlooking the mouth of Little Horse Creek.

But McCain had to go back to the house first and get Pearl. He'd promised he would take her out with him tonight, keep her from whining about being cooped up all day and night with nobody to talk to. He would let her ride along and sit in the car while he talked with Mister Big-Money. Maybe he'd even stop someplace with her and buy her a bottle of pop before he took her back home.

Jordon glanced at Slim Hall, who had propped himself against the doorframe again. "No pool players tonight?"

Slim shook his head. "Deader than Methuselah's dick."

"How about dealing a few hands? I want to take a break."

Slim seemed surprised, but pleased. "Sure."

Jordon had been spending some time with Slim when he could, teaching him about running a game. The young man knew the basics of poker and blackjack and craps, knew them well, but the basics were just enough to get you in trouble unless you knew more.

Slim took over and Jordon walked outside into the warm night air. Moody McCain had left. Just as well, Jordon thought. He didn't want or need a fight with this man, but there had been something about him, right from the start, that Jordon disliked.

Maybe it was his cold arrogance, which, as it turned out, seemed to just barely conceal a hot, seething anger always waiting to flare up.

Or maybe it was something about the way he lounged around cleaning his fingernails with a long-blade pocket-knife, stroking his hair, seeming to delight in finding a chance to make some slighting comment about somebody.

Jordon wondered where the man got his money. He certainly was no more than a mediocre gambler.

Jordon strolled across the lot to Della's Place, where he could hear the record player making music.

Inside, he sat at a table and asked a waitress to bring him

a cup of coffee. The only other people in the place were two younger couples in conversation at a table in the corner. Once in a while, the girls would shriek with laughter.

Della was nowhere to be seen. Since the other night in Corbin, she had not said a dozen words to Jordon, nor had he seen her except for an occasional glimpse as she hustled around looking after every last detail, it seemed, of her thriving business enterprises.

Oh well. He had things to do now. HR Buxton had given him three names of people to talk with. Asher Jennings, Myra Chastayne, and Pennyrile Gruber. Jordon knew none of them personally, but all by reputation. He knew they were coal operators.

Asher Jennings had come from someplace outside the mountains and started his coal mines.

Myra Chastayne had inherited her operation when her husband, who had started it many years ago, died suddenly.

And Pennyrile Gruber was a native of the mountains, a poor boy who had clawed his way up the heap and along the way had earned a name as a ruthless entrepreneur, a buccaneer, a woman chaser, a libertine, you name it. A man devoted to making and spending money, who asked for no favors and gave none. From what Jordon had heard, Pennyrile seemed to revel in his reputation.

"Go talk to these people," HR Buxton had said. "Use my name anywhere you think it will do any good. Ask them to give you whatever help they can. Hell, you know what to say. I don't know what you can learn, but it's a start. Also, go see Sheriff Trumble. Find out if he's learned anything. In the meantime, I'll make some calls, ask some questions myself."

By saying he was calling at HR Buxton's direction, Jordon had found the three coal operators willing to see him. He had appointments with all of them tomorrow. And since he had not yet been able to catch up with the sheriff, Jordon figured he'd try that again tomorrow, too. It would be a full day. The big question was, would it lead to anything?

Jordon felt that if he didn't catch the man or men behind

Willis's death, he would explode. Call it vengeance or whatever, but he knew he would never draw another peaceful breath until he settled this debt.

Della came out of the back, saw him, and strolled over. "Things okay over there?" she asked, glancing toward the poolroom.

He nodded. "Just taking a break. Sit down for a minute."

She looked at him for a moment. "Sorry. I can't. I'm in the middle of something in my office. I just came out to get a cold bottle of pop."

He took a sip of coffee and smiled at her. "I was thinking about what a good time the other night was. I thought we might get together again."

She glanced away, then back at him. "Actually, I'm too busy to play right now. Some big things brewing." Her facial expression and the sound of her voice came across very cool.

Jordon was stung. It was not just a passing thought he had given to their night together in Corbin. He had caught himself more than once fantasizing about it. He could close his eyes, as he had been doing, and see her there beside him on the big soft rug with its blue circles.

He stood up, making an effort to seem unconcerned. "Well, I've got work of my own to do." He turned and started toward the door.

From behind him she said, "I may want you to go with me to another meeting in the next few days."

He stopped and glanced back at her. From the look on her face now, which was not cold, but not warm either, he wasn't sure whether she really meant a meeting . . . or something else. And at this moment, he wasn't sure he gave a good goddamn. "Let's see," he said and stepped out into the darkness.

Back in the poolroom, the tables were still idle. Jordon went to the telephone, took the receiver off the hook, and cranked the handle. When the operator came on, he said, "Does Emerson Calhoun have a telephone?"

The operator said, "Yes, he's on a party line."

Jordon asked her to ring it.

When Emerson answered, Jordon identified himself and said, "Could I see you for a few minutes after while? About midnight, say."

"The mines ain't running tomorrow. I don't have to get up early," Emerson said. "You can come by my house. If that suits you."

"It does."

"You know where I live?"

Jordon said no, and Emerson told him how to get there. It was over on Muscadine Ridge.

"I'll wait up," Emerson said.

Moody McCain drove with his left hand while he stroked Pearl's thigh with his right. Maybe, he thought, this little drive would keep her quiet for a while. "See?" he said. "I don't get a chance to take you anywhere very often, but when I do, I do."

Pearl's strange, off-center, almost-pretty face was lit up in a smile. "It'll be interesting to see this man's big house, from what you say about it."

"You'll only get to see the outside. We'll be talking business."

"You mean I've got to stay in the car while you go inside?"

"I don't expect to be too long. And I'll take you someplace for a Coke and a sandwich before we go home."

She didn't try to hide her disappointment. "I thought I'd get to see the inside."

"Hey, Pearl. It's not like it was a goddamn castle or something."

Pearl said no more, apparently hushed by the rising impatience in his voice. As he steered the car through the darkness along the winding road up the mountain, he smiled. She was learning at last not to press him too far.

Some five miles out of Buxton, near the top of the mountain, McCain turned into a paved driveway as he'd been instructed to do, and threaded his way through a thick grove of tall straight pines. The light from the house shone through the trees, creating long shadows and giving the whole scene an unreal look. Soon they reached a large parking area at the side of a huge red brick house that was lit up inside and had floodlights trained on the parking lot. Several great old oak trees surrounded the house, and evergreen shrubs and a meticulously kept lawn rounded out the picture.

"Oh, Moody," Pearl said. "Isn't this beautiful? Just like I've seen in magazines. God, it must be something inside." She shivered with excitement. "Like a movie star's house."

McCain shook his head in disgust. Movie stars again. "It's just business, Pearl. That's all."

"Your union business?"

"That's right. My union business." He got out of the car and said, "I don't expect to be too long."

McCain stepped up to the door and rang the bell. Almost at once the door opened and a big man with a bulldog face and a loose gray suit said, "McCain?"

"That's right."

The man stepped aside. He looked to be maybe forty, and to weigh well over two hundred pounds. To McCain, he appeared to be granite hard. But McCain went through life with the comforting knowledge that physical strength or toughness was nothing, less than nothing actually, against just one well-placed bullet. Nobody awed McCain. Not since he'd overcome his fear of his father so many years ago. The biggest, meanest, wealthiest, strongest, most important man alive collapsed like a punctured balloon when a bullet entered at the proper place. Maybe God had made men or maybe he hadn't, McCain reflected, but Mr. Colt had certainly made them equal. Assisted by Smith & Wesson, and Remington, and, in McCain's case, the good people at the Springfield Armory. He had learned his profession early and well, honed it as a sniper in the war in France, and no man gave him cause for concern.

The big man led McCain down a broad hallway to a closed door. "In there," the man said.

McCain opened the door without knocking and stepped inside.

Pennyrile Gruber stood up from a well-padded brown leather chair and said, "By God, you're here."

Jordon pulled his car in at the front of Emerson's house and cut the lights and motor. All the houses on the dirt road that ran along the crest of the ridge were dark. Jordon got out and closed the car door quietly. He went through the gate and into the yard. He was almost to the front steps of the little frame house when, out of the corner of his eye, he saw the silhouette of a man step from behind a big tree at the side of the yard.

"Over here," the silhouette said in a low voice.

Jordon altered his course and walked to him.

"With party lines and everything else the way it is, no telling what's liable to happen anymore," Emerson said. "I decided to wait for you out here." He took Jordon by the arm and led him around the house and through the backyard to a big flat rock. "Let's set here."

The two men sat quietly for a little while before Jordon asked, "Did you and the others decide yet on whether or not you're going to help me try to find out who killed Willis?"

"We did."

"What's it going to be?"

"We're generally agreed to help you."

"Generally?"

"Not everybody trusts you."

Jordon was silent for a few moments, then asked, "How do you feel personally? The same as before?"

"Like I told you before, Willis was my nephew. Turner Lott, too. I feel responsible for both of them. And I can trust you if Willis could."

"Good. What can you tell me?"

"Not a whole hell of a lot, when it actually comes down to it. And, before I say what I know, there's something else we got to clear up."

"What?"

"If I'm going to help you, I want this understood: Whenever a showdown comes, I aim to be in on it."

"In on it? In what way?"

"Just what it sounds like. If you or us or all of us together find out who killed Willis and Turner, then I aim to be one of the ones who takes care of them."

"You'll be helping to do that if you can steer me toward who it was."

"That's not enough for me. I want to be there. To have a di-rect hand in it. Ain't nothing short of that will pacify me."

"I just can't promise it will turn out that way, Emerson."

"Why not?"

"Well, it might not unravel that way, that's all. I might find myself in a situation when you're not there, and I have to do something by myself. You see what I mean?"

Emerson seemed to be pondering it. At last he said, "All right, if it comes out that way. But if you're going to set something up where there's a head-on fight, I expect to be in on it. Do we understand one another?"

Jordon thought about it. Finally he nodded. "If things develop so that's how it is, and if I can, I'll get word to you." This was as far as he was willing to go.

Emerson must have sensed it from Jordon's tone of voice, for he said, "All right. Now here's all I've got right now. It might not be much, but it might be a whole lot. There's a feller living in Chambers in one of the company's houses, who ain't working at nothing, but who's got money, and who's supposed to be a union man, sent in here to help organize a local."

"And?"

"Ain't none of us ever heard of him before."

"What does that mean?"

"It means at least that he's lying about what he's doing here. And it could be that he's who we're looking for."

"How'd you find out about him. He surely didn't say anything to you about being an organizer?"

"No. That part come through Curly Bunch's old lady. Curly lives right next to them, and Curly's wife got to jabberin' out in the backyard with this feller's woman the other day. She told Curly's wife that her man was a union organizer. Course, Curly's wife told him and he told me. The thing is, this man ain't got nothing to do with the union."

"Who is he?" Jordon asked.

"Fellow name of McCain. Moody McCain. His woman's called Pearl. Pretty little thing, young and blond and curvy, Curly's wife said. Said the way the girl looks, it's a wonder McCain don't stay holed up with her all the time. But he don't. Said he's in and out of the house all hours of the day and night."

Pearl snuggled back in her seat in the darkness as Moody drove back down the winding road from Mr. Pennyrile Gruber's mansion on top of the mountain. She didn't want to talk, just to remember and relive the excitement she had just experienced at seeing the inside of the big house. The other thing that happened, well, it made her so mad she could hardly stand to remember it. This was the first time in weeks that she'd been anywhere outside of the little miner's shack, except to gossip once in a while with that Bunch woman next door, who didn't know anything worthwhile to gossip about.

Tonight, however, just a few minutes after Moody had gone inside the big house, he had come back out and said, "Mr. Gruber invites you to come inside."

Pearl couldn't hide her surprise. "Are you sure?"

Moody nodded. "Says he won't hear of you sitting out here by yourself while we talk."

"You told him I was here?"

"He asked me why I didn't bring you. I said you were out here. He remembers seeing you from over at Della's the other night."

When they got inside, she was delighted at the expensive surroundings. The plush carpets, the lovely furniture, the paintings. And when he greeted her, she immediately recognized him from Della's. She had caught him looking at her several times that night, and when their eyes met, he never looked away. Now, up close, she could see why Mr. Gruber had wanted her to come in. He had the unmistakable look of a highly sexual man. He had wanted her in here to look her over, to make a close inspection of the kind of woman Moody had. God, how she knew the signs. And Pennyrile liked what he saw, she could tell that, too. He smiled warmly at her, showing a couple of glittering gold teeth, and said, in a smooth, charming voice, "How wonderful to meet you, Mrs. McCain." It was a mountain accent, she knew at once, but his voice was strong and easy and confident. He reached out and took her hand, and she shivered a little at his touch.

"Call me Pearl, Mr. Gruber." It didn't tell him whether she and Moody were married or not, but it put things on a friendly basis.

"Ah, Pearl. A lovely name for such a lovely woman. A Pearl of great price, as they say. And you, my dear, must call me Pennyrile." He chuckled. "Everybody does."

Out of the corner of her eye, she could see Moody watching her and Pennyrile, knew Moody did not like the way the older man was paying attention to her, nor her response to him.

"I regret to say that Mr. McCain and I have some business to discuss for a few minutes, Pearl. But perhaps you could have a drink and just wander around the house and keep yourself amused. I have collected some interesting curios over the years, and you'll see them throughout the place. What would you like to drink?"

"I love peach brandy."

Pennyrile pushed a button, and the man with the bulldog face appeared. "Get Mrs. McCain some peach brandy," Pennyrile said. "And then she's going to wander around while we talk." To Pearl he said, "Why don't you go into the library? That's where some of my most interesting things are. Luther will show you where it is."

Pearl had loved the attention. She knew well what Pennyrile wanted. She'd seen it in enough men's faces in her short life. And it was written all over this one. Moody knew it, too, she could tell. Well, what of it? A man like that would certainly appreciate her. Wouldn't keep her penned up all day like a chicken in a coop. He'd be proud to be seen with her. Would take her to Hollywood. Or Broadway. Or wherever she wanted to go. She had no doubt about that. With what she knew, she could do things to him that would make him come across with anything she wanted. And she wouldn't be afraid of him all the time either.

Yes, it had been a thoroughly interesting time. Except for the old things in his library, which was kind of stuffy. Some old iron suits like they used to wear in battles, and helmets, and axes, stuff like that. And some big ugly masks like witch doctors wore. And guns, lots of guns, pistols and rifles both, mounted on the walls and in glass cases, some of them real old looking. The strangest looking thing, though, in Pennyrile Gruber's collection was a little brown thing about the size of a baseball, sitting in a glass case on the table. It looked like it was made out of leather, and it had the squinched-up face of a man on it, with his lips tied together with little leather thongs, and it had hair on its top, just like a real head.

After a while Pearl wandered out of the library and strolled down the hallway, looking at the paintings that hung there. They were mostly outdoor scenes, stuff that didn't interest her much.

As she got nearer to the room where she had left Moody and Pennyrile Gruber, she could hear them talking through the door that stood partly open. It was Moody's voice she heard.

". . . carry the damn things along with them when they travel from one village to another," he was saying. "Down there, of course, in all the South American countries, it's pretty much the same. I was in several of them. It's hot as hell, and meat spoils right quick. Yeah, they'd take a live chicken or two right along with them. Wanted to have fresh meat when they got where they were going. So they just tied up the wings and the feet and carried them along and ate them when they got ready for them."

Pearl stood there listening. Moody had told her once he'd been in South America, but he'd never said why or anything else about it. She wondered why he was telling Mr. Gruber this stuff about chickens now.

"Yes, well . . ." Pennyrile Gruber said.

"What I was getting at," Moody said, "is, that's the way it is with me. I need a woman with me all the time. Learned that about myself early in life. And rather than be troubled with trying to find one when I get where I'm going, I just carry one with me wherever I go." She heard him laugh. "You know, have my fresh meat when I want it. Just like they do in South America." He laughed again.

Suddenly Pearl realized he was talking about her. She felt her stomach roll, and almost gagged. She clapped her hand to her mouth so she wouldn't be heard. That's me! That's what I am to Moody McCain. Fresh meat that he takes along so he won't have to look around for it when he gets where he's going. Oh, God. That's all I am.

She ran back to the library where she sat down in a chair and wept silently. When she had finished, she sat with her hands clasped in her lap and waited for Moody and Pennyrile.

When they came to get her, she was in full control of herself. But when she looked at Moody, she saw someone she had never seen before. None of the physical cruelties he had inflicted on her before, painful as they were, had affected her like what she had overheard him saying tonight. But she didn't let on that anything was different.

Pennyrile asked what she thought of his collection.

"Fascinating, just purely fascinating, Mr. Gruber."

He beamed. "Pennyrile, my dear. You must call me Pennyrile."

She smiled back. "If you insist. Pennyrile."

"I do insist." Pennyrile turned to Moody and said, "You are a fortunate man, Mr. McCain. A fortunate man, indeed."

Moody had put his arm around her shoulder then, had

squeezed her a little. She knew it was more a signal of possession than affection. When he turned the full intensity of those icy blue eyes on her, she could tell. "She's a prize, that's for sure," Moody said.

Now, scrunched down in her seat in the dark car, Pearl glanced furtively at Moody out of the corner of her eye. He didn't seem very happy.

She knew he had been irritated at the way Pennyrile had looked at her. And she knew that Moody would drop her like dirty underwear when he got tired of her, and that he'd surely kill her if she tried to leave before then.

He had made that clear to her more than once. And she had no doubt that he meant it.

That was the only cloud on Pearl's horizon. And there might be a way to solve that if she just gave it enough thought. Moody had always treated her like she was dumb. And he had hurt her physically in ways she didn't even like to think about.

But the talk tonight about her being nothing more to him than a live chicken was the worst thing he had ever done to her. Maybe I am dumb, she told herself. But I'm more than a piece of fresh meat. And maybe I'm not as dumb as he thinks I am.

Jordon checked his watch. It was just past eight-thirty in the morning.

He was on his way to see Mrs. Myra Chastayne, one of the coal operators HR Buxton had said he ought to talk with.

He was having a little trouble with his Model A. It didn't want to idle right, for some reason, even though he adjusted the spark the way you were supposed to. He needed to take time to get somebody to look at it. It wasn't the kind of thing he did very well himself. If it was mechanical and got beyond the very simplest level, Jordon was lost.

He reflected on last night's meeting with Emerson Calhoun.

This fellow McCain's name kept coming up. Jordon and Willis had wondered about him that first night he came into the casino. And Jordon's later experiences with him at the poker table were certainly not in McCain's favor.

Now, this pretending to his woman to be a union organizer. But he'd told the poker players he was a timber buyer. It was all just speculation, but it looked like it might add up to something.

Jordon wished now he had not agreed to let Emerson know in advance and let him be in on it if a showdown was in the making. He hadn't done so completely, only if it turned out that he could work it out. But he wished he had not done that, even.

Jordon wanted to take care of this himself. He wanted the satisfaction of settling it on his own.

Emerson had gone along with Jordon's plan, though, and both of them thought it might bear some fruit. Emerson would get some of his group to shadow McCain, watch his comings and goings, see who he met with and talked to.

And one of the men would go to McCain and pretend to be a Buxton spy. He would tell McCain that he had learned Jordon was snooping around, that he suspected McCain of being involved in the murders.

Maybe this would smoke McCain out, get him to make a move on Jordon. It was risky, because if McCain was the sniper, and if he got spooked, he might just decide to kill Jordon from ambush.

But there was no time to play it safe. Friday was only two days away. Keeping the peace and saving the hides of some big-shots was not Jordon's main concern, though he felt some sense of responsibility to do his part in the deal with HR Buxton.

What Jordon wanted most, however, was to know for sure the identities of the men responsible for Willis's death.

It was almost more than Jordon could bear to think of Willis being dead. He tried to keep it out of his mind so he could think and do what he had to do. But it kept creeping back in.

And times when it hit him with its full force, it overwhelmed him. Which happened now. He felt his eyes begin to sting and water. He pulled his car over to the side of the road and gripped the steering wheel, staring at the tight white skin stretched across his knuckles.

Bowing his head forward and leaning it against the wheel, he set his jaw and gritted his teeth until he thought they might break. He felt like screaming his rage and frustration to the hills.

Goddamn, damn, damn it.

Grief flooded over him and he wept, and through the hot blur he could see the teardrops as they fell onto his pant legs. I still haven't been to the dry cleaners, he thought, as though it made any difference.

At last, he took a deep shuddering breath, pulled his handkerchief out of his pocket, and wiped his eyes and face, blew his nose, and started the car.

Somehow, someway, he would learn the truth, if it was the last thing he did on this earth. And if it was McCain, or whoever it might be, the score would be settled. And whoever was behind it, had hired it done, he, too, would pay.

$\triangledown$

16

JORDON PULLED HIS MODEL A into the wide place beside the road in front of Myra Chastayne's house.

It was a massive, two-story redbrick, crowned with a steeply pitched, gray slate roof, twin gables in front and others on the side, a round, windowed turret guarding each corner, and a broad covered porch running all the way across the front and around the sides. There was not another house even remotely similar to it in the entire county.

Jordon's eyes scanned the neatly clipped lawn and shrubbery in the level front yard, which covered more than an acre. He figured the house must contain at least a dozen rooms. It was, he decided, the kind of place he would not live in if somebody gave it to him. Which was the least of his worries.

He checked his watch. Two minutes before nine. The morning sun was already beating down on Stanton County, and no air was stirring. Dog days were not yet over. Jordon was supposed to be here at nine. He liked to be on time. And from what he'd heard about Myra Chastayne, she expected no less from anyone.

Jordon got out of the car and stretched, putting his hands on the small of his back and arching his spine.

He stepped up on the porch of the old Chastayne house and gave the handle of the mechanical bell on the door a sharp twist. He took off his wide-brim felt hat, ran his hands through his hair, and smoothed his mustache.

A stolid young woman of maybe thirty answered the door. She wore a plain gray dress and white apron and looked out at the world through sad, bovine eyes. Without a word, she stood aside and motioned Jordon to enter.

From inside came a strong, clear, "Come in!"

Jordon stepped into a well-lighted foyer, and the girl who had opened the door quickly disappeared back into the house. To Jordon's left a double doorway was open, leading into a parlor where Myra Chastayne sat in the center of the room in her wheelchair.

Her expression, Jordon thought, was one of unamused skepticism, as though she were a queen on her throne, prepared to receive one of her ministers and hear some excuse about why he had failed to carry out some command or other. As Jordon looked at her, *imposing* was the word that came to his mind.

"You may sit down, sir." Her voice was gravelly, but friendlier than he'd expected, judging from her appearance and what he had heard about her.

Jordon thanked her and took a seat in a well-stuffed chair nearby. He sat up straight, waiting for some signal as to her attitude. An electric fan in the corner of the room hummed benignly as it moved the air around in the room, which seemed surprisingly cool considering the temperature outside. His nostrils caught the aroma of something minty, pennyroyal maybe, in the air.

"Make yourself comfortable," Myra Chastayne said. "Lean back and stretch your legs if you feel like it."

Jordon grinned a little, then extended his legs and crossed his feet.

"Something to drink?" she asked.

"Coffee would be fine, if it's convenient."

"Nothing stronger? Bourbon, maybe?

A little early, Jordon thought, but he said, "What are you having?"

She picked up a little silver bell from the table beside her and gave it a vigorous shake. The young woman in the apron appeared from another room. "Bring glasses and ice and bourbon, Lorene."

"Yes, ma'am," the girl said in a quiet little voice and quickly left the room. It was the first time she had spoken. She returned almost immediately with a tray on which were two glasses, a silver bucket of ice, and a cut-glass decanter two-thirds full of a brown liquid Jordon hoped and expected was as good as it looked. He figured the tray must already have been prepared in anticipation of his saying yes.

"Put it here on the table next to me, Lorene."

"Yes, ma'am." Lorene disappeared again back in the house.

"So," Myra Chastayne said, and reached for the decanter, pouring generous drinks for both of them. "Ice?" she asked.

"Just plain," Jordon said.

"Me, too," she said with a smile. "Isn't it nice Prohibition is finally over and we can take a drink knowing deep down in our hearts that we are decent, law-abiding citizens?"

"We're still living in a dry county, of course."

She smirked. "Some dry county."

When he had his drink in hand, she lifted her glass and said, "Here's to money and power and a long life in which to enjoy them." She put her glass to her lips and drained it.

Jordon did the same. It was good bourbon. As good as it looked.

Myra Chastayne set her glass down and opened a box on the table and took out a cigarette. "Smoke?" she asked Jordon.

He shook his head.

She lit up, took a deep drag, and blew the smoke out in a long fine stream. She looked at Jordon for a moment and said, "You said you're doing something for HR Buxton and you needed to see me. So what is it?"

Jordon was glad to get right to it. "I'm trying to find out who killed Willis Dobbs."

She poured herself another drink of bourbon and extended the bottle toward him. He let her pour him another three fingers or so as well.

"And how do you think I might help you?" Myra Chastayne said.

"I'm not sure. I thought maybe you could have done some

speculating as to who might have hired the gunman that killed Willis and Turner Lott." Jordon had no real idea why HR had thought he should talk with Mrs. Chastayne.

"Why would you think that?"

"Everybody else is. Speculating, that is. Actually, I came to see you because Mr. Buxton suggested it."

She studied him for a long time. "Do you think I might have had something to do with it?"

Jordon chose his words carefully. "I have no reason to think that."

She was quiet for a long time. "How well did you know Willis, Mr. Jordon?"

"He was the best friend I had."

"What about his early life? Did you two ever talk about that?"

Jordon thought about it for a few moments. "Not really, except for a few things."

She watched him closely as she spoke her next words. "You didn't know Willis was my sister Annie's boy, did you?"

Jordon was dumbfounded. "No."

"Let me tell you something. I was a McDonough before I was married. Born and raised in Whitley County. My father was a merchant. Right well-to-do. I graduated from the Williamsburg Academy. One of my sisters, Annie, married Logan Dobbs, Willis's daddy. When Willis was eight years old, his mother died of consumption. Logan had always been a heavy drinker, but after she died, he took to it with a devilish thirst. And before a year was up, he was found dead in his bed. They weren't sure what killed him. Some people thought it was bad liquor he got ahold of. But I've always believed it was caused by him just plain not wanting to live after Annie died. He just gave up and died."

"Willis never talked to me about any of this."

"Did you ever ask him?"

Jordon shook his head. "We just always took one another for what we were, and never asked a lot of questions."

"Like most men," she said, looking disgusted. "Afraid to

talk about yourselves even to your best friend." She took a sip of her bourbon. "With Willis's mother and daddy both dead, I took him into my home. He was just nine then. My first husband, Jacob Wells, had been dead about two years at that time. He was a hotheaded man, full of passion and quick to anger. Killed in a gunfight just outside Middlesboro. My son Clayton was seven years old when Willis came to live with us, and the two boys played together. Then, a year or so later, I married again. To Adam Chastayne. He was a businessman, and a damned good one. Timber and coal. And he made a lot of money before he got killed in an accident in the log woods in 1917. He left me a widow again, but he left me rich."

"So Willis lived with you all that time?"

"No. Willis left my home in 1900, after staying with me for about six years. He wanted to take care of himself, so he got a job in the mines. He was about fifteen at the time."

Jordon tried to digest all this new information about his buddy, wondering how it might help him somehow in his search for the killer.

"The reason I wanted you to know these things, Mr. Jordon, was to give you an idea how I felt about Willis. If I could help you, I would. If I knew who killed him, I'd have the slimy sonofabitch killed myself."

"What about Turner Lott? Was he related to you, too?"

"No. Turner and Willis were related through Willis's dad."

"I see." Jordon could think of nothing more to ask her. He felt like a fish flopping around out of the water.

"Who else did HR Buxton tell you to talk to?"

Jordon hesitated for just a moment. "Pennyrile Gruber and Asher Jennings." Then he added, "And Sheriff Trumble."

"And have you? Talked to them?"

"Not yet. But I aim to."

She nodded. "Do you need anything? Is there any help I can give you?"

"You have no thoughts at all about who might be behind this?"

"None that you don't already have if you've talked to HR Buxton."

"I'm curious about one thing, Mrs. Chastayne."

"What's that?"

"How come you aren't any more upset than you are about Willis's death?"

"You want to know why I'm not weeping and wailing and sniveling about it?"

"Or showing any feeling at all."

"Because I'm a realist. And because, for a woman, showing feelings is often interpreted as a sign of weakness. I learned very early that life is filled with problems, things we can't control. So I take it as it comes. I'm seventy-three years old. Have lost two husbands. And watched Willis, who I loved like a son, leave my home, go to war, lose his leg in the mines, and now get killed by some sneaking sharpshooter. My son Clayton left home when he was eighteen. Last I ever heard from him, he was in New Orleans. Both of them, and a lot of other folks, always saw me as a domineering, meddling female with too little feeling and too much money. Well, by God, maybe I am. But I don't sit around twisting my hankie and crying about things beyond my influence. I do what I can, which most times is sufficient. And the rest can go to hell."

"That's plain enough," Jordon said.

"Remember this much, young man: I'm a very rich woman. If there is anything money can buy that will help you find who killed Willis Dobbs, you come to me. You hear?"

"This is one of those times when it takes something besides money to get the job done."

She shook her head. "That's a goddamn shame. You think you've got what it takes?"

"I don't know. I hope so."

She gave him a last hard look before he turned to go. "So do I, Mr. Jordon. Because I have a feeling you're going to need it."

*   *   *

Jordon was due at the the mountaintop home of Pennyrile Gruber that morning at eleven o'clock. He was five minutes early. When he parked and got out of his car, he could hear dogs barking somewhere behind the house. As the sound didn't come nearer, he assumed they were penned or chained up.

He rang the bell, and the door opened at once. A big man with a face that looked like it had been bigger once but had been crunched together, stood looking at him. "What is it?" His voice was not friendly.

"My name is Jordon. I have an appointment with Mr. Gruber."

"He's not here."

"But we had an appointment at eleven," Jordon said, looking at his watch to make sure of the time.

"He had to go out. Said for me to tell you you'll have to see him another time."

"You know where he went?"

The man's voice was not quite a snarl. "If I do, I'm not about to tell you. You'll have to see him another time."

Jordon started to respond, but instead simply turned and went to his car and headed back to Buxton. His appointment with Asher Jennings was at two o'clock this afternoon.

Pearl took a final look at her face and dabbed at her cheek with a powder puff. The bruises still showed through, in spite of all she could do. Her eyes were red from weeping, and her hand shook at she applied the talcum. Last night when she and Moody had got home, the bad feelings between them had erupted into a fight. Moody had hurt her worse than he ever had before. He was furious at the attention Pennyrile Gruber had shown her, and at her response to him. Tears welled in her eyes as she remembered what he had said and done to her, things she wondered if any man had ever done to a woman before. Especially a woman he pretended to care about. She would never forget how the broomstick hurt.

Now, it was almost noon and Moody had been gone since early morning on some kind of union business. Thinking about her situation all morning, she had finally decided on what she would do.

She had called Pennyrile Gruber about ten o'clock and told him she had to see him about something urgent. She had made her voice sound as promising as she knew how. He didn't hesitate. "Meet me at the fork of the road outside of Chambers," he'd said, "at noontime. Just walk on past the commissary, past the tipple, and around the curve. Wait at the side of the road. I'll pick you up."

"What if Moody comes along?" she'd asked.

"Stay hid in the woods till you see my car," Pennyrile told her "It's a gray Packard sedan. You'll know it. I'll stop and wait for you to come out."

Pearl was watching the road from behind a big oak tree when she heard a car coming. She wore a pretty, white form-fitting dress and carried a small white purse. As the car came into view she watched and waited until it rolled to a stop near where she stood. The window on the driver's side was down and she could see that Pennyrile Gruber was driving and that he was alone. He glanced around both sides of the road, looking for her. Pearl ran from her hiding place toward the car. As soon as he saw her, Pennyrile said, "Get in, honey." She ran around the car and jumped in.

She had been crying again as she waited, and she knew her makeup was ruined. When Pennyrile saw her he said, "What happened, Pearl?"

She started to cry again, and he said, "Never mind. I reckon I know already. We can talk about it later."

Between sobs she said, "Will you help me?"

Pennyrile said, "You're not married to him, are you?"

"No."

Pennyrile nodded. "Good. I never mix into trouble between a man and his wife. Learned about that the hard way when I was a young feller." He rubbed a small crescent-shaped scar on his right cheek. Then he reached over and patted Pearl on the shoulder. "What is it you want, honey?"

"Will you help me get away from him, from here?"

He hesitated only a moment. "If that's what you want."

"Can I stay with you till I go?"

"You can."

She began to cry again, without restraint. "You go ahead, sweetheart. Let it out." He started the engine and began to turn the car around there in the middle of the road.

"Where are we going?" she asked.

"To my house. Why?"

"I have to go back home first. There's a few things I got to get."

He studied her for a moment. "Why didn't you bring 'em?"

She looked at him and wiped her eyes and nose. "I didn't know if you'd help me."

"Something you got to have?"

"Stuff I want."

"Where's McCain?"

"I don't know. He left early this morning. Some business with his union friends, he said."

"Union friends?"

She sniffled and nodded. "I guess I can tell you. He's here to help organize the miner's union."

"He told you that?"

She nodded again. "I'm not supposed to talk about it, but what difference can it make now?"

Pennyrile shook his head. "What difference, indeed. Well, let's get your stuff and get out of here. I don't much think it would be a good idea to be around here when he comes back."

He straightened the car and drove on into the camp and to the house she directed him to. As they passed down the single cinder-covered street that ran alongside the railroad, women in several of the houses looked out their front doors at them. A couple of them even came out on the porch and stared openly.

"You can come inside with me if you want," Pearl said. "But I won't be long either way."

"I'll come."

Inside, Pearl pulled a large tan fabric-covered suitcase from under the bed and began to throw clothes, cosmetics, earrings, bracelets, shoes, and magazines into it. She looked around the room, trying to remember if there was something she was forgetting.

Pennyrile pulled a chair over to where he could watch out the front window and see the street. "Don't worry about anything you might leave," he said. "We'll get you new stuff. For that matter, you can leave all this." He waved his hand around the room.

"I want my things," she said. "They're mine." To herself she said: They cost me enough, and I intend to keep them.

As she closed the lid on the suitcase and started to snap it shut, she heard the back door open. She sucked in her breath and her hand went to her mouth as a wave of terror rippled through her.

She heard a couple of footsteps and then saw Moody McCain appear in the doorway to the bedroom, smiling as though he was pleased to have company.

Pennyrile Gruber started to stand up, but McCain motioned him back down with his hand.

Pearl was speechless.

McCain looked at the suitcase, then at Pearl, still smiling. "Going someplace?"

Pearl was still holding her hand to her mouth. She took it away, but said nothing. She looked from McCain to Pennyrile and back again.

"Cat got your tongue?" Moody asked.

She tried to say something, but it was just a noise, more of a croak.

Again Pennyrile started to stand up, but this time McCain put his hand into his pocket and came out with his short-barreled .38 Smith & Wesson special. "Just sit there and make yourself comfortable, Mr. Gruber. I'll let you know when to get up." McCain let the hand with the gun in it hang loosely at his side.

Pennyrile said, "Let's talk about this, McCain. This is no time to do anything crazy."

"Don't use that word with me!" McCain said. "It was one of my daddy's favorites."

Pennyrile nodded. "Sorry. But let's talk about this. We're both reasonable men. Pearl wants to leave. Why don't you let her go? We won't cause you any trouble. After all, you and I have business to be done."

"You won't cause *me* trouble?" McCain laughed. "Seems to me it's the other way around. What the hell do you mean coming into my house and trying to steal my woman?"

Pennyrile rubbed on his right thigh, scratched it a little, then left his hand near his pocket. "She wanted to go," he said. "And I agreed to help her. That's all."

"Aw, come on now, Pennyrile. That's surely not all," McCain said, his voice heavy with sarcasm. "I saw how you looked at her last night. Like a hungry boar hog at slopping time."

"I just wanted to help her," Pennyrile said. He moved his hand closer to his pocket.

Again McCain laughed. It was cold and harsh. He turned to Pearl. "You feel like talking now, honey? You going to try to make me believe you really want to leave your sweet Mooooooody?" He shook his head, as if it saddened him. "And after I've been as good to you as I have?"

McCain turned suddenly and pointed the gun at Pennyrile. "Stand up. Face the wall. Put your hands over your head."

Pennyrile said, "Wait a minute, now. There's nothing here we can't work out."

"Do it!"

Pennyrile stood up, faced the wall, raised his hands.

McCain stepped over to him and began to frisk him, feeling his right pocket first. McCain reached into the pocket and took out a small pistol. "Lookee here. Thirty-two squeeze-handle," he said. "I thought you had a mighty itchy leg."

"I carry it all the time," Pennyrile said.

"Not any more," McCain said with a little laugh as he dropped the pistol into his own pocket. "Just stand there and keep watching the wall."

"What about our business?" Pennyrile said.

"We have no business," McCain replied. "Just talk up to this point."

"Well, I promise you, there's business for you. And plenty of money for it. Let's don't let this stuff today get in the way of that."

"Shut up," McCain said. He turned to Pearl and said, "Come over here to me."

Pearl felt her heart thumping as though it would burst from her breast. "Please, Moody. I didn't mean anything. I was just mixed up. Scared. I'll stay, and do whatever you want me to."

"Come, Pearl. Come to me."

She stepped closer. "Please?"

He motioned with his hand. "Come."

She came closer and suddenly McCain lashed out with his left hand, so fast it was like a blacksnake whip flicking a fly off a mule's rump, and slapped her hard across the face, sending her sprawling across the bed on top of the suitcase.

She shrieked and started to wail.

Pennyrile Gruber moved as if to turn around and look.

But McCain took two quick steps and hit him across the back of the head with the .38. Pennyrile groaned and collapsed on the floor.

"Like a sack of shit," McCain said. He bent down, rolled Pennyrile over, took a handful of his shirt, pulled him to a sitting position, and propped him against the wall. "I told you to keep watching the wall. You been on top of the dung heap so long you've plumb forgot how to listen."

Pennyrile shook his head. Looking half dazed, he reached around to touch the back of his head. He brought his hand away and looked at the blood on his fingers.

McCain was still bent over, only inches from Pennyrile's face.

Suddenly, Pennyrile made a grab for McCain's gun hand, wrenching it around until it pointed toward the wall.

With his free hand, McCain went for Pennyrile's throat, pushing him back to the floor.

As the two of them struggled, Pearl jumped from the bed and stumbled out the front door and ran down the street, not looking back. She crossed to the other side of the dirt street and kept running all the way down to the swinging footbridge that spanned the creek, then across it toward the handful of houses on the other side.

She kept on running, past the houses, through the woods. She wasn't sure where she was running to, but she had no doubt what she was running away from. Her life with Moody McCain.

As she ran, she heard the crack of a single gunshot echo from the camp.

She altered her course and began to claw her way up the side of the mountain.

$\triangledown$

17

JORDON STRODE UP THE broad front steps of the Stanton County Courthouse in Kings Mill two at a time. He'd only been back inside the building a couple times since the election last fall. If he had won, he'd be spending much of each day here now.

Surveying the dimly lit halls that stank of disinfectant and stale tobacco smoke, he wondered if he ever had truly wanted to be high sheriff. He certainly had not lusted after it enough to pay the price to win. Which also was true of most of the other goals he'd watched others struggle to attain in life.

His goal now, however, was simple and straighforward: to catch up with the men responsible for Willis's death. It was clear and enticing, even if the path to it was obscure. He knew what he wanted to do, and he didn't allow himself to question the rightness of it. He would do what he had to do, which was the same as what he wanted to do. If he could just figure out how to do it.

Down the hallway on the left was the sheriff's office. Jordon stepped inside and asked the office deputy behind the counter if Sheriff Trumble was in. The deputy was a man Jordon didn't know.

"What's your name and your business with the sheriff?" the deputy asked from his desk.

"My name is Jordon. And my business with the sheriff is private."

The deputy, a skinny man who looked to be around forty, gave Jordon an unfriendly once-over and said, "Wait here."

He went into the sheriff's private office, a room Jordon was quite familiar with from the months he'd spent working out of it under Sheriff Noble Treadway.

The skinny deputy came back out and said, "He'll see you." He sounded as though he was not pleased about it.

Jordon went through the open door and found Sheriff John Bill Trumble propped back in his chair, his large relaxed body dressed in faded khakis, his booted feet on his desk top. He fixed his droopy, hound-dog eyes on Jordon and made a small movement with his lips. It was not a smile. Maybe, Jordon thought, he's adjusting his false choppers. They always seemed to be clicking around in his mouth when he talked. Trumble made no effort at friendliness or even ordinary courtesy.

Jordon remembered the trouble he and Trumble had had during the election campaign last fall, how Trumble's men had heckled Jordon, told lies about his record as a deputy in other counties, and contributed in large measure, Jordon was sure, to his ultimate defeat. The dirty politicking had been done, Jordon was also sure, at Trumble's direction. Jordon could still hear Trumble's words on election night: "Elections is about winning and losing, boy. Truth ain't got nothing to do with it. A feller ain't learnt that, he's better off staying home with the women and chillern. He don't know enough yet to be out in the world by his self."

Now, having triumphed over Jordon at the polls, Trumble sat here enjoying the fruits of his victory. "What is it you want?"

Jordon took a deep breath and expelled it slowly. "HR Buxton suggested I talk to you and see what you might be able to tell me about the death of Willis Dobbs."

"What business is it of yours?"

"Willis was my friend. I'm trying to learn who killed him."

"What's that got to do with Mr. Buxton?"

"For reasons of his own, Mr. Buxton would like to see me find the man who shot Willis."

"What reasons?"

"You'll have to ask him that."

"I'm asking you."

Jordon shrugged. "I really can't say. I can say, however, that he and I are after the same thing: finding whoever it was killed Willis Dobbs and Turner Lott."

The sheriff stared coldly at Jordon a moment. "I'm the high sheriff of this county. It's my job to find out who killed them men. It's none of your business."

"It's a very personal matter to me," Jordon said.

Sheriff Trumble picked up a piece of paper from his desk and began to study it. "If and when I get information I think ought to be passed on, I'll get it to the people I figure it ought to go to."

"Who are you talking about?"

The sheriff glared at him. "Who, hell. Your feet don't fit no limb, boy. I ain't got nothing to tell you."

Jordon looked him over for a few seconds, a sardonic little grin playing at his lips, then slowly shook his head.

"What?" Sheriff Trumble asked.

"Nothing."

"What, goddammit?" His voice had a sharp edge.

Jordon turned to go, then looked back over his shoulder. "You really are a low-down sonofabitch, John Bill."

Moving with surprising speed for a large man, Sheriff Trumble was on his feet, pointing a finger like a pistol at Jordon. "Some people around this county are afraid of you, Jordon. They think you're bad. But I'm not one of them. You come into my office and talk to me like this, you could find yourself up shit creek without a paddle."

Jordon grinned at him and walked out. In the outer office, the skinny deputy was watching Jordon closely. As Jordon went by, the deputy looked up with a little grin. And a tiny nod.

It was a few minutes before one in the afternoon when Jordon left the sheriff's office. He decided to stop in the court clerk's office where Cassie worked and say hello. He still had plenty of time to get to Asher Jennings's home by two.

Cassie had her head buried in a stack of papers when he stepped inside. Another woman who stood near the counter said, "Can I help you?"

"I'd like a word with that lady," Jordon said, pointing toward Cassie.

At the sound of his voice, Cassie looked up and smiled warmly. She got up and came around the desk to where he stood. "It's good to see you, Berk. How are you?"

Jordon felt his pulse quicken. She looked marvelous, standing there in a simple pale blue blouse and dark blue skirt that showed off her mature, totally feminine figure. He remembered how good she looked with nothing on, as the two of them would sometimes loll in her big feather bed for hours at a time during the days when things were good between them. He looked at her full head of dark hair swept back in a loose wavy style, and thought, she may be forty-one, but to me she's like a girl. Her big soft brown eyes and her bright smile, with the little crooked place in her front teeth, brought back memories almost too painful for him to bear.

"I'm okay," he said. "Had some business with the sheriff, and just stopped by to say hello on my way out."

She came around the counter. "Come on, I'll walk you outside."

As they stepped out onto the front steps of the courthouse, she said, "Dog days this year seem worse than any time I can remember."

He looked at her. "They don't seem to be having any effect on you. You're as fresh and pretty as ever."

He thought she blushed, but he couldn't be sure.

She gave him an anxious look as they made their way slowly down the steps. "You feeling any better about Willis now?"

He gave his hand a little wave. "Aaah." He sighed. "It follows me around like a hungry dog."

She stopped and touched his arm. "I know how it feels to lose someone you love." She looked down.

"Your husband, you mean," he said.

She looked up at him and said nothing.

He cleared his throat and said, "Ah, well, I better keep moving." After a moment he added, "Got to see a man named Asher Jennings over on the other end of the county directly."

She nodded. "Thanks for stopping in."

He tried a little smile, but it didn't work too well. "Yeah."

She took his hand and squeezed it. "Be careful, Berk."

He said, "Sure," and started on down the steps. Near the bottom he looked back.

She was still standing there, midway, watching him go.

Suddenly he blurted, "Cass?"

"Yes?"

"Would you be interested in going out with me for supper sometime? Maybe take in a picture show?"

She smiled at him for a moment, then said, "Call me."

He tried a smile again, and this time it came better.

She turned to go, then glanced back at him and said, "That's not a maybe, Berk. That's a yes."

Before he could reply, she ran up the steps and back inside, reminding him for the world of a schoolgirl who's just heard the bell ring, signaling the end of recess.

Jordon knocked on the front door of Asher Jennings's home and waited. It was a medium-size, two-story, white frame structure, set on a large level lot that had been graded away at the foot of a hill near the paved highway a couple of miles outside Buxton.

The house appeared to be well built and maintained, and the grounds showed the effects of continuing care, but the place was nowhere near as imposing as the homes of HR Buxton or Myra Chastayne. Jordon knew that Jennings, while he was a coal operator, was not in the same league as either HR or Myra. Jennings owned several smaller mines and generally conducted his business in Stanton County with little fanfare.

Asher Jennnings himself answered the door. "Mr. Jordon? Come in."

Jordon stepped inside. The house was much cooler than the temperature outside, made so apparently by cross breezes stirred by a couple of large fans. Also, the house itself was shaded by two huge oak trees.

Jennings took him into a small officelike room where there was a desk, a couple of file cabinets, and two plain chairs. "Sit down."

Jennings took his place behind the desk and said, "You said on the phone you were doing something for HR Buxton. How can I help you?"

Jordon watched Jennings closely as he began to fidget with a letter opener, blinking his bulging eyes through his thick-lensed glasses. In spite of the heat, he was wearing a starched white shirt and florid tie.

Jordon said, "Mr. Buxton suggested that I ought to ask you if you could give me any information about the murders of Willis Dobbs and Turner Lott."

Jennings's eyes blinked even more. He seemed irritated. "Why me?"

"You're one of several people he said I ought to talk to."

"I'm afraid I can't help you. I know nothing about this matter."

"Have you even speculated about who might want to have it done? And why?"

"I really don't have time for such speculation, sir. My days and nights are fully taken up trying to keep my business from going under during this damned depression."

"I know things are bad," Jordon said. "It's affecting us all."

"You're not a businessman, are you, Mr. Jordon?"

Jordon shook his head.

"Well, then there's no way you can possibly know what I'm going through." Jennings waved his hand. "As I've already told you, I have no time for speculating about the violence that goes on around here all the time. And I have no time for further discussion of it." He stood up. "Unless there's something else, I need to get back to work."

The telephone on Jennings's desk rang, and he picked up the receiver. "Yes?" He jotted something on a pad and said, "I'll get back to you." He listened for a moment, then repeated, "I said I'll get back to you." He listened again, then said, "Yes. Soon. Right away." Again he paused, then said, "That's right," and hung up.

Jennings stood up. Once more he said, "I have to get back to work."

Jordon, too, stood. "Thank you for seeing me. If you should think of anything, you can reach me by calling Della's Place and leaving word. I'll get back to you."

Jennings said nothing. He guided Jordon through the house and out the door.

18

Moody McCain watched Pennyrile Gruber roll his head back and forth, trying, it seemed, to clear his mind and make some sense of what had happened to him.

"You're going to be fine," Moody said. "No real damage done to you. You're lucky I took pity on you and shot into the wall instead of your head. Hell, it missed by at least two inches. Just a warning, old man, that's all. And you're being smart. Just keep on being smart and you might come out of all this in one piece."

Pennyrile looked at himself. He was sitting on the floor propped up against the wall, ankles bound together with rope, hands tied behind his back. He looked back at McCain. "What is it you want from me?"

McCain waved his pistol toward Pennyrile. "Right now, just keep your mouth shut while I think a few things through. Then I'll let you know."

Pennyrile said nothing more.

McCain looked at Pearl's things on the bed—the partially filled suitcase, the dresses, the makeup, the magazines. He pushed everything off onto the floor and lay down, propping his head up on both pillows.

He lay there looking at the telephone, wondering how soon Asher Jennings would call back. Somebody had been in Jennings's office when McCain had called before. Suddenly everything's changing, McCain thought. This morning, in town, a miner McCain had seen around but didn't know had taken him aside and told him that Jordon had been poking around all over the county asking about Mc-Cain, trying to learn if he'd had anything to do with the killing of Lott and the one-legged fellow, Willis. "Who the hell are you, and where'd you pick this up?" McCain had asked the man. "I do some things for Mr. HR Buxton, unbeknownst to anybody," the man said, "and I'm supposed to let you know about what Jordon is doing." McCain didn't know whether to trust the man or not, but somebody sure as hell knew something.

And then, coming home and finding Pearl fixing to take off with Pennyrile Gruber. A dumb-assed cunt and a sneaking, sniffing old sonofabitch still following his dick wherever it led. It had made McCain so angry he'd almost lost all control. He came within an ace of killing them both. But now he was glad he had not. Pennyrile was worth a lot more alive than dead. And Pearl, well, McCain would take care of her later, in his own good time. She knew too much to be left alive.

He rubbed his finger along the scar on his face as he tried to sort out what was going on, make some kind of plans. Jennings had told him there could be more work, high-priced work. If so, McCain wanted to do it and get the hell out of here.

Jennings had already paid him for Lott and Willis. If there was more to be done, for an even bigger fee, then he wanted it now. Or to hell with it.

The telephone rang and McCain went to the wall and picked up the receiver. "Yes."

It was Jennings. "I can talk."

McCain and Jennings had discussed early on about how careful they had to be on the telephone. McCain replied, "Lots of things happening."

Jennings said, "Yes."

"I may be traveling soon."

"Can we meet tonight?"

The hour and place for their meetings were prearranged, but McCain said, "I think not."

Jennings was silent for a moment, then said, "Somebody was here. We need to talk."

McCain thought about it for a moment, then said, "An hour from now?"

Jennings hesitated, then said, "Yes."

McCain replaced the receiver on its hook and sat studying Pennyrile Gruber. "How would you like for things to be back just like they were before this morning?"

Pennyrile said, "I'd like that very much, indeed."

McCain studied him for a moment, then said, "Is it worth twenty-five thousand dollars to you?"

Pennyrile's hesitation lasted only a moment. "Yes." Then he added, "If I can get it together."

McCain laughed. "Don't shit me. I'm going to call the Bank of Buxton, and you can talk to the president and tell him you want twenty-five thousand in fives, tens, and twenties got ready for you. Tell them you'll arrange for picking it up later. Then we'll take it from there."

"I'll try." ·

"No. You'll do it. You'll do it because you want to see the sun come up tomorrow morning."

McCain backed Pennyrile Gruber's big Packard sedan into the bushes off the narrow trail that led away from the dirt road. Satisfied that the car could not be spotted from the road, McCain took a last look at Pennyrile, who lay trussed up and sweating on the floor behind the front seat. "Rest easy, now. We ain't going to be here long."

McCain checked his watch. Still a good ten minutes before Jennings was supposed to be there. McCain walked down the road away from Pennyrile's car. He didn't want Jennings to see it when he arrived.

McCain reflected on the plan he had set in motion in the past hour. He had called the operator and asked for the bank, then listened to the conversation with his head stuck next to Pennyrile's as the bank president, a Mr. Bertram, had gone through some routine about "This is highly irregular" and some other shit. To a banker, everything was irregular except making money. "It's an important business deal, damn it," Pennyrile had said, just as McCain had instructed him to do. "I need the cash and I need it right away." Bertram had agreed to get it together. He insisted he would not release it to anyone, however, without Pennyrile himself signing for it. McCain had nodded, then whispered to Pennyrile, "Tell him we'll call back and let them know where to deliver it. And that you'll be there to receive it and sign for it." Pennyrile, of course, followed the instructions to a T, and the arrangements were completed. The old bastard did, indeed, want to keep on living.

McCain had untied Pennyrile then, and they had walked side-by-side, for the benefit of the neighbors, to Pennyrile's car, where Pennyrile got into the driver's seat, and McCain sat next to him. From the time they had left the house, McCain's gun was pointed through his trousers pocket at Pennyrile.

They had driven away from Chambers and out a gravel road about a mile and a half from Buxton, where they had parked and walked to a clump of big rocks and sumac bushes where McCain retrieved his long leather bag from a hole back under one of the rocks. So what if Pennyrile knew where McCain's hiding place was? He wouldn't be using it anymore after today.

Then, McCain had tied Pennyrile up and driven here to his meeting with Jennings.

Soon, Jennings came driving up in his 1933 Plymouth. No showy machine for him, McCain thought. Uses his money for important stuff, like investing in coal mines and eliminating enemies.

Jennings got out of the car and wiped his forehead with a clean white handkerchief. "You know this man Jordon?" Jennings asked.

McCain nodded. "Some."

"I think he knows too much. More than is safe for us."

"Is he the one was there when I called?"

Now Jennings nodded. "He said HR Buxton told him to talk to me about the two killings. He acted to me like a man who knows more than he was letting on."

McCain digested this. Added to what he had heard from the miner this morning, it sounded like Jennings could be right. Somehow Jordon had got on to something solid.

"What are you thinking?" Jennings said. "That maybe it's nothing to worry about?"

McCain shook his head. "No. I think you're probably right. He's got a whiff of something."

"If he has, there's no stopping him until he gets to the bottom of it."

"You know him?"

"Know of him. He was the one in a murder case here last fall. The sonofabitch dug and dug until he finally dug up who it was killed a young girl. Stirred up a lot of shit, trouble for HR and Young Harry Buxton. Not to mention the man that killed her."

"What do you want to do about him?"

Jennings stared at him. "I would think you'd want to be rid of him."

McCain shook his head in dismay. "I don't believe this. He's breathing down your collar, got you so nervous you're shaking like a dog shitting peach seeds, and you want me to get rid of him for nothing."

"It's not my money, you know, that I've given you. It's other people I've got to answer to. I can't . . ."

McCain held up his hand, silencing Jennings. "First, you ain't give me anything. I've done work for it. And second, if the sonofabitch causes trouble for me, that's trouble for you, believe it. And third, if you don't want to pay me, piss on it. I've got other stuff to do."

McCain turned around as if to go. "By the way, how about the other job you said might be coming up? Something very big, you said."

"I haven't heard for sure yet. It's still up in the air." Jennings took out his handkerchief and wiped his face. "All right, all right. Five hundred for Jordon. Same as for Lott."

McCain glared at him. "This Jordon could be a tough nut to crack."

Jennings blinked rapidly. "I could get somebody around here to do it for a lot less. A hell of a lot less."

"And run the risk they'd fuck it up, and then come back to you wanting more money, try to blackmail you, who knows what? I don't fuck things up. And once I'm finished here, I'm gone. You never have to see me again. My fee is worth every cent it costs you. I'm still not sure I ought to do Jordon for five hundred." He paused, as if thinking it over. He hated this goddamn quibbling over money. It was not professional. Not at all. "I'll do it. But I want my money now."

"What makes you think I've got it with me?"

"Because you are smart enough to know I'd expect it. And you were going to pay it all along. And you like to be prepared. Right?"

Jennings nodded. "I'll get it." He went to his car and brought back an envelope, which he handed to McCain.

McCain put it in his pocket without looking inside it.

"You don't want to . . . ?"

Moody grinned as he watched him, standing there blinking his big eyes like a frog in a hailstorm. "You wouldn't shortchange me, would you?"

Jennings kept blinking. "Of course not."

Pearl stood at the counter of the country store and said, "Can I use your phone?" The air in the place was heavy with the aroma of cheese and baloney, leather and coal oil, tobacco and cow feed.

The thick-bodied middle-aged woman storekeeper had her lips compressed in a tight line as she gave Pearl a thorough inspection.

Pearl glanced at herself. She was a mess. How could she not be, after crawling up the side of the mountain and walking through the woods for miles. Her once-white dress was filthy and torn, she had deliberately broken the high heels off her shoes so she could walk better. And her arms and legs, probably her face, too, were scratched from bushes and briars. Then there were the bruises she already had, from last night.

"I'll be glad to pay you," Pearl said. "I just need to call somebody."

The woman's face softened a little. "Are you hurt? Did some man mistreat you?"

Pearl knew what she meant. "It's not that," she said. "I just had some car trouble and decided to take a shortcut through the woods." She tried to smile. "It turned out to be a bad decision."

"You can use the phone. There's no charge."

Pearl went to the telephone. The storekeeper stood nearby watching and listening.

"Would you mind if it was private?" Pearl said.

The woman gave her a cold look, shrugged, then turned and went back through the store. Pearl could see the two men and several boys on the porch outside peering through the windows at her.

Though she had been trying to think about what to do as she trudged through the woods, Pearl still had not made up her mind what was best. She didn't want to do anything that would make Moody do something real bad to Pennyrile. Kill him, maybe, if he hadn't already done it. She worried about the shot she heard when whe was running away. But if Pennyrile wasn't dead already, once Moody was out of the picture, Pennyrile would take care of her. She knew he would. Otherwise, he wouldn't be where he is. He had to have known he was taking a chance when he came to meet her, but he took it anyway. For her. She thought about calling the sheriff. Maybe that would be best. Let him straighten it out. Moody wouldn't want a shoot-out with the law.

She took the receiver, cranked the phone, and said, "Sheriff's office."

That's what the man who answered said. "Sheriff's office."

"Can I talk to the sheriff, please?"

"He ain't in right now. I'm the office deputy, Hixon. What is it you want?"

Pearl wasn't exactly sure. "I've been hit, hurt."

"What's your name?"

"Pearl . . . McCain."

"What's your problem, now, Miz McCain? You say you've been hurt?"

"I . . . my husband . . . hit me."

"Is he drinking?"

"No. He doesn't drink."

The deputy was silent for a moment. "What did you do that made him hit you?"

"Nothing."

She could hear the deputy take a deep breath and sigh. "A man don't hardly ever hit a woman unless he's been drinking or got some other real good reason to. You sure you didn't do nothing to give him a reason?"

"No. But Mr. Gruber . . . he's . . . I'm afraid for him."

"Pennyrile Gruber?" The deputy chuckled. "You and Pennyrile Gruber and your husband, involved in some kind of fracas? I think I'm beginning to understand."

"No you don't."

"I know Pennyrile Gruber, lady. Most folks around here do. Sounds to me like what we've got here is a family matter. The sheriff don't get involved in family matters."

"Does that mean you won't do anything?"

The line was silent for a moment. "If your husband has reason to believe that you and Pennyrile Gruber were . . . being specially friendly with one another, you know what I mean? . . . and he decided to do something about it, then the law would stay out of it. Unless somebody got killed. And maybe then, too, depending on who was on the receiving end."

"You don't understand all of it—"

"I believe I do. If I was to find out my wife was messing around with Pennyrile Gruber, or some other man, I'd probably shoot him and beat her within an inch of her life. Maybe shoot her, too. You understand? And the law wouldn't do nothing about it. Never has. Never will, I hope."

"That's not the way it is." Pearl stumbled on. "This man's . . . not actually my husband."

"McCain's not? But you been living with him, is that it?"

"Yes. We're . . . planning on getting married later."

"It's against the law to live with a man you're not married to. You know that, don't you? That's illegal."

Pearl didn't know what to say.

"Where you all living, Pearl?"

"In a house in Chambers. Rented from the Buxton company."

"Well, living with this here McCain like you admit you been doing, I'd say you've got even less legal rights than a wife, don't you reckon?"

"I guess so," Pearl said. Her voice sounded weak, even to her. And she was tired.

"Was there something else, Pearl?" the deputy asked. For some reason, he sounded tired to her as well.

"No. That's all."

"This here's free advice, for whatever it's worth to you, Pearl. You might give some thought to marrying your man McCain, instead of just living with him." He paused. "Most men ain't likely to buy a cow as long as they're getting all the milk they want for free. You know what I mean? And if I was you I wouldn't expect too much from old Pennyrile Gruber. He's not exactly the steady type when it comes to women. No, I'd say McCain's your best bet."

Pearl broke the connection and stood there holding the hook down. She considered her choices for a moment, then made up her mind. She would call Moody, try to reason with him. "The Pearl Schaeffer residence in Chambers," she told the operator. Moody had had her put the phone in her name, why she wasn't sure.

The phone rang. And rang again. And again. The operator came on and said, "There doesn't seem to be anybody home, ma'am. Is there another call?"

Pearl thought for a moment. "Ring Curly Bunch's residence, please."

"Yes, ma'am."

When Lulumae Bunch answered, Pearl said, "It's Pearl. From next door."

"Are you all right? Where'd you run off to, honey?"

"I'm at a store. Have you noticed, is Moody at home? Do you see his car?"

"Oh no, honey. Him and the other man, the one come with you? They left a while ago. Just walked out and got in that big gray car you all come in and drove off, pretty as you please."

"And nobody's there now? You're sure?"

"I'm sure, honey. The place is empty as my pocketbook."

Jordon took a cue from the rack and broke the balls. Sometimes shooting by himself helped him get his thinking in order. He still wasn't much closer to anything substantial than he'd been in the beginning. Nothing worthwhile from Myra Chastayne, except encouragement. Nothing from John Bill Trumble. Nothing from Asher Jennings. He had seemed kind of nervous, is all, like he might be trying to hide something. But maybe he was just worried about his business, like he said. And Pennyrile Gruber, hell, Jordon still hadn't seen him.

The phone rang and Slim Hall put down the deck of cards he was practicing with and answered it. He listened a moment and said, "For you."

Jordon left his cue on the table and went to the phone. "Jordon."

"This is HR Buxton. You talked to any of the people I suggested?"

Jordon told him which ones.

"Learn anything?"

"Nothing of any value, I reckon."

"You didn't mention Pennyrile."

"I tried to see him. Had an appointment with him this

morning, but when I showed up, he wasn't at home. His man said he had to go somewhere."

"I know what he was doing, at least part of the time. Pennyrile Gruber called the bank this afternoon and ordered twenty-five thousand dollars in small bills to be prepared for him. Said he'd call back later and arrange for getting it delivered."

Jordon whistled through his teeth. "He's got that kind of cash?"

"And more."

"You know all this for a fact?"

HR's voice sounded disgusted. "I own the bank. I know everything that happens there, especially anything unusual. And twenty-five thousand dollars cash is unusual, believe me. That's as much money as a coal miner would earn in about fifty years, at current wages, if he could work that long. Give or take a decade or so, of course."

Jordon thought about it for a moment. "Any ideas about what the money's for?"

"Just what my imagination can come up with is all."

"And what's that?"

"Well, you put it with something else I just learned today, and it's mighty interesting."

Jordon waited.

"I was told that John L. Lewis will be here in Buxton tonight."

"On his way to that big union rally in Pineville."

"That's it."

Jordon thought maybe things were beginning to take shape. "You know anything about a man named Moody McCain?"

After a moment, HR said, "I think I've heard his name mentioned. Why?"

"He may be one of the ones I've been trying to get a handle on."

"You know where he is?"

"Not at the moment. I know he lives in one of your houses in Chambers with some young woman."

"Well, what are we going to do about John L.? He ought to stay out of sight."

"I'll think about it. You know when he's coming in? And how?"

"On the train, I imagine. But I may be wrong. There's the southbound passenger due in at six-twenty-two. I'll have somebody watch for him."

"Good. And call me back if you hear anything else. Okay?"

HR said he would, and they hung up.

Slim Hall stopped dealing and said, "Something about to happen?"

"Could be."

"Anything I can do?"

"That could be, too. Would you mind going with me later if it comes to it?"

"Anytime."

"It could turn out to be right dangerous."

"Say the word."

Jordon nodded and grinned a little. He liked this boy.

It was less than half an hour later when HR called again. "A new development," he told Jordon.

"What?"

"Pennyrile called the bank again. Wants his money delivered to him at the Buxton Hotel at nine tonight."

"Is he registered there?"

"Not yet. But I'll know when he is."

"You're a good detective. Keep me posted."

"If it weren't for the seriousness of it," HR Buxton said, "I'd by God enjoy this stuff."

"You know what I can't figure out?"

"What?"

"Unless Pennyrile Gruber is a complete fool, which I doubt, he wouldn't be taking out a bundle of money like that right when he was about to pay somebody to shoot John L. Lewis. That's like advertising he's mixed up in something."

"Maybe so, but what else could he be doing?"

"Just business of some kind?"

"We don't ordinarily do business around here with that kind of cash, boy."

Boy? Jordon thought. Where was HR getting this "boy" stuff?

It was after dark when McCain pulled Pennyrile's Packard up to the Buxton Hotel. His watch said ten after eight. He parked in the shadows, well away from the entrance.

The hotel was a striking big wood-frame building, painted white and trimmed in black, that stood on a hillside, away from the street, situated so that guests in rooms on two sides could see Buxton's town square, most of the main street, the drugstore, and the Buxton Office Building.

Surrounding the hotel were half a dozen majestic old oak trees and a beautifully kept lawn with evergreen shrubbery here and there and winding flagstone walkways from the parking lot and through the parklike setting. It had four floors, more than sixty guest rooms and suites, and a large dining room reputed to be the best in several counties, some even said the best in all of Eastern Kentucky.

McCain glanced over the back of his seat and said to Pennyrile, "I'll be back soon. Just be comfortable, now. You wouldn't want anything to go wrong. Believe me, you wouldn't."

Inside the hotel, a couple of men sat in big comfortable chairs reading papers. Neither of them looked up. The clerk, a pudgy man of maybe forty with a thin reedy voice and a mottled complexion, said softly, "Yes, sir? May I help you?"

McCain said, "I'm with Mr. Pennyrile Gruber. He wants a small suite, on the second floor if possible, one where he can see the town square."

The clerk made a show of looking at his board, but McCain could see that most of the pegs had keys on them. "Why, yes. I can give you something on the second floor, right at the corner. One bedroom and a sitting room. Will that be satisfactory?"

"Fine," McCain said. "We'll be back in a little while. I'll take the key now."

"Would you like to sign in, sir?"

McCain took the pen and signed "J. C. Jackson for Mr. Gruber."

"Thank you, sir," the pudgy clerk said. He handed the key to McCain and said, "Mr. Gruber has been our guest many times, sir. So I know he'll enjoy his stay. Ah, how long will that be?"

"We'll let you know."

"That will be fine, sir."

McCain thought the clerk must have been an honors graduate from some ass-kissing school. But he liked the way there had been no difficulty.

Outside in the car, McCain spoke to Pennyrile. "This next part is important, Pennyrile. If you do it right, you're going to be okay. Tomorrow morning all this will seem like a dream. And not even a very bad one. If you don't, tomorrow morning folks around here'll be getting ready for slow walking and sad singing over your remains. Before I take the gag off, I want to know if you hear me and understand me completely. Just nod if you do."

Pennyrile nodded vigorously.

McCain took off the gag. "Now, before I untie your hands and feet, remember this thirty-eight I'm carrying. The one that put a bullet in the wall a couple of inches from your head today. I won't hesitate to kill you wherever it might become necessary. Right in the middle of the hotel lobby, if that's what it comes to. I hope you understand and believe me. You ought to."

"I do, I do," Pennyrile said. His voice sounded strange and cracked from the gag and from not talking for hours.

"We're going to walk into the lobby, up the stairs to the second floor, down the hall to our room, and go inside. You are not going to say anything to anybody, not going to speak to anybody if you are spoken to. Just nod. And if you do that, and do not slow down or stop on your way through the lobby and up the stairs, you'll be fine. Just walk like you're going to some important meeting that's all ready to begin. Do that and you'll make it." He paused a moment, then said, "Okay, let's go."

That's exactly the way it went. Into the lobby, across to the stairs, up them and down the hall to room 208, where McCain opened the door and steered Pennyrile inside, then followed him in and locked the door.

"Turn around and put your hands behind you," McCain said. As he tied Pennyrile up again, he said, "I'm sure you can see I'm a reasonable man. I wish this wasn't necessary, but you know that it is."

When he had finished binding and gagging Pennyrile again, McCain checked his watch. He still had to go back outside to take care of a couple of small chores. According to the instructions he had made Pennyrile give the banker, the man with the money would be at the hotel at nine sharp. That was only about thirty-five minutes from now.

Two boys were shooting sixty-one at the far table, and Slim Hall was reading a book behind the cash register at his high-counter station. Jordon stood looking out the screen door at the still August night. Two big fans humming in the poolroom moved the air around, but brought no real relief from the heat.

The phone rang, and Jordon got it.

It was HR once more. "Jordon? Pennyrile just checked in at the hotel."

"By himself?"

"No. This fellow McCain you mentioned, is he tall, blond, got a scar running down the left side of his face?"

"Right."

"That's him, then. He and McCain came in the hotel together. They've got a suite on the second floor, room two-oh-eight, facing the square."

"I'm on my way to the hotel."

"I'll walk over there now and get a room. Any particular place?"

"Yeah. On the second floor. Across the hall from McCain's. Move somebody if you have to. But be quiet about it."

"I'll see you there."

They hung up and Jordon looked at Slim Hall. "You ready?"

Slim nodded. "Do I need to take my pistol?" He reached behind the counter and pulled out an old-looking long-barreled .44 Smith special. "My daddy's old gun," he said. "But it'll shoot where you hold it."

"Bring it," Jordon said.

They told the boys at the far table they were closing up for the night.

Outside, Jordon said, "Wait for me in my car. I have to get something from my room."

Inside his little bedroom, Jordon unlocked the big wooden trunk where he kept most of his personal belongings, and in which he packed everything when he moved. Down in the bottom, wrapped in a towel, was a Stevens 12-gauge double-barreled sawed-off shotgun with a stock that some-body had cut away so that only the pistol grip remained. Jordon had confiscated the fierce-looking weapon after an arrest he had made several years ago,. He had kept it for himself and had used it from time to time when going up against men he knew to be especially dangerous. The tough-est man alive became as gentle as a puppy when he stared into the deadly black holes of the twin barrels. Jordon loaded it now with two rounds of double-aught buckshot and took it outside and put it under the rumble seat of his car.

"I need to talk to Della for a minute before we go," he told Slim Hall.

"Take your time. I'll be here," Slim said.

Della was sitting at the front counter of the restaurant, watching a few couples having supper. Her Victrola was play-ing a song about having another cup of coffee.

"We're closing the poolroom for the night," Jordon said. "No business to speak of. And Slim and I've got something to do."

Della seemed excited. "I was going to ask you, do you have anything planned for early in the morning?"

Jordon wondered what tomorrow morning would be like. "I'm not sure right now."

"Well, how would you like to meet an important politician who's coming to town?"

Jordon dreaded to ask. "Who is it?"

"Lieutenant Governor Happy Chandler." Della made no effort to conceal her excitement. "I've been invited to have breakfast with him and a few others at the Buxton Hotel. I can take you along if you want to come."

Oh, shit, Jordon thought. "I'll have to let you know later, I guess."

"Well, I'm supposed to be there before seven. So I'll leave here at six-thirty."

Jordon nodded. "Why does Chandler stir you up so much?"

"Because he's ambitious. He wants to be governor. I'm betting he's going to make it. Maybe more, before he's through. And I'm going to do what I can to help him." She paused, then added, "Ruby Lafoon's political career is about over. He can't run for governor again. He's weary from butting heads with President Roosevelt and the New Dealers. He's old and tired, and his health's not that good from what I hear. All he's looking forward to is going home to Madisonville and sitting under a shade tree with a cool drink and a fan."

"How do you know all this?"

"Friends tell me things," she said with a knowing smile. "And one of the things they tell me is that Happy Chandler has the earmarks of a winner. So, in this case at least, I'm listening to what they tell me."

"Purely a matter of making a good bet, then?"

She nodded. "As far as I'm concerned, that's what politics is all about."

"Well, lady, you know a lot more about such things than I do."

She smiled and nodded. "I surely hope so. If I'm right, and Happy gets to the governor's mansion, I intend to make

damn certain he remembers who I am when it comes time
for him to start passing out favors to his friends."

"That makes sense, I guess."

"Believe me, it does. By the way," Della said, turning the full
intensity of her smile on him, "I was thinking, maybe you and
I could get away together for a while tomorrow night."

Jordon looked at her, acutely aware of the excitement she
was showing. He chose his words carefully. "Actually, I'm too
busy to play right now. You know how that is." He saw the
astonishment on her face, but before she could recover and
reply, he turned and walked toward the door.

From behind him he heard her say, in a low voice that
sounded like it was fighting its way through clenched teeth,
"Sonofabitch."

In a back booth by herself in the Buxton Drugstore, where
she had been for the past couple of hours, Pearl sipped at a
Coke. Her mind was a jumble of doubts and fears. She had
no idea where Moody and Pennyrile might be. When she'd
called a taxi at the store and gone back home to get her stuff,
she'd found it scattered on the floor. She had prayed that
Moody would not come back and find her there.

While the taxi waited, the first thing she'd done was look
for the pair of brown shoes she'd hidden her emergency stash
of money in. It wasn't a lot, but it added up to more than a
hundred dollars, enough to get her on a train and somewhere
far away from Buxton if that's what it came to. Some of it
she'd had when she met Moody, and some she'd saved. A
dime here, a quarter there, changing it from time to time for
dollars and fives and tens as it accumulated. She had known
all along that an emergency could come up where she would
need it. And Moody never gave her money for herself. He
liked the control of making her ask for it.

The money was there, just where she'd left it. She hur-
riedly packed her things, jamming and cramming them in
as well as she could, then sat on top of the suitcase while
she locked it shut.

She had the taxi driver come in and carry it out for her, then take her to the drugstore in Buxton. She figured she would wait here for a while, at least. And maybe she'd see somebody she could ask about Moody. Or maybe see Moody and Pennyrile. She didn't really know. But this place was near the railroad depot, and if she wanted to get away on a train in a hurry, it would be easy to do it from here.

She was starved, so she ate two ham sandwiches and two glasses of milk. Plus a dish of chocolate ice cream. She bought a movie magazine and sat reading it, looking up from time to time as people came and went. Poor Fay Wray. The magazine said she'd had nightmares about King Kong. Oh, Pearl thought, how I'd love to go to Hollywood.

She kept looking up as folks came in, but she never recognized anybody. How could she, though. She had hardly been out of the house since she'd been here. Anyway, nobody seemed to be paying any attention to her. Even though she was rushed at the house, she had taken the time to quickly clean herself up, fix her hair a little, and put on a clean, pretty bright blue dress, fresh makeup, and another pair of heels. Thank God her face was not scratched up from her trip through the woods. She knew she looked good, in spite of her bruises. She had been able to cover them up real good. And she had put finishing touches on things in the ladies' room at the drugstore.

Now it was getting late, and she was tired. She decided what she would do for the time being. She went to one of the taxis parked in front of the drugstore and asked him to get her suitcase and drive her up the hill to the Buxton Hotel. She would take a room for the night and figure out what to do next when tomorrow came.

As the taxi pulled into the hotel parking lot, Pearl opened her purse to take out the money to pay her fare.

She was comforted by the sight of the shiny little pearl-handled double-barreled .41 Remington derringer pistol that lay there like a deadly jewel, staring up at her from the purse.

The little pistol had been a gift from her mama before she

died. "Take it, honey, and remember," her mama had said, "it might turn out to be the last and best friend you ever have. Lord knows you can't depend on most men . . . women neither, when it comes right down to it. You've got to look out for yourself. Get somebody to take you out and learn you how to shoot it. And then always keep it with you, like I've done. If you ever have to use it on somebody, aim for the middle of his chest, unless you're close enough to be sure you can shoot him in the head. The closer you are, the better, with a little gun like this. Then turn around and walk or run or ride as far away as you can get. Don't look back. Don't even think about turning yourself in. If your aim is good, there'll be nobody left to tell the tale, and there's always a good chance they'll never know who done it. At least not so they can prove it."

Pearl remembered asking her mama if she'd ever used the derringer on anybody. She would never forget her mama's reply. "Nobody that's left to tell the tale," her mama had said with a sly grin. "I'm a good aimer."

Pearl had got one of her boyfriends, long before she met Moody, to take her out in the woods and show her how the little derringer worked. She had learned how to break it open and load it, how to cock it, aim it, and pull the trigger. She had fired it a number of times to get used to how it felt. Like her little bundle of personal money, she had kept it hidden where Moody couldn't find it. She prayed she would never be pressed into a place where she would have to use it, ever. But like her mama told her, it might be her last, best friend in the world. It was one of the most valuable things her mama had ever given her.

Jordon, Slim Hall, and HR Buxton sat in suite 207 of the Buxton Hotel, across the hall from Pennyrile Gruber's suite.

HR poured coffee. "Cream?" he asked Jordon.

"Just black."

Slim held up his hand and said, "Pass."

HR, dressed in his usual navy blue suit, white shirt, and

tie, took a small gold pocket watch out, pressed the stem to open the cover, and looked at the time. "Ten minutes till nine. Bertram will be here with the money soon."

Jordon scratched his head. "Let's try to sort out what we know for sure from what we think might be so," he said. "When it gets right down to it, all we know is Pennyrile Gruber and McCain are in the room across the hall. Your bank is bringing Pennyrile a bundle of his own money. McCain is an arrogant asshole, but we really don't know that he's done anything except lie about being a union representative. Does that about cover it?"

HR thought it over. "That's about it. We know that John L. Lewis is supposed to be here tonight."

"And Happy Chandler, too, I hear."

HR said, "Where did you hear that?"

"Some of the local politicians are going to have breakfast with him here in the morning."

HR shook his head. "For once, at least, your sources are better than mine. Do you think I better say anything to the sheriff? Or to Ike Sewell?"

Jordon nodded. "I think it would be best if you told them to stay away from the hotel. With either one of them around, there's no telling what might happen. And if McCain's got something planned, seeing them just might be enough to spook him into being foolish."

"I heard from somebody that he's supposed to be a cool character."

"He tries to give that impression," Jordon said. "But from what I've seen of him I think underneath his put-on, he's as fractious as a filly at breeding time. He's strung a little too tight."

HR sighed and shook his head. "I'm beginning to wonder if we can keep things from getting out of control. I got a call from a fellow I know over on the other side of Leslie County today. A man who owns a few small mines over that way. It's turning ugly."

"How?" Jordon asked.

"He said they brought a man in to the doctor yesterday, almost beat to death with a leather belt. He was a miner, a holdout who wouldn't join the union. Some fellows caught him and took him out into the woods and held him and whipped him till he said he'd join. Then they took him to the creek and baptized him in the name of John L. Lewis."

"Why'd they do that?"

"Why? Because they didn't want to kill him, I suppose."

"You believe that story?" Jordon asked.

"Why would the man lie about it? I know this story is true: The coal operators association over there just brought in another carload of gun thugs from out of state. The sheriff deputized them and turned them loose on the union men. The fellow I talked with said it's coming to bloody war, any day now. Men have to choose sides when it gets like that. A beating with a belt is not the worst thing that can happen by any means."

"Your friend, the operator over there, what's he going to do?"

"He's already done it. A bunch of men went to one of his tipples and set dynamite under it a few nights ago. They called him at daylight and told him he'd better come down and talk to them. They held a carbide lamp an inch from the fuse while they negotiated with him."

"And?"

"He signed." The old man shook his head. "Let's hope it doesn't come to that here."

Jordon said, "Personally, I think keeping Ike and the sheriff out of the way will help."

HR picked up the phone and told the operator, "See if you can find Ike Sewell and have him call me. And put me through to the sheriff's office." HR motioned Jordon over to listen in.

The phone rang twice and the voice said, "Sheriff's office, Deputy Hixon."

"This is HR Buxton. Is Sheriff Trumble there?"

"Yes, sir, he sure is. Just a minute."

A moment later, Trumble came on the line. "Yes, sir, Mr. Buxton. What can I do for you?"

"There's some business going on at the hotel tonight and tomorrow. I think it would be best if you and your men stayed away until I let you know."

"Nothing we can help you with, sir?"

"Just do what I said is all, Sheriff. Stand by. And if I need you, I'll call."

"Yes, sir, if that's what you want." Sheriff Trumble hesitated a moment, then said, "Mr. Buxton, is it possible any of this has got anything to do with Mr. Pennyrile Gruber?"

HR said, "Why do you ask that?"

"Well, sir," the sheriff said, "my deputy Hixon got a call this afternoon, a woman said she was afraid something might be about to happen to Mr. Gruber, some fuss between him and the man she's been living with. Hixon didn't think there was anything to it, but when he reported it to me, I tried to check it out. Sent a man to a house in Chambers where Pennyrile was supposed to have been. Wasn't nobody there. Checked by his house. He's been gone all day. Nobody seems to know exactly where he's at. But they expected him back by now." The sheriff chuckled. "Course you know old Pennyrile, he could be holed up somewheres with some pretty little thing. Maybe the one who called in here, for all I know."

"Who was she?"

"Said her name was McCain. Pearl McCain, according to my man here. Let me put him on and you can talk di-rect to him."

"I'm going to put Jordon on and let him talk with Hixon."

"Jordon? What's he doing in this, if you don't mind me asking, sir?"

"He's . . . working with me. Put Hixon on the line."

"Yes, sir," Sheriff Trumble said. His voice sounded to Jordon somewhere between sad and mad.

Jordon took the phone. "Hixon? How did this Pearl McCain sound to you when she called in?"

"Well, she was right upset, it seemed to me."

"She say where she was calling from?"

"Nope. Just told me where she was living is all."

"And you decided it wasn't too important."

"Tell the truth, I thought old Pennyrile had just followed his pecker into a thicket. Sure wouldn't be the first time, would it? And probably not the last, either. I figured he'd call us his self if he needed us."

Jordon said thanks and hung up. He thought for a minute. "I need to talk to this woman Pearl. I met her the other night at Della's. Pretty little blond. I wonder . . ." He got up and started for the door.

"Where are you going?" HR asked.

"Down to the drugstore. See if any of the taxis might have hauled her anyplace today. If she and Moody were having some kind of trouble over Pennyrile, then she'd have probably needed a taxi."

"It kind of looks like Mr. Pennyrile Gruber just might not be in that room of his own free will, huh?" Slim Hall said. It was the first time he had spoken since passing on the coffee.

Jordon looked at him and nodded.

"Want me to come with you?" Slim asked.

Jordon shook his head. "Stay here with Mr. Buxton. I won't be long."

"You sure there's nothing I can do?"

"Not now. You getting fidgety?"

"I was just wondering why you brought me along."

"I guess I'm not sure, to tell you the truth."

"Would you rather I go?"

"No. I've got a feeling things are going to get a lot hotter before they cool down. I'd rather have you here and not need you than the other way around. If that's all right with you."

"You call the shots. I'll stay."

Yes, sir, Jordon thought, he was liking this boy . . . young man . . . more and more.

On the way down the stairs, Jordon saw a man coming up with a bulging black briefcase in his hand. He wore a suit and tie, round steel-rimmed glasses, and his magnified eyes darted furtively around as he approached Jordon. Jordon figured it must be Bertram from the bank on his way to Pennyrile's room.

"Bertram?" Jordon said.

The man drew back, jerking the briefcase away from Jordon and looking as if he might break into a run at any moment. "What do you want?"

"Take it easy. I'm working for Mr. Buxton. When you get through with Pennyrile Gruber, knock on the door across the hall, number two-oh-seven. Mr. Buxton's there. Wait till I get back, will you?"

Bertram drew himself up stiffly now, evidently sensing he was out of danger for the moment. "I already know to do that," he said curtly. "Mr. Buxton called and told me."

As he strolled down the hill toward the drugstore, Jordon thought about the irony of himself working hand in glove with HR Buxton. He would have laid heavy odds it never would have happened. And it probably would never happen again. But right now, it wasn't too bad having the old man, with his brains and balls and power, seeking the same objective as Jordon. Not too bad at all.

19

WHEN JORDON GOT BACK to the hotel room, Bertram the banker was sitting, stiff-backed and prim, waiting for HR Buxton to come out of the bathroom. The banker had returned from delivering the money to Pennyrile and was waiting to tell HR about it.

Buxton came out drying his hands on a towel and said, "So tell us what happened with Pennyrile."

"He was angry. Very angry," Bertram said.

"Why?" Jordon asked.

"Because I didn't bring all the cash he wanted, that's why. He wanted twenty-five thousand dollars. And I brought ten thousand." He held the receipt in his hand and waved it a little as if proof were required.

"Why did you do that?" Jordon asked.

"I instructed him to," HR said. "At the time, I thought it was a good idea. I figured on it delaying Pennyrile till morning, give us more time to figure out what the hell was going on, and what we're going to do."

Jordon shook his head. "Seems to me we'd be better off if Pennyrile and McCain got out of here right now, wouldn't we?"

"I'm not so sure," HR said. "We know where they are now. That's something in our favor."

Jordon thought about the situation. He didn't like it, but, as HR pointed out, at least they had some kind of handle on things as long as the two were in a known location, however dangerous it might be.

HR spoke up again. "I did what I thought best, based on

what I knew at the time." His voice had taken on a little edge of irritation, apparently his normal reaction to having his judgment questioned.

Jordon nodded. "You were probably right."

That seemed to please HR, though God only knew why he wanted Jordon's approval.

"Now what?" Jordon asked. "When's the rest of the money due?"

HR said, "We'll deliver it in the morning. At ten, I told him, is the earliest we can get it to him. He didn't like it much, but he seemed to believe my story that we had to get the rest of the amount in small bills from the bank in King's Mill. He knows we keep a lot more scrip than currency on hand."

"I wasn't aware the bank dealt in scrip," Jordon said. "It's not legal tender."

HR smiled a little. "Since it's my bank, it tries to accommodate us. Holds on to our scrip in safe deposit till we need it. Kind of like a box you put your papers in."

Jordon nodded. "So what about McCain?" he asked Bertram. "Did he say or do anything?"

The banker shook his head. "He just sat there, kind of behind and off to one side of Mr. Gruber, where he could see what he was writing. Never said a word the whole time."

"Could you see his hands?" Jordon asked.

"His hands?" Bertram seemed puzzled. "Why no, now that you mention it. He kept his hands in his pockets all the time. Is that important?"

"Maybe," Jordon said. "Did you notice anything else unusual?"

"Like what?"

Jordon sighed. If I knew, I wouldn't have to ask, he felt like saying. "Just anything you might have noticed."

"Well, you asked about the other man's hands. I noticed Mr. Gruber's hands seemed stiff when he signed the receipt and looked at the money. And his wrists look rough and red. One of them raw, even."

"Anything else?"

"Not that I can think of now. Except Mr. Gruber looked awfully tired. Exhausted."

HR looked at Jordon, then said, "Thank you, Bertram. I'd like you to go home now. Get some rest. Stay by your telephone until you go to the bank in the morning. And right up until you leave to bring the money at ten." HR paused, then said, "And, not a word about any of this to anybody."

Bertram stood and drew himself up to his full height of perhaps five five. He gave HR a stern look. "Sir," he said, "as a banker, one of my first responsibilities is to respect and protect the confidentiality of my customers' dealings."

HR smiled at him. "I know." He dismissed the banker with a little wave of his hand.

When Bertram had gone, HR said, "A pretty good clerk." He looked at Jordon. "Learn anything from your walk down to the square?"

Jordon nodded. "Pearl spent a couple of hours with a big suitcase in a booth in the drugstore this afternoon. Then she got a taxi to haul her and her bag up here to the hotel less than an hour ago."

HR reached for the phone.

Jordon held up his hand. "I already checked at the desk. She's in room one-twelve." He stood up. "I'm going down and see what I can learn from the lady."

"Before you do that," HR said, "what do you think about just calling Pennyrile in his room and asking him is everything all right? You know, mention I know about the bank transaction, and offer to help him if he needs it."

Jordon pondered it for a moment. "I don't think so."

"Why?"

"If McCain's holding him prisoner, he can't tell you the truth. And if he's there because he wants to be, he won't tell you the truth. Or at least anything that will help us. And, we could stampede them into doing something stupid."

"You keep worrying about that."

"It's a legitimate worry. You're the one kept telling me a

little while back about a powder keg. I agree that's what this is. And it's getting hotter all the time. But I think we ought to try to learn a little more about it before we move. Keep in mind, *they* don't know that *we* know anything yet."

"You are a more deliberate man than I've ever given you credit for being," HR said. "I'd always had you down as a hothead."

Jordon gave him a sidelong glance. "Don't fall in love with me," he said. "I'm spoke for already."

HR laughed.

The phone rang. HR Buxton picked it up, then motioned for Jordon to listen in.

"Mr. Buxton?" It was the clerk on the desk. His voice sounded breathless. "Mr. John L. Lewis just checked in. You wanted me to let you know."

"Who's he with?" HR said.

"Two men. You want to know their names?"

"Yes."

"One of them is a Mr. William Turnblazer. The other one's name is . . . a Mr. John Wesley Stoner."

"Where did you put them?"

"Why, right down the hall from you. Rooms two-oh-one, two-oh-three, and two-oh-five."

"What for, for Christ's sake?"

"I thought you-all were going to be having a meeting or something. And I thought it would be more convenient for you-all to be on the same floor, with Mr. Gruber and all."

"Ah, well," HR said, shaking his head.

"You want me to move them?" the clerk said anxiously. "I can do that."

"No, no, don't move them."

After a moment, the clerk said, "Is there anything else you want me to do, sir?"

"Nothing, thank you. Just don't think anymore tonight."

Jordon smiled a little and said, "I'll be back," and left the room.

*   *   *

When Jordon had gone, Slim Hall said, "Mr. Buxton, is there anything else you can think of that I ought to be doing?"

Buxton hesitated for a moment before answering. "Does it bother you so much just to sit and wait?"

Slim nodded. He felt restless just sitting here, waiting for something unpredictable to happen. "My Uncle Ben says doing nothing gets nothing done."

"Sometimes the most important thing you can do is wait. Patience is a virtue a young fellow ought to cultivate." HR sighed. "But I confess to you, I've had a tough time learning that myself."

"That's another thing Uncle Ben says. But he says getting shot helped it sink in."

HR looked at him closely. "Ben Hall? He's your uncle?"

"Yes. Why? Do you know him?"

"I remember when he was shot and became paralyzed." After a moment HR said, "Then your father was Ben's brother Jim? And your name is John?"

Slim nodded. "John Pennington Hall is my full name. But these days folks mostly call me Slim." They were silent for a little bit, then Slim said, "You knew my dad?"

HR Buxton had a faraway look in his eyes. "Oh, yes. I knew him. I was very sorry when he lost his life."

"I just barely remember him," Slim said. "I was only about four when the slatefall caught him."

"Yes, I know," HR said, looking at Slim closely. "You favor your mother a lot. Same eyes, same hair, same complexion."

"That's what folks tell me." Now Slim gave HR a curious look. "You knew my mother, too?"

HR nodded. "Beth Pennington used to work for me. In my office. Before she and your father were married. A long time ago."

HR's voice sounded odd, and somehow sad. Slim wondered why.

"What have you been doing lately, son?" HR asked.

"Went to Cumberland College for a while. And taught some. Right now, I'm working with Jordon at Della's Place."

HR seemed to be thinking this over. "And what do you think of him? Jordon."

Slim had not expected the question. But after a moment he answered it. "From what I've seen of him, I can't think of another man I respect more. Except maybe my uncle Ben."

HR smiled and sighed. "It's interesting you feel that way."

Again Slim thought the old man seemed sad. "Why do you say that?"

HR shook his head slowly. "Maybe because I'm beginning to feel a little like that myself about Jordon. And it surprises me some to hear myself saying it. The man's never done much except drink and gamble and scuffle around the edges of things."

"That may be so, but there's a wide streak of something in him that I'd like to find a little bit of in myself. It's not something you see in a man every day."

HR nodded. "You are a young fellow wise beyond your years, it seems."

Slim grinned. "Maybe it just seems that way because I try to pay more attention than most folks."

HR cocked his head a little. "And maybe it's more than that."

Room 112 was a small room with a single bed. Jordon sat on a straight-backed chair across the room from Pearl and studied her face. He had not paid a lot of attention to it the other night at Della's, but now he noticed it was somehow out of kilter. Not unattractive, just different. Her body, though, from what he could see of it, was something to behold. She couldn't be older than her mid-twenties, he guessed.

She looked tired and drawn. And the bruises on her face and arms were a sign that somebody had hurt her in the not-too-distant past.

"You said you were working for Mr. Buxton?" she asked Jordon.

"A special assignment."

"Are you a detective or something?"

"Not exactly. I was a deputy sheriff until the election last fall. And I've been a deputy other places before that."

"What do you want from me?"

Jordon's voice was gentle. "I want to know what you know about Moody McCain, who he is, what he's up to. And what business Pennyrile Gruber's got with him."

"I don't know the answer to all them questions," Pearl said.

"But you know some of them," Jordon said quietly. "Is McCain the one left those bruises on you?"

She looked at the floor. After a few moments she nodded.

"You and McCain live together in a Buxton company house in Chambers?"

She nodded again.

"How long?"

"A few weeks now."

"What does McCain do for a living, Pearl?"

She hesitated. "What's going to happen to me?"

"What do you mean? Have you done something that could get you in trouble?"

"I don't think so. I guess what I really meant is, what's going to happen to Moody? Is he going to get in some kind of trouble?"

"You want to protect him? Is that it?"

She shook her head vigorously. "I'm scared about what he might do to me. And to Mr. Gruber."

"Why don't you tell me all you know about it, Pearl. I'll see that McCain doesn't bother you anymore."

"How can you say that?"

Jordon thought about it and sighed. "Well, I'll do all I can. And I've got no reason to think that won't be enough."

Her voice cracked a little. "I don't know."

"I don't want to see him hurt you or anybody else anymore, believe me."

She dabbed at her eyes with a handkerchief. "Who else has he hurt?"

"I'm not certain. But I'm beginning to think maybe a lot of people."

She looked at Jordon a long time before she answered. "You promise you won't forget about me?"

"Yes," he said, "I do." He waited as she dabbed at her eyes again. "Now you want to tell me about it?"

She did. About the visit to Pennyrile's house last night, about how she saw that Pennyrile liked her. Then about the way Moody had treated her at home later, not spelling everything out in words but hinting at it until her voice cracked and her eyes overflowed. Then, after a pause, she told Jordon about her calling Pennyrile this morning, how he met her in the woods, and how Moody came in and caught them together at the house as she was packing to leave.

"I don't know if Mr. Gruber . . . Pennyrile . . . is dead or what," Pearl said. "I heard a shot while I was running away." She looked straight into Jordon's eyes and said softly, "I've been worried to death about that. I don't know how I could stand it if he got killed over coming to help me."

Jordon believed her. Her lip was trembling, and he thought she was going to start crying again. "Don't worry about Pennyrile," he said. "He's not dead."

"How do you know?"

"He's in this hotel. Upstairs. With McCain. In room two-oh-eight."

This seemed to take Pearl totally off guard. "They're here? Right now?"

"The thing is, we don't know if they're cooking up something together, or if McCain is holding Pennyrile against his will."

"Pennyrile's not cooking up anything with him."

"How can you be sure?"

"I believe the only reason Pennyrile asked Moody to come to his house was because he wanted to see me. He kept looking at me the whole time Moody and me were at Della's the other night. He must have got word to Moody that he wanted to see him, figuring maybe he'd bring me. And then

I saw the way Moody treated him just before I ran away. And I saw the way Pennyrile looked at him. I don't believe Pennyrile ever planned to do any business with Moody."

"That's something to consider," Jordon said. "Anyhow, you ought to stay out of sight until this business is cleared up and we know exactly what's going on. Who knows you're here?"

"Just me and the taxi driver, I guess. And whoever you've told."

"Let's keep it that way," Jordon said.

"Tell me something," Pearl said. "Do you believe Pennyrile is in real danger?"

"You know McCain better than anybody else around here. What do you think?"

She stared out the window for a while, then nodded her head slowly.

"I'd have to guess that he is, too," Jordon said. "He's got the bank bringing him money, quite a lot of it, apparently to buy McCain off. But that doesn't mean McCain will let him go. Probably just the opposite. With Pennyrile dead, who'd be left to testify against McCain? He could say everything Pennyrile did was voluntary, blame his death on somebody else. Once McCain's through here, I don't think he'll have any more use for Pennyrile."

"I see," she said, nodding her head slowly. "You think you can get him away from Moody?"

"I'm sure going to try," Jordon said. "And also stop Moody from doing anything else that might start a war around here."

"What do you think Moody's done already?"

"Did you ever see Moody with any guns, Pearl?"

She nodded. "He's got a pistol. A thirty-eight, I think."

"How about a rifle. Ever see him with one?"

"No, not since I've known him."

"Has he got any long skinny cases of any kind?"

She thought about it a minute. "He had a long leather bag, but it wasn't skinny."

"Long enough to hold a rifle?"

She thought for a moment. "Yeah. And a lot of other stuff, too. But I haven't seen it for a while. I don't know what he could have done with it. Maybe sold it or something."

"Or maybe hid it out away from the house?"

"I guess so," she said. "Yeah, he could have done that. Why?"

"It's possible he killed two men from ambush the other day."

Pearl was silent. Then she said, "Ambush?"

"Pearl," Jordon said quietly, "you've spent a lot of time with Moody McCain lately. Do you think he's the kind of man who could ambush somebody and kill them? Somebody he didn't even know? For money?"

Pearl looked at the ugly bruises on her arms, then gingerly brushed her fingers across her left cheek where the worst discoloration had settled. "Mr. Jordon, I guess it took me a long time to learn this, but I think he's the kind of man who could do the worst thing a person might imagine."

Jordon pondered this for a moment. "I think he already has, Pearl."

After Jordon left, Pearl lay across her bed, thinking about all she had been through in her short life. It had not been easy.

She thought about her mama, remembering again what she used to say about men and women when she'd get to drinking too much gin. It embarrassed Pearl a little even today to remember it.

"Don't ever forget the difference pretty women make in this world, honey. And you're one of the pretty ones. I used to look better myself, but never like you. Remember. The power of pussy. Never underestimate it." Pearl could still see her mama the day she had first talked about the subject. Pearl was barely fourteen. And Mama at that time was living with the steelworker, more or less. "There are times when a man will do anything for a particular woman. Pussy power has started wars and revolutions, it's brought down empires, cost rulers their thrones. By God, I even read once where it was behind the start of the Church of England. If it wasn't for pussy, the British would still be bowing down to the pope of Rome."

Pearl never said anything when her mother was like this. She just sat and listened.

"You see this?" Her mother pointed to one of the books she was always borrowing from the city library a few blocks away. "Books, honey, books. If it wasn't for books, and this"—she held up a glass half filled from the bottle of gin on the table—"I'd have gone crazy a long time ago. I never would have made it to see you grow up." She'd started to weep, as she often did by the time the gin bottle got low. She wagged a finger at Pearl. "Read, read. That's how you learn things." She took a swig, wiped her mouth and nose with the back of her hand, and waved her finger again. "And never, ever, underes . . . underestimate the unbelievable, wonderous, world-moving power of pussy."

If it was so powerful, Pearl wondered, why hadn't it brought a better life to her mama? She had wondered about that, more than once, but she was always afraid to ask.

Pearl never forgot the words, though, and she had let them guide her in her fight for survival. She had long since come to think of her body as both a blessing and a curse. It attracted men to her, that was true. But it brought her enough trouble from them that sometimes she thought she'd have preferred to look a little less attractive. Lately, she'd found herself hoping more and more that there was something to life other than sex and the struggle over it that went on constantly between men and women. Something more lasting than that.

She thought about this morning, how Pennyrile Gruber had come after her, without question or promise of any kind from her. He'd just come. She knew part of why he'd come, of course. The same reason men had been coming after her ever since she'd been twelve. What her mama had been talking about.

But when Moody had surprised them today, Pennyrile had not abandoned her, had not blamed her, had still tried to help her. Couldn't it be true that there could be feelings between men and women that were a mixture of selfish and unselfish? Did it have be to all one way or the other? Couldn't you want somebody to please you and want to please them, too? And not just for sex? Was it just pussy power like her mama had said? And money and fear and meanness, like with Moody?

She was worried about what was going to happen. It might turn out that Moody would kill Pennyrile for trying to help her. She knew next to nothing about Pennyrile Gruber, of course. Except that he was rich, and liked toys and curiosities, kind of like a little boy. Also, he seemed to care something for her, had tried to help her at considerable risk to himself.

She knew this much, too: Whatever else he might deserve, he did not deserve to die for what he had done for her. If there was a chance she could help him escape, she had to make the effort. And as she turned the thought over and over in her mind, she began to think there might be a chance. Even a good chance.

She started to work out the details of a plan in her mind. If it was successful, it could get Pennyrile free, and maybe it could get her out from under the control of Moody McCain once and for all.

She took a sheet of hotel stationery and an envelope from the drawer of the little table by her window and started to write. When she finished, she folded the paper, sealed it in the envelope, wrote on the outside, and took it out and left it with the clerk on the desk.

Then she went back and lay on her bed for a little while.

She traveled in her mind once again to the table in her mama's kitchen as her mama drank gin and told her about how it was with women and men. Pearl had never read many books. Just magazines mostly. But she had never really believed that a woman could make a king give up his throne for her, like her mama said. Some things, maybe, but not that.

Then Pearl sat up and reached for the telephone.

Moody McCain sat staring out his window on the town square of Buxton and the floodlit grounds of the Buxton Hotel. The drugstore had closed. The picture show was over. The town slept. Most of it.

McCain was still furious at the way the man from the bank had only brought part of the money. He wondered if maybe there was some way Pennyrile had signaled the man on the phone not to bring it all at once. But Pennyrile had seemed genuinely upset at what had happened. And he had no reason to delay, unless he had thought McCain might be satisfied with only part of it. Moody doubted that. Pennyrile must have figured he'd be free and off in some safe place comforting Pearl by now.

McCain watched Pennyrile, sitting there with his hands and feet tied up, dozing in a stuffed chair. What had made the sonofabitch think he could just walk in and take Pearl and walk away with her?

Last night at Pennyrile's place, McCain could see the old man lusting after her. Could see the wheels turning in his head. Knew old one-eye was stirring and twitching at the thought of the sweetness of Pearl. But McCain was surprised that Pennyrile had moved so soon.

And that fucking Pearl. Ungrateful bitch. It wasn't that she was that important to him. He could get another like her. But the brazen, open insult of having her leave him for somebody like Pennyrile. Or for that matter, leave him for anybody until he was goddamn good and ready to let her go.

As it had turned out, however, Pennyrile's lust had become a blessing. McCain had turned it into an opportunity to acquire more money than he had ever envisioned having at one time. The only thing was, he had to be careful about leaving evidence that he had violated the Lindbergh kidnapping law. He didn't want to get the G-men after him. Frying in the electric chair for kidnapping an old bastard like Pennyrile Gruber was not part of McCain's plans for the rest of his life.

Last night, Pennyrile never had got around to saying specifically what he had wanted McCain to do for him. "I heard from a confidential source," the old man had said while Pearl was poking about in his library, "that you were a man who could handle very specialized kinds of . . . assignments . . . if the price is right. And that you do them quiet and clean and leave no tracks." Moody had smiled and said, "Your confidential source has good information." But that's about as much as ever got said. Pennyrile seemed reluctant to go further at the moment, although he did give McCain a hundred-dollar bill, "As a token of my appreciation for your time in coming up here to see me, and your patience in standing by for a brief time. It's very possible we'll have business to do in the not-too-distant future."

Then Moody had talked about Pearl. And chickens.

Through the open window, now, McCain heard voices from below. Scanning the area outside, he saw two men walking across the hotel grounds, coming closer and chatting as they apparently took an evening stroll before bed.

One of the man was barrel-shaped, wore a dark suit and a wide-brimmed hat tilted forward, and puffed on a cigar. He gestured with the cigar as he spoke, and his voice was deep and rich. There was something very familiar about him.

McCain could not quite make out what he was saying, but as the two men walked closer, he could pick out a few words.

Suddenly, he recognized who it was. John L. Lewis, the big shot over the United Mine Workers! Anybody who went to the picture show had seen him in the newsreels. Hell, he was as famous as Roosevelt, and here he was, taking a bedtime turn across the lawn of the Buxton Hotel.

This must be the big job Asher Jennings had been talking about. Jennings was right, this was big time.

John L. and his companion were close enough now so that Moody could hear them. They stopped, and John L.

stretched and tossed his cigar away. "Well, Bill, tomorrow we'll see. Calhoun says the men will be ready at nine. I think down by the depot is as good a place as any to address them. Then we can drive back up the street with the top down and make a show of confidence. It'll do our men good. And I have a feeling it may take some of the starch out of old Buxton."

John L. and the other man went around the hotel toward the entrance, and McCain sat there staring into the night, thinking about what he would do in the morning. At last he decided he would try to get a little sleep. He got up and made sure Pennyrile was well tied for the night. Then McCain slid down in his easy chair and stretched his long legs out before him. He tried to relax.

His thoughts went to Pearl. He would sleep a hell of a lot better if she was here to service him beforehand. He cursed himself for permitting his thoughts to drift to her. If he wasn't careful, he'd never get to sleep.

But as he made an effort to let his muscles relax, he began to feel sleep might be near. He closed his eyes, let his breathing slow, felt the muddle of thought just before going under.

The jangling sound jerked him awake, and his hand automatically grabbed his pistol off the floor by his chair. It was the telephone. Who the hell could be calling?

He let it ring again, decided he'd better answer.

"Yes." He could see the ringing had disturbed Pennyrile's sleep, and he moaned and tried to roll over, which was difficult for him with his hands and feet tied.

"Is that you, Moody?"

"Pearl?" He thought for a moment maybe he'd drifted into sleep and was having a dream. "Where are you?"

"I'm calling from the phone at the depot," she said.

"How'd you know where I am?" he asked.

There was no delay before she answered. "A taxi driver said he saw you turning in the hotel drive tonight. The desk clerk told me Pennyrile was registered."

"Listen, Pearl. We need to talk. Come on up here to the hotel."

"No, Moody. I don't want to be with you anymore."

"Listen, goddammit, I said . . ." He suddenly decided this was not the way to do it. "Hey, Pearl. I'm sorry about today. And last night. It was a misunderstanding." He had to get hold of her. It was too dangerous for her to be out on her own, and mad at him as well.

"I called to see about Mr. Gruber. Is he all right?"

"Him. Oh, sure, he's fine. We've got that all patched up. He's sorry. Me, too. And we've got some business to do together. Then you and me, we're going to get the hell out of here. How about that trip to California? You know, Hollywood? How would that suit you?"

"I don't know, Moody. You really hurt me."

"Oh, come on, Pearly, that won't happen again. You can depend on it. Never again. I don't know what got into me. Just couldn't face losing you, I guess. It just made me a little crazy, thinking about being without you."

She said nothing.

McCain tried again. "Why don't you come up here to the hotel? We can just talk, see if we can work things out. It's going to be different from now on. Okay?"

She was still silent, but finally said, "I'll meet you in the hotel parking lot. We can talk out there. Then I'll decide."

"The parking lot?" What the hell, I'll have her then, he thought. She'll have no choice once I get my hands on her. "Sure, Pearly. The parking lot. Right away, okay?"

"It'll take me about ten minutes to get there," she said.

Pearl's feet made no sound as she ran down the carpeted hallway on the second floor to room 208.

She had hidden in the hall on the first floor near the bottom of the stairs until she had seen Moody come down and head out the door to the parking lot, expecting to see her coming from the depot. He hadn't waited more than a couple of minutes after her call. Evidently he wanted to be there when she arrived.

But she wouldn't arrive. Not unless the door to 208 was

locked. She had figured it was a fifty-fifty chance. If it was unlocked, she would go in and get Pennyrile out. She was sure he must be tied up or something. He wouldn't switch back to Moody and turn his back on her. She was counting on that. Moody must be holding him.

If the door was locked, well, then she'd have to go to the parking lot and talk with Moody, end up going to the room with him, wait and watch for a chance to get Pennyrile loose and get away. What other choice did she have?

The door was unlocked.

As soon as she stepped inside, she saw the sitting room was empty. The small table lamp in the bedroom enabled her to see Pennyrile dozing there in a big chair. And she saw at once that she had been right. His feet were tied together, and his hands, too, behind his back. And he had a gag in his mouth. She ran to him and started working at the ropes, trying to untie them.

Pennyrile roused up. She took the gag out of his mouth. He looked confused. "Pearl? What's going on? How'd you get here?"

"I'll have you loose in a minute," she said. "And we'll get out of here."

Her fingers pulled at the ropes, trying to get them loose.

Then she heard a small movement behind her, and sucked in her breath sharply as she heard a click that sounded like the door shutting.

She spun around, and there was Moody McCain, long and loose as a snake, standing with his hands on his hips, shaking his head and smiling.

"Ah, Pearl, Pearl, Pearl," he said softly.

20

JORDON, SLIM HALL, AND HR Buxton entered the dining room of the Buxton Hotel together. It was a little before seven.

The morning sun streamed in through the windows with their filmy lace curtains, the rays reflecting off the pristine white tablecloths and the sparkling vases of fresh-cut flowers on each table.

Large wooden fans whirred gently overhead, but they were no match for the sluggish, sultry air of dog days. Jordon could feel a thin film of sweat already beginning to form on his forehead.

"Bring us a pot of coffee first," HR said to the waitress. They were still on their first cup when John L. Lewis came down the stairs and into the dining room with two other men.

Jordon recognized John L. from having seen his picture in the papers, and from watching and hearing him in the newsreels. But the other two men were unfamiliar. He glanced at HR, who whispered, "That's Bill Turnblazer with him. He's the United Mine Workers District Nineteen president. An old friend of John L.'s, but not much of a leader himself, they say. I don't know who the younger fellow is."

John L. glanced toward their table, and HR stood up. Jordon and Slim followed suit. "Welcome to the Buxton Hotel, Mr. Lewis," HR said.

John L. said, "Thank you, sir. I don't think I've had the pleasure." His powerful voice filled the empty room, though he seemed to be making no special effort to project it. He walked toward them and extended his hand to HR, smiling a little. His barrel-like body and shaggy eyebrows, with his great thick mane of dark hair and massive jowls, made him a figure so distinctive that most of the nation, and all in the coalfields, recognized him on sight.

HR put out his own hand. "HR Buxton."

John L.'s little smile faded. As they shook hands, the two men eyed one another like game roosters circling in a cock pit.

"Will you join us for breakfast?" HR said.

John L. studied him for a moment before saying, "Most gracious of you to invite us, sir. We'd be pleased to."

HR motioned to the waitress who was hovering nearby, and she came at once and began to push two tables together. Slim Hall helped her.

HR and John L. introduced the others, by name only, before everyone sat down.

Once everyone was seated, more cups and coffee were brought and orders taken for eggs, country ham, red-eye gravy, sausage, and bacon. Another waitress came at once with baskets of large, hot fluffy buttermilk biscuits, little crockery pots of strawberry and blackberry jam, apple butter, and sorghum molasses, chilled bowls of fresh white butter, and pitchers of cold, fresh sweet milk.

HR and John L. sat across the table from one another. As the men all drank coffee and some went after the biscuits and jam, HR asked the labor leader, "To what do we owe this unexpected pleasure?"

John L. looked at him for a moment, then gave a small grunt. "Surely, sir, that's a question to which you already know the answer. But for the record, we are merely stopping over here on our way to Bell County, where we shall hold a great rally of the coal miners of the area in the city of Pineville."

Here John L. paused for effect, and his voice turned weighty. "And where we shall make final plans for our all-out assault on the bastions of unbridled power and privilege here in the mountains," he said, waving his arm in a sweeping

gesture that seemed to take in at least thirty or forty counties. Another pause. "None of this is news to you, of course."

HR smiled back at him. "Of course." He took a sip of
coffee. There was more than a hint of sarcasm in Buxton's
voice when he spoke. "It seems that there is no end to the
parade of famous men we are seeing here in the mountains.
Some time back it was Mr. Theodore Dreiser and John Dos
Passos and some other literary lights of the big cities who
graced us with their presence. Now you. And we hear of
others poised to leap into the fray. We know there must be
important things afoot when such important men take time
out of their busy lives to descend upon us."

John L. looked at him squarely. "Mr. Dreiser and Mr. Dos
Passos and the others came to conduct public hearings into
the outrageous conditions working people here in the mountains are trying to survive under, sir. And the thanks they
got was a trumped-up charge of fornication against Mr. Dreiser by the authorities at Pineville. I can assure you, Mr.
Buxton, that neither ridiculous charges of sexual miscon-
duct nor anything else that can be dreamed up is going to
stay us from our mission."

"Which is?"

"A contract under which Kentucky's coal operators will
be legally bound to guarantee their workers a fair wage for
their labor, along with just treatment and decent working
conditions."

HR sipped his coffee. "As you yourself might say, there is
the rub."

Lewis permitted himself a little smile, but said nothing.

HR sighed. "You have the words and the precepts right.
But how can men, even reasonable men, ever agree on what
constitutes fairness and justice and decency?"

Lewis's eyes bored into HR's. "That, sir, is what we intend
to find out. If agreements cannot be reached, you have my
solemn promise that no coal will move, and the great wheels
of industry in this nation will grind to a complete halt." He
set his jaw like a bulldog.

At that moment another gathering of people appeared at the dining room door.

Jordon looked over to see Della standing alongside Lieutenant Governor A. B. "Happy" Chandler. Both of them were smiling as if they were expecting the newsreel cameras. There was a man on Chandler's other side Jordon didn't know. And there were a couple more smiling men Jordon took to be politicians. And Stanton County Judge Ethelrod Treadmore, a Democrat who had been elected on a fluke last time, simply because he was personally liked by a lot of people, aided perhaps by the fact that his father had spent a small fortune buying chain-ballot votes for him and handing out free moonshine on election day.

Also, in what seemed to be a separate group, there were Emerson Calhoun and two other men Jordon recognized from the night he had met with them under the cliff, when the talk ran high about scabs and gun thugs. The three of them were dressed in overalls, clean white dress shirts buttoned up to the neck, without ties, but wearing suit coats in spite of the heat.

"Excuse me for a moment, gentlemen," HR said as he rose and called out, "Mr. Lieutenant Governor, will you join us for breakfast? All of you, please come and eat with us."

Happy Chandler bestowed his winning smile on all of them and said, "We'd be delighted to."

Jordon caught Della staring at him. There was an expression of amazement on her face. Jordon figured he and Slim Hall were the last two people on earth she had expected to find here this morning.

There was much scraping of chairs and fussing with napkins as everyone stood and introductions were made all around.

Another table, and still another, were brought over. Della managed to get a seat right next to Chandler without too much difficulty, and Emerson Calhoun and his friends sat next to one another. Judge Treadmore and the other politicians fended for themselves as best they could, jockeying for positions as close to the the lieutenant governor as possible.

Two more waitresses came and busied themselves with cups and coffee and biscuits and jam. HR Buxton leaned over to Jordon and whispered, "Catch one of the waitresses when you can and tell her to send the bill for all this to my office." Jordon nodded.

"Did one and all enjoy a good night's rest here in Mr. Buxton's renowned establishment?" Happy Chandler asked with a big smile. "I know I did, even though I arrived after midnight."

Around the table several people smiled and nodded and murmured gracious comments about the accommodations. HR Buxton was beaming, Jordon noticed.

In a strong, dignified voice everyone could hear, Emerson Calhoun said, "We slept at home. We've got no money for hotels. Nor anything else."

In the dead silence that followed, a cloud of discomfort seemed to settle on the group. Nobody made any response to Emerson's remark. It was as if someone had broken wind during a religious service.

Then one of the men at the other end of the table said, "Would you pass the biscuits?"

Emerson said, "Sorry if I spoiled anybody's appetite. But the truth is, I'm ashamed of myself for sitting down to a meal like this when I know what my friends and neighbors and their families are putting on their tables today. That may or may not bother some of you, but that's the way it is."

John L. Lewis cleared his throat and spoke up. "It's the way it is, indeed, Brother Calhoun. But be assured, my friend, it's not the way it's going to remain."

John L. turned to Happy Chandler and said, "You, young man, have come to Buxton, but your leader, Governor Lafoon, has not seen fit to do so. Why is that? And will he come to Pineville?"

Chandler was not smiling now. "Governor Lafoon is not my leader. He has his schedule, and I have mine. You would be better informed if you were to ask him personally why he is not here. And what his plans are."

"You carry no message from him, young man?"

Chandler's expression was stony. "I am not Ruby Lafoon's messenger boy, Mr. Lewis. I am here on behalf of the good citizens of the Commonwealth of Kentucky—the greatest state in the forty-eight as far as I am concerned—who have seen fit to elect me their lieutenant governor."

Della, smiling, spoke for the first time. "And in another year, our governor, if I may be the one to say it."

All heads turned to look at her. Chandler smiled at her, then at the others, as if his mood had changed that quickly. "I have a supporter, it seems."

"You do indeed," Della said. "And many more here in the mountains, I can assure you."

John L. looked at Chandler intently, as if reassessing him. "How old are you, sir?"

"Thirty-six."

"A remarkable career you have underway, it seems, for one so young."

Chandler grinned. He leaned back and looked at the ceiling, then closed his eyes and recited:

> Gather ye rose-buds while ye may,
> Old Time is still aflying,
> And this same flower that smiles today,
> Tomorrow will be dying.

John L. watched him and when he was finished, gave an appreciative nod. "So it will," he said.

Chandler still sat with his eyes closed.

John L. fished in his plate for a piece of ham. "Well, sir, since you have decided that you are going to be governor of Kentucky, perhaps we should sit down sometime and have a visit with each other. Who knows, if you have the best interests of the working people of the state uppermost in your mind, we might find ourselves becoming friends."

"The people of this state know I am *their* friend," Chandler said. "That's why they elected me. My position against the sales tax, and my record on other matters of concern to working people, speak for themselves. I have no hesitation to stand before the people at any time."

"Nor I, sir," John L. said. "Be assured of it."

Little else of substance was said as they all served themselves from the great steaming platters of country ham and sausage and bacon and other things that were were passed around. As they ate, the room was filled with the rich aroma of the delicious food for which the hotel was so well known. Waitresses hurrying to and from the kitchen kept the supplies replenished.

When he had finished eating, John L. lit a large cigar and stood up, making a final pat at his mouth with his large white linen napkin, which he continued to hold in his hand like a scepter. "An exceptional meal," he said. Scanning the table, he spoke in his strong, portentous voice. "Lord Acton once observed that, 'In every age, liberty's progress has been beset by its natural enemies, by ignorance and superstition . . .' "

Here he turned to stare at HR Buxton, " '. . . by lust of conquest and by love of ease . . .' "

Now he glanced at Chandler, " '. . . by the strong man's craving for power . . .' "

And at last he looked at Emerson Calhoun and his friends, " '. . . and the poor man's craving for food.' "

Pausing for effect, he dropped his napkin to the table and said, "Now, lady . . . and gentlemen . . . if you all will excuse me, I have business which must be attended to. It's been a pleasure."

The others began to stand, and HR Buxton stepped close to John L. and said, "May I have a word privately with you and Mr. Chandler?"

John L. studied him. "Of course."

To Chandler, HR said, "Will you take a moment to speak with Mr. Lewis and me?"

Chandler looked at John L., then said, "At your pleasure, sir."

HR started out of the dining room with the two of them.

Jordon stood where he was. HR turned to him and said, "Would you come with us, please?"

The little party of four left the others standing in the dining room and made their way down the hall to one of the first rooms.

Inside HR didn't bother to sit or invite the others to do so. "Gentlemen, Mr. Jordon is helping me out in connection with a very delicate situation we have here in Buxton. I'm going to ask him to tell you about it."

Jordon looked at Chandler, then John L. "It's hard to be certain just what's going on, but we think there may be a sniper here who could be planning to assassinate one or both of you."

John L. looked surprised. "On what kind of evidence, sir, do you make such a statement?"

"A lot of little things. As I said, nothing for certain. But we had two men killed by a sniper here a few days ago. We think the same man could be set up for you."

"You know who he is?"

"We're not sure."

"You know where he is?" Chandler said.

"Here in the hotel, if he's the one."

"Why don't you arrest him?" Chandler asked.

"He may be holding a hostage that he would kill if we try to take him."

John L. thought about it for a moment. "Let me see now. You think a sniper may be here in the hotel, but you're not sure. You think he might be holding a hostage, but you're not sure. You think he might be the same man who killed somebody a few days ago, but you're not sure. So the man actually may have done nothing, and may plan to do nothing, as far as you know for sure. Are you sure of anything, Mr. Jordon?"

Jordon took a deep breath and said, "Not much. I know it sounds pretty vague, but I don't think either one of you ought to be out in the streets here until this thing is cleared up."

"Exactly who are you, Mr. Jordon?" John L. asked.

"A gambler, sir. And, I hope, a pretty good one."

"Is that your only area of expertise?"

"I've been a peace officer from time to time. And done a few other things."

"I see," John L. said with a nod. "And you believe it's that risky for us around here today?"

"I do. If something should happen to you, either one of you, who knows where it would stop, how many innocent people would die."

John L. seemed to be considering Jordon's words. Then he shook his head. "I'm sorry, but that won't do for me. Chandler can speak for himself. I personally am not going to huddle back in my hotel room or go slinking around back streets and alleys because of some threat that might or might not exist. If I behaved like that, how could the men I lead have any respect for me?"

"You could be staring assassination in the face," Jordon said.

John L. waved his arm. "I won't be intimidated from doing what I came here to do. I'm going to speak to our people at the depot at nine o'clock. And I'm going to let them see me in the streets of Buxton. They deserve no less, and they will get no less from me."

Jordon looked at Chandler.

"I'll take my chances as well," the lieutenant governor said. "If there is an assassin, and if he tries something, then we'll deal with that when the time comes." He looked at HR Buxton. "I trust you gentlemen will be trying to get to the bottom of this business this morning anyhow, won't you?"

"Of course," HR said.

John L. looked at his watch. "It's a quarter after eight," he said. "Mr. Buxton, if you have some time available before nine, I'd like to spend a few minutes talking with you about what our men would expect in a contract with you. Is that possible?"

"It is. Let's go to my office."

"I have business of my own," Chandler said to no one in

particular. Then, to John L. Lewis, "But I'll be on hand for your speech to the men at nine."

"Would you like to say a word or two to them? Just a greeting?"

"I would. And I would be grateful for the opportunity."

"Let us see how it goes," John L. said.

In the hotel lobby, the others who were at breakfast were waiting in little clusters when the four emerged from the room. Jordon saw Della look at him with an expression he couldn't quite characterize. Was it envy? Or hostility? Hell, maybe it was indifference.

As they began to break up and re-form in groups to leave, Emerson Calhoun approached Jordon. "Is something happening I ought to know about? Remember what you promised me if you found who killed Willis and Turner?"

"All I know for sure is McCain is here at the hotel. I'm going to try to figure some way to keep him from doing anything. But if I were you, I'd make it my business to stick next to John L. Lewis until he gets out of town. You'll be doing more for your cause that way than anything else I can think of."

"He's got men with him."

Jordon shrugged. "Well and good. But he needs all the protection he can get right now."

Emerson gave him a long hard look, then turned to go with John L. and HR Buxton and the others.

Jordon caught up with HR and said in a low voice, "I'll be in the hotel room when you're through."

"How about thinking of something," HR whispered, "to get this goddamn mess under control?"

Jordon said, "You're the brains behind the mighty Buxton empire. Why don't you think of something?"

As they parted, they exchanged dirty looks.

Then, just before he started up the stairs to the room, Jordon glanced back over his shoulder at HR Buxton, who was headed for the door with John L. and his group.

HR was pressing his fist on the center of his chest.

21

JORDON SAT IN ROOM 207 wondering what was going on across the hall in 208. He'd heard no sounds of any kind since he'd been there, either last night or this morning. It was almost as if the room was unoccupied.

He picked up the phone and waited for the hotel desk. "This is Jordon in Mr. Buxton's suite. Would you send somebody up with the key to room two-oh-six." It was next door to McCain's suite, and the window there would let Jordon see the square from the same angle that McCain saw it.

"Yes, sir," the clerk said. "By the way, you have a message here. Shall I deliver it to you?"

"What is it?"

"I really can't say, sir. It's a sealed envelope."

"Who left it?"

"It doesn't say."

"When was it left?"

"There's no indication. But I think it must have been sometime last night. It was here when I came on at six this morning."

"Why didn't I get it sooner?"

"It has 'Deliver to Mr. Jordon in the morning' written on it."

Jordon told the clerk to send the message with the key, right away.

In a couple of minutes he had both.

Jordon tore the envelope open.

Written on a sheet of hotel stationery, in the same neat script that was on the outside, was the following message:

> *Mr. Jordon,*
>
> *If you are reading this, I have failed. I am writing it just before 10 o'clock in the evening, a little while after we talked in my room. I know Moody's holding Mr. Gruber, I have made up my mind, I am going to try to get Mr. Gruber away from Moody. I have a plan. You'll only see this if it does not work. Do whatever you think is best then. And don't worry about your promise to try to protect me. I'm relieving you of that by what I'm doing. Thank you for your kindness to me.*
>
> > *Pearl*

Jordon sat there shaking his head. Well, she didn't make it. But at least, goddamn it, she did something. Which was more than he could say at this point for himself or HR Buxton.

"Damn it all to hell," Jordon said out loud. Now Moody must be holding both Pearl and Pennyrile across the hall. To burst in on him and try to take him by force was almost certain to get them all shot, Jordon felt. He had no doubt McCain would kill all or any of them with no hesitation if he was cornered.

The phone rang and Jordon picked it up. It was Cassie. "Berk," she said, "I'm glad I found you."

"How'd you track me down?"

"It took a little doing. I called Della's. They said she was at the hotel. Nobody knew where you were. I knew there were some big shots in town, so I figured you might be there. I kind of got an idea you were involved in this business when we talked the other day at the courthouse. Anyhow, the hotel clerk told me you had been meeting with HR Buxton."

"Yeah," he said. Somehow, it pleased him to know she'd gone to that much trouble to find him. "Is there something you need?"

"No. I just want to tell you something I found out. I got to thinking after we talked the other day."

"What's that?"

"You said you were going to see Asher Jennings. Well, I don't know if you're aware of this, but he's been buying and taking options on a lot of little coal and timber tracts around the county lately. Looks like he might be trying to put together some of kind of big package deal or something. His options and deeds and land contracts keep coming in here for recording every little bit."

Jordon didn't know quite what to make of it just now, but it seemed to fit into the picture someway. "Thanks, Cass. I appreciate it."

For a few seconds she was quiet. Then she said, "Are you okay?"

"I'm fine. Why do you ask?"

"You seem kind of distant."

"It's not that. I'm just sort of wrapped up in something."

"Anything I can do?"

He sighed. "I guess not. But thanks for asking."

Again she was silent for a moment. "Be careful, Berk. I still haven't had that supper and show you offered me."

"You'll have them, lady. Soon."

They hung up, and he sat there thinking about her. Wondering if what he'd just promised her would turn out to be true. He was making a lot of promises, it seemed. He sure hoped he could keep the one he'd made to Cassie. A nice quiet evening at the picture show with her looked damn good to him right now.

He had no idea how all this was going to end up, but the next hour or two were not something he was looking forward to. He had a bad feeling about it. That damn white mare had stayed after him it seemed like all night long.

He picked up the key to room 206, then walked across the hall and went inside. He put his ear to the wall, but could hear nothing from McCain's room on the other side of the partition.

He looked out the window and saw that the town square was extraordinarily busy. Model A's, Model T's, a scattering of newer model Fords, Chevys, and Plymouths, an occasional Buick or other big car, a few horses and wagons.

It seemed as if every coal miner in the county had turned out. They meandered along the street or chatted in small groups. Many had brought their wives and children along to see the great John L. Lewis in the flesh. The party lines must have been busy last night and this morning, Jordon figured, once it became known for sure that John L. was here.

Jordon pulled up a chair and sat next to the window, trying to figure out what to do now. The people milling around in the square had to be oblivious to what was going on behind the scenes. They were only aware that the UMW leader would be speaking.

Jordon saw Lieutenant Governor Chandler and the man traveling with him come down the steps of the Buxton Building and cross the street to the drugstore, seemingly unconcerned about anything.

The telephone rang and Jordon picked it up.

"Jordon?" It was HR Buxton.

"What is it?" Jordon said.

"The clerk told me he'd sent you the key to this room. What's happening?"

"Looks like McCain's got the girl, Pearl, now too."

"What? How?"

"I got a note from her a little bit ago. She left it for me sometime last night, it seems. Said she was going to try to lure McCain away from the room and try to get Pennyrile out. I guess she didn't make it."

"What a frigging mess!"

"I'd figured that much out by myself."

"Anything else?"

"No. I was just trying to get a look at what Moody McCain can see from here."

"Everything, right?"

"That's it."

"So what's next?"

"I guess we wait and see. You have any better idea?"

"I'm going down to the drugstore and see if I can talk to Chandler and John L. again, get them to stay out of McCain's range of fire."

"How can they do that, unless they get out of Buxton?"

HR sighed. "Jesus, I don't know."

Jordon put the receiver back on the hook and sat looking out the window, wondering when and whether and against whom McCain would strike. And trying to think of some way he could get Pennyrile and Pearl out of captivity so McCain could be taken.

Moody McCain awoke sitting slouched down in his chair, his long legs stretched out before him, his pistol in his lap. Across the room, Pearl lay on the bed, her hands tied behind her back and her ankles tied together, held with strips of cloth torn from a bedsheet. Her mouth was gagged. She did look like one of those South American chickens now, McCain thought, smiling as he looked at her.

Over in the corner, on the floor, Pennyrile was trussed up the same way.

Moody stretched and yawned. "I'm going to take your gags off now," he said. "If you holler out, nobody will hear you anyway, and I'll have to hurt you and gag you again. You both understand?"

They nodded, and McCain removed their gags.

He looked at his watch. It was a few minutes before nine. He'd been unable to sleep until almost daylight, then had finally dozed off and slept for a while. Even though he had insisted that Pearl relieve his sexual pressure after he had found her trying to untie Pennyrile last night, McCain had still been unable to relax. This situation had somehow become a little complicated.

He wasn't exactly sure yet how to resolve it. The man from the bank was due at ten o'clock with Pennyrile's other fifteen thousand dollars. After that, he could leave the hotel with Pearl and Pennyrile. One at a time, he figured. Could walk Pearl to the car, tie her up, come back and do the same with

Pennyrile, then drive out of town, down toward Knoxville and do whatever seemed best at that time. Find the right place and get rid of them both. Even set it up like Pennyrile had shot her and then killed himself. A lover's dispute turned ugly. Or just bury the bodies good and let time take its course. Or maybe something else. Whichever way he decided to go, that part didn't seem too difficult.

He wondered, though, what to do about John L. Lewis. He was sure this had to be the big job Asher Jennings had mentioned. Who else could it be?

McCain figured there had to be a huge fee involved for getting rid of the great John L. The money Asher Jennings had paid McCain was being put up by others, according to Jennings. He was just the go-between. How much might they pay for Lewis?

McCain wondered if he should call Jennings and let him know what the situation here was. The thing could be done with no problem from this window if John L. let himself be seen again anywhere in the town square of Buxton.

McCain picked up the phone and when the operator came on, he said, "Get me Asher Jennings."

Jennings answered after the first ring.

"It's me," McCain said.

Jennings was silent for a few moments. "Why are you calling me?"

"You know the big job you mentioned?"

Silence again. Then, "I don't know who you are or what you are talking about."

It was a moment before McCain understood. The telephone. "It's all right. Everything's under control."

Jennings was silent.

"The big job. I can do it. But I want to know how much."

"I told you I don't know what you are talking about. Whoever you are, you're crazy."

"Don't say that to me, you sonofabitch. I hate that."

"I'm obviously talking to a lunatic. There's been some

mix-up," Jennings said. "I don't know you. Leave me alone." His voice was icy.

"Goddamn you," McCain said through clenched teeth, "I'm in place."

"You are stark raving mad," Jennings said, and hung up.

McCain felt the fury boiling up from his gut. That white-livered sonofabitch. Too chickenshit even to talk in code. Well, fuck him. McCain would wait for the rest of the money from the bank. Then take it and leave. In the meantime, watch the proceedings down in the square. He sat looking out the window, and as he did he imagined what it would be like to get John L. Lewis in the cross hairs and squeeze off a shot. Just to see him wilt.

And maybe, McCain thought, I'll see Jordon down there. Get a chance to drop him. Not for that goddamn queer Jennings, but for me. For my own sweet satisfaction.

McCain took a deep breath and relaxed. Nobody who mattered knew he was here. Just Jennings and the banker. And in an hour, he'd be out of here and on his way. Maybe back to South America. Brazil this time. He'd heard Rio was a good place to go if you had money. And he'd have plenty when he left here.

On the other side of the partition, Jordon sat looking out his window, wondering what McCain was thinking less than ten feet away. When Pennyrile's money was delivered by the banker, would McCain just take it and leave? Would he take Pearl and Pennyrile along? Or turn them loose? Had he been paid and assigned to shoot John L. Lewis or Happy Chandler? Or both? Or maybe somebody else? Me, for instance? As had been the case all the way through, there were plenty of questions. And no answers.

The telephone rang. It was HR Buxton. His voice sounded a little strange to Jordon when he said, "Can you come down here to the drugstore, please? Right away?"

Jordon hesitated a moment to see if any further information was coming. Hearing none, he said, "I'm on my way."

The Buxton Drugstore was packed with people. Jordon pushed his way inside and through the crowd, looking for HR. He found the old man sitting in a booth by himself, his hands folded in front of him, looking ashen.

"Sit down," HR said, and Jordon slid into the booth on the other side.

"What's up?"

HR looked around the room and lowered his voice to a whisper. "I'm not feeling very well."

"What is it?" Jordon asked. "Your gallbladder?"

HR studied him for a moment. "It was never my gallbladder."

Jordon looked at the old man's face and saw the strain on it. "Your heart?" he said softly.

HR nodded. "Nobody knows about it except me and Doc Klein."

"And me."

"And you." HR reached into his pocket and took out the little box he carried his pills in. He slipped one into his mouth surreptitiously.

"Don't you think it would be a good idea if we called Doc and you went someplace to rest?"

"I can't do that now." HR tried to take a deep breath, but seemed unable to do so. "I just wanted to tell you, if something happens that I can't carry on here, you do whatever you think is best. I'm delegating to you whatever authority you need to do what has to be done."

Jordon thought, that kind of authority doesn't amount to much if HR's not around to verify it, but he decided not to bring it up. "I'll do what I can."

As if reading Jordon's thoughts, HR took a pen from his inside coat pocket and said, "You have a piece of paper?"

Jordon produced the little notebook he carried with him all the time.

HR turned to a blank page and wrote, "Berkley Jordon has complete authority to act for me in all security matters until further notice." He signed it. Then, glancing at the big grandfather clock near the front window, he wrote the time and date.

HR handed the notebook back to Jordon, who read his note and nodded.

At that moment, two somber-looking men in dark suits and ties and felt hats approached the booth. "Mr. HR Buxton?" one of them said.

"Yes," HR said. "What is it?"

One of the men reached into his pocket and produced a small leather folder and flipped it open to show a badge. "I'm Special Agent Milburn. This is Special Agent Rutledge. We're with the FBI."

"G-men?" Buxton said.

Milburn gave him a tight little smile. "That's what they're calling us nowadays."

"What do you want?" HR asked.

"We've been looking for a man named Moody McCain for some time. And we have reason to believe he may be here in Stanton County."

HR looked at Jordon, who shook his head slightly.

"What is it you want this man for?" HR asked.

"We're not at liberty to say," Rutledge said.

"Like that, huh?" HR said.

"We can say it's in connection with a felony investigation involving serious violation of federal statutes."

HR laughed. "Oh, well, that makes it all very clear. I'm sorry, gentlemen, I can't help you. I don't know the man."

"We thought maybe you had heard of him or something about him, where he might be. We've received information he's in this area. We'd like to talk to him."

"I told you, I'm sorry." HR's face was white and strained, and he was pushing on the middle of his chest.

The federal agents looked at Jordon, then back at HR. "Do you mind if we look around?"

HR seemed to be thinking about it for a moment, then said, "As a matter of fact I do. This is not the time to have you wandering around asking questions and stirring people up. Call my secretary, make an appointment to see me tomorrow, and we'll talk then." The words were clipped and coming faster, as if he was trying to get it settled with them quickly.

Jordon was glad HR was going to get them out of here. With things as delicate as they were, he didn't want a couple of J. Edgar Hoover's G-men running around with their guns drawn the way the papers and newsreels had reported they'd been doing.

"Are you saying we can't look for him here?" Milburn asked.

"I'm saying this is private property, my property, that you're standing on. This town and everything in it belongs to me. If you don't want to wait until tomorrow to talk to me as I offered to do, then go to London and get yourself a warrant or a court order from Judge Ford in the federal court over there and come back and see me then. I should tell you, though, that it might take you a little longer that way. In the meantime, I'll let my legal staff know you're here."

Jordon figured from the way they looked that they were not accustomed to being treated so, but there was little they could do, it seemed, for as he watched them turn and walk away, they said nothing more.

When Jordon looked back at HR Buxton, he gave a little gasp and collapsed across the table.

Jordon scanned the room full of men and spotted Young Harry Buxton, wearing a seersucker suit with his collar unbuttoned and his tie dangling down. He was standing at the soda fountain, laughing and talking with some of his cronies. "Harry!" Jordon yelled. "Harry!" When Young Harry looked over, Jordon motioned to him.

Harry came swaggering across the room, taking the path that opened up for him. Then he saw his father lying facedown across the table. "Oh, God! What's wrong?"

"He just collapsed," Jordon said. "Stay here with him while I call Doc Klein. And don't let a crowd of people push in here around him."

Young Harry looked stricken himself as he sat down next to his father, picked up his hand, and began to rub it.

Half an hour later, the crowd had moved to the railroad depot to hear John L. speak. A few people were left in the drugstore, those who despised John L. Lewis so much they wouldn't permit themselves to go see him, and a handful of others.

Jordon sat across from Young Harry in the same booth in the drugstore where HR had collapsed. After Doc Klein had come and had some men carry HR Buxton to the doctor's office down the street, Jordon had brought Young Harry to the booth and filled him in on what was going on, including the fact that McCain was holed up in the hotel in a room overlooking the square, and that he was holding Pennyrile and Pearl.

"What I want to know is what you're doing in the middle of all this?" Harry said. "You have no authority around here."

"Your dad asked me to help him," Jordon said. "He thought maybe we could keep a lid on things here, maybe prevent a lot of bloodshed. He gave me the authority to do whatever needs to be done."

"You?" Harry said with a sneer. "Why would he choose you?"

"That's something you can ask him . . . when he's able to talk," Jordon said.

"I don't believe you."

Jordon took out his notebook and turned to the page where HR had written the note a few minutes earlier. He handed it to Young Harry.

Young Harry read it, sat silently for a moment, then laid it on the table in front of Jordon.

"That note means nothing. It isn't witnessed, the powers you say it delegates are far too broad to be taken seriously,

and for all I know, somebody other than my father wrote it,"
Young Harry said.

"Is that the kind of stuff you learned before you flunked
out of law school?"

"Screw you, Jordon. As of right now, I'm taking over. Doc
Klein said he's going to put my father on the next train out
of here and get him in the hospital. I'll run things while he's
gone. Do you really believe anybody in this county would
back you up in this thing against me?"

Jordon remembered HR Buxton's comment from a while
ago: What a frigging mess.

At that moment, Asher Jennings walked in the front door
of the drugstore, went to the soda fountain, and ordered
something to drink. Young Harry saw him and said, "I have
an appointment." Turning to Jordon he said, "Whatever ar-
rangement you claim you had with my father is terminated.
I've sent for Ike Sewell and Sheriff Trumble. We'll handle
whatever needs handling."

Jordon drew a deep breath and expelled it slowly. He shook
his head but said nothing. Young Harry hadn't inherited the
old man's brains, but it appeared that he had got his share
of the Buxton balls. Jordon watched the young man in his
seersucker suit strut across the room to talk with Asher
Jennings.

Jordon looked at his empty coffee cup. He picked it up and
started to stand and go to the counter for a refill when he
saw Cassie come in the door. She walked over to him and
said, "Are you all right?"

"I'm fine," he said. "But you shouldn't be here."

"Why not? I wanted a Coke." She smiled.

"It's kind of touchy around here," he said. "And it could
get worse right quick, I'm afraid."

"I thought something was going on," she said. "Sheriff
Trumble went tearing out of the courthouse a while ago like
a bat out of hell, and I decided I'd come and see what's going
on. I heard John L. Lewis is going to speak."

"He's speaking now, down at the depot."

"Why aren't you there?"

Jordon shook his head and sighed. He decided to tell her the whole thing, which he did, as briefly as he could. "So stay off the street outside, will you?"

She nodded. "How about you? What are you going to do?"

"It looks like there's not much I can do. Young Harry just told me to mind my own business. HR is out of it, maybe even dead by now. McCain is sitting up there holding Pennyrile and Pearl, probably with a gun to their heads. And John L. and Happy Chandler are determined to go on with their show, it seems."

She looked at him for a moment. "It's not just a show, is it?"

"Whatever it is," he said. "I wish to hell it was over."

She glanced around the room. "There's Asher Jennings," she said. "Did you have a chance to think about what I told you? Is he mixed up in this?"

"I've had a funny feeling about him since I first talked with him. With what you told me, I think it could be he's been trying to stir up trouble around here to drive the price of coal and timber property down even further. If things get nasty enough, people who own the stuff will be virtually giving it away. He can pick it up for a song and sing it himself."

She nodded. "I think you could be right. Prices are already low, but more violence could only make property here less desirable."

"Well, if that's what he wants, it looks like he's getting it." Jordon was silent for a moment. "You reckon he could have hired McCain to kill Turner Lott and Willis?"

"He could be a go-between. And a straw buyer. I never thought he had that much money of his own, from what I've heard around the courthouse."

They looked at Asher Jennings and Young Harry as they talked. "Sit here for a few minutes, Cass. I'm going to talk to him."

She took him by the arm. "For God's sake, be careful what you do and say."

"Who, me?"

As the two men saw Jordon approaching, they turned and stepped out onto the street. Jordon, ignoring the snub, followed them.

Outside, Jordon saw Ike Sewell striding up the street toward them.

$$\nabla$$

22

F ROM HIS ROOM IN THE HOTEL, Moody McCain watched what was happening in the square. He kept far enough back from the window that he couldn't be seen from down below.

He had watched the crowd move toward the depot, out of sight down the street. He could barely hear someone speaking there, John L. Lewis he assumed, the oratory punctuated from time to time by the faint sound of applause.

Now he saw Asher Jennings come out of the drugstore, along with a stocky young man dressed in a seersucker suit. As they talked, Jordon came outside and stood near them. And from down the street, Ike Sewell made his way toward them. Very few others were on the street, most apparently having gone to hear the speaking.

The little group seemed to be debating about something. Asher Jennings, the sonofabitch, stood there like he owned the world.

McCain still felt the burning fury that had flared up in him when Jennings had called him crazy. That's what the old man used to say about me, McCain remembered. "Crazy." When he sent me to Baylor to try to get me educated for the ministry, and I ended up in trouble all because of that hot-assed little music student. And when he tried to get me a commission in the Army Signal Corps and I chose instead to become a sniper. "Crazy, boy. You're crazy." And when the old man would come home after conducting the Sunday night service at the church and drink himself senseless, he'd still say to Moody, "Crazy, boy. I don't know why I ever named you after Dwight Moody. You never had in you what it takes to lead a flock." And finally, that night when Moody came home from Wheeling to visit his mother lying on her deathbed, too weak from cancer to move, and found his father on the sofa in the front room of the big rambling house "counseling" the widow Honeywell, his hand up her dress and his mouth all over her.

The widow had run from the house, and Moody had beaten the old man until his face was a bloody, shapeless mass. Moody turned to leave, without even looking in on his mother, and the last thing he heard his father say was the bloody, blubbery word, "Crazy."

Now McCain picked up his Springfield, rested the barrel on the windowsill, found Asher Jennings in the lens of the scope, and set the cross hairs on his face.

In front of the drugstore, Young Harry turned to Ike. "Can you take a couple of men and get some dynamite, then get around to the other side of the hotel and get in without being seen?"

"Easy," Ike said.

"And put a charge in the room underneath where this McCain is supposed to be holed up?"

"How much you want to put?"

"Enough to blow the whole goddamn hotel to kingdom come, for all I care. Just as long you make damn sure it gets McCain."

Jordon said, "Think about what you're doing, Harry. You've got no reason to do this."

Young Harry said, "I don't need any more reason than I've already got. I'm in charge of this situation. And this company and this town. I'm going to blast his ass out of there."

Jordon could see it had come down to a matter of Young Harry exercising his authority. He seemed determined to make an impression on John L. Lewis and Happy Chandler and everybody else in town, show them who he was and what he could do if he wanted to.

Still, Jordon had trouble believing what he'd heard. He tried once more. "You're not just talking about McCain. I

couldn't care less about him. But what about Pearl and Pennyrile? You're not going to blow them up? That's murder."

Harry laughed. "You think I'd ever come to trial for getting
rid of a man who's threatening to assassinate our important
visitors? Weighed against that, the others won't matter. I'm
going to do what I have to do. The commonwealth's attorney
won't even look twice at it."

Asher Jennings spoke up. "For all we know the girl and
Gruber are already dead, if they're even in there. We don't
know that for sure."

"That's right," Harry said. "They're probably already long
gone. Or maybe dead."

Jordon glared at him. "If we're going to speculate, maybe
McCain's dead, too, and you can forget the whole thing."

"I saw him moving up there just a minute ago," Jennings
said. "Harry's doing the right thing. It's exactly what I'd do."

What bad days this community is in for if old man Buxton
does die and this arrogant young bastard takes over for real,
Jordon thought. By comparison, HR was starting to look like
Albert Schweitzer.

"Like you said, you're doing the right—" Asher Jennings
never finished his sentence. His face took the bullet and the
back of his head disintegrated.

A fraction of a second later Jordon heard the crack of the
rifle. He hit the ground, as did Young Harry and Ike. All of
them scrambled for the door of the drugstore and made it
inside, but there was no further shooting.

Inside, as they got to their feet, Cassie came running to
Jordon. "Are you all right?"

"Yeah," he said. "But looks like that's it for Asher Jennings."

"Was it McCain?" she asked.

He nodded. "It had to be."

Young Harry looked at Jordon. "Satisfied?" To Ike he said,
"What are you waiting for?"

"I'm gone," Ike said, and headed out the back door of the
drugstore.

Jordon took a last long look at Young Harry. "Maybe if Ike hurries, you can get rid of me at the same time," he said.

"What's that supposed to mean?" Harry asked.

"I'm going up there," Jordon said.

Harry smiled and shrugged. "You're a free man. It's your ass."

"So it is."

Cassie pulled Jordon to one side. "You can't go up there. McCain will kill you. And if he doesn't, Ike and his dynamite will. What the devil is wrong with Young Harry Buxton?"

"What's wrong with him is as old as human history—or at least the Bible. A beggar on horseback. A third-rate man in a first-rank position. I watched fools like him get men slaughtered by the thousands in the war. They're not only a pain in the ass. At times, they're deadly as a rattlesnake."

"Looks like this is one of those times."

"Oh, yeah. I'd say it is."

She took him by the arm. "Do you have to go up there? Isn't there some other way?"

"I promised Pearl I'd do everything I could to protect her," Jordon said. "I can't just stand here and watch her be blown to smithereens without trying."

Cassie looked at him. "She's nothing to you, is she?"

He looked directly into her eyes. "Just somebody I made a promise to."

Cassie studied him for a moment more, then said, "Go ahead. You've got to be you, I guess, Berk."

He didn't reply.

She took him by the arm. "But you listen to me: I've got to be me, too. And you might as well know this. I'm not staying away from you any longer. I've tried to, but what's a person's life worth if it means being away from the one you love?"

He pulled her to him and hugged her.

"Does that scare you, what I said?" she asked.

"A little," he said with a small grin.

"Well, maybe a man as tough as you can stand it."

"Maybe," he said.

He turned and went out the back door and sprinted off in the direction of the depot. He would cut up the hill, through the little patch of woods there, then circle around behind the hotel and get to the entrance without exposing himself to McCain's fire.

As Jordon approached the depot, he could see a gathering that looked like a couple of hundred or more, mostly miners, but some women and others. A few people noticed him trotting, but most were too intent on what John L. was saying to pay more than a passing glance to Jordon.

John L. was in splendid oratorical form. "The Great Commoner William Jennings Bryan once said, 'You shall not press down upon the brow of labor this crown of thorns, you shall not crucify mankind upon a cross of gold.' Well, my friends and fellow workers, I say today to the coal operators of Eastern Kentucky and the rest of the nation, 'You shall not crucify the men . . . who mine the coal . . . that turns the wheels . . . of this nation's industry . . . upon a cross of *greed!* Cold, heartless, pitiless greed. Untold, unmeasured wealth comes from under these mountains, and the men who dig it out with their bone and sinew and their very lives shall have their fair share of it. As almighty God is my witness, it . . . shall . . . be . . . a . . . fair . . . share!"

The crowd whistled and applauded loudly.

Old man Plato Egan, who had to be in his nineties, had shown up, wearing his tattered blue uniform coat and cap from the Civil War, and waving his sword in the air as he marched round and round in a little circle at the edge of the gathering singing, "We'll hang Jeff Davis to a sour apple tree, a sour apple tree, a sour apple tree. . . ." He did the same thing at every public gathering of any kind and had for as long as folks could remember. Nobody paid any more attention to him than he paid to what John L. was saying.

Jordon trotted on past and headed up the hill and through the little patch of trees toward the hotel. He loved the sound of the great rolling cadences of John L.'s rich, mesmerizing voice, and wished he could have listened to the rest. It was almost like having the King James Bible or a Shakespearean play spring to life and begin to speak.

But Jordon knew time was running out.

The last thing he heard before he was out of earshot was John L. saying, "It was old King Lear who said, 'How sharper than a serpent's tooth it is to have a thankless child.' But, oh, my brothers in the great family of labor, how much sharper it is to work your heart and soul out in the bowels of the earth and have a thankless and greed-consumed employer who sups on pheasant under glass while you do without the meat and curse the bread you cannot find to fill your babies' empty bellies. No more, I say. It shall be thus no more!"

Even from a distance, Jordon heard the crowd's response come as a roar torn from the throat of an angry beast.

When he got to the hotel parking lot, he ran to his car, unlocked the rumble seat, and grabbed the sawed-off shotgun, checking to make sure he had loaded it. He had. Double-aught buckshot.

A large young man with a plain, open face stood in front of the hotel entrance. He wore clean overalls and a blue work shirt. A .44 Smith rested in a holster on the heavy leather belt strapped around his middle.

As Jordon came near, still moving at a trot, the young man held up his hand. "Sorry, mister, but if you're thinking about going in there, think again."

"Son," Jordon said, sucking in great gulps of air, "I'm here on orders from Mr. HR Buxton. I've got things to do inside. I'm going in, with or without resistance from you. I don't have much time."

The young man looked unsure of what to do. He eyed the shotgun. "I've got my orders not to let anybody go in," he said. But he made no move of any kind.

"You call it, son," Jordon said. "But make it quick."

"You know they're on their way up here with dynamite?"

"I do know that. But there are things I've got to do in there before it blows."

The young man studied Jordon for a moment, then stepped aside. "It's your funeral."

"That well may be."

Jordon sprinted inside the hotel, grabbed the extra key to 208 off the board behind the desk, then hurried up the stairs to the second floor. Though the inside of the hotel looked the same, he could feel the emptiness, knowing the people had all been moved out. All except those in 208.

Now that he was here, Jordon was unsure exactly what the best way was to move against McCain. He just knew he had to try. He wasn't going to leave Pearl and Pennyrile to be blown to bits along with McCain, without even trying to get them out. And damn it, he had to admit to himself even now that he was as driven by wanting Moody McCain for himself as by anything else. He didn't want the sonofabitch sent to hell by the likes of Young Harry Buxton and Ike Sewell. Not after Willis. Maybe I'm crazy, he thought, but it's the way I feel. There's only one small problem. I don't have any idea how I'm going to do it.

One thing was certain, though. He didn't have a lot of time to chew it over.

He stood for a minute catching up on his breathing, getting ready for his move. Then he walked softly down the hall to 208 and gently tried the knob. It was locked. He inserted the key, turned it, then twisted the knob. It turned, and he pushed the door open a crack, standing back out of the way in case McCain was watching it and fired a shot through it.

Peering through the cracked door, Jordon could see the suite was arranged very much like the one he'd stayed in last night across the hall. A sitting room and a bedroom off to one side. Maybe another on the other side, too.

Pushing the door open a bit more, he stuck his head inside. No one was in the sitting room. One of the bedroom doors was open, and Jordon could see Pennyrile Gruber sitting in the corner by the bed, his hands tied behind him, and his ankles tied together with rope. Pennyrile had no gag on.

Jordon eased the door the rest of the way open and stepped

inside, holding the shotgun in his right hand, finger on the trigger, hammers cocked. He was watching Pennyrile, but from this position he could not see either Pearl or McCain.

Pennyrile must have heard some sound from Jordon, or sensed the movement, for he turned slightly to look in Jordon's direction. Pennyrile's eyes widened, but he made no sound or other move. Then he cut his eyes to one side and gave a little jerk of his head.

McCain came into Jordon's view in the bedroom at the same time that his pistol exploded and Jordon made a dive for the floor. Jordon landed on his left shoulder and side and felt a shrieking pain slice through his upper body, simultaneous with a sharp crack.

Jordon held on to the sawed-off shotgun and as he fell, he squeezed off one of the rounds, ripping a jagged hole in the wall near the door.

McCain had jumped back out of Jordon's line of vision after he got off his round. "So you finally came, did you?" McCain said. "The mighty Jordon. Well, you've arrived just in time. But unfortunately you can't see the fireworks that will be coming as soon as John L. stops spouting bullshit down at the depot and heads up the street. Too bad you won't be alive to witness some history being made."

Jordon started to reply, but when he breathed, it felt like he'd torn something up pretty bad inside his chest. He realized now that McCain's shot had missed him, but he knew he had broken something, his shoulder probably, and maybe some ribs, when he hit the floor. He was getting too damned old and his bones too brittle for this kind of stuff.

His left arm was getting numb, and it was all but useless. He could barely move his fingers. And anything other than a shallow breath sent a sharp, knifelike pain shooting through his chest.

"Stick your head around the corner of the doorway a little, Jordon. You can see Pearl and Pennyrile. And we can talk."

"We can talk this way," Jordon said. "Tell me, it was you, wasn't it, that killed Willis and Turner Lott?"

"It was no big deal," McCain said. "Lott never knew what hit him. And your buddy Willis, the cripple. I let him watch Lott for a little while, then I shot him. But in the chest, so it would take a few minutes. Then I watched him die there on the porch, bleeding like a stuck hog. You'd have been proud of him, though. The sonofabitch never squealed. At least not loud enough that I could hear it."

Nobody said anything. McCain laughed. "Come on out, Jordon. Let me see you."

Jordon lay there. He swallowed hard, and he felt his eyes filling. "McCain, this whole place is going to blow sky-high in a minute or two. Young Harry Buxton's got men right now setting a dynamite charge in the room below. The fuse may already be lit."

"Good gamble," McCain said. "But it won't work. Buxton would never blow up his own hotel."

Jordon tried to breathe deeply, but started coughing. When he finally stopped, he spit and saw foamy blood. "It's not Buxton that's doing it. The old man just had a heart attack. It's his son running things."

"Bullshit."

Jordon tried again. "Before you shot him, Asher Jennings was egging Young Harry on to blow you up. He was dying to see you get blown to hell. You got any idea why he wanted that?"

McCain hesitated a moment, then said, "You're a fucking liar."

"It's true. Could it be he was the one that's been paying you? He sure wanted you dead. With you out of the way, nobody could ever have tied anything to him. Well, too late for him now. But not for you."

"You're crazy."

"Well, it wasn't Myra Chastayne, I'm sure of that. And it wasn't HR Buxton. He's got other ideas about how things ought to be handled. And, I don't think it's old Pennyrile there. If it was, the two of you would still be doing business. Am I right?"

McCain didn't answer.

"So, it looks to me like it must have been Asher Jennings. I've got a theory or two about why. But one of the things that made him look the most suspicious to me is how bad he wanted you to get blown up. Hell, if it hadn't been for him, Young Harry's men wouldn't be lighting that fuse downstairs."

Again, McCain was silent. Then he muttered, almost to himself, "That low-down, back-stabbing sonofabitch. I'm glad I took care of him."

"Why'd he pay you?" Jordon said. "Did he tell you?"

"He never told me, and I never asked. If he was still alive and you were going to be, you could ask him yourself. Too bad you won't ever find out why. I never cared. Don't you understand? It's none of my business. It's a job to me. I'm a professional." His high, crazed laugh burst out again. "I'll tell you this much, though. Nobody paid me anything for killing your buddy, Willis. I did that for my own personal pleasure."

Jordon squinted his eyes and swallowed. In a moment he said, "It's the truth what I said about the dynamite, Mc-Cain. It could go anytime."

McCain made no response. Jordon figured he must have gone around the bend completely. Nothing he was doing made sense.

McCain spoke again. "Come on, Jordon, look in here. I'll show you something. Maybe you'll want to watch this. Come over here, Pearl."

Pearl's voice was trembling. "I can't, Moody."

"Just crawl over here, girl. I want you to do something for me."

"Don't, Moody."

"Pearl?" His voice was low and menacing. "Come on, Pearl."

Jordon saw Pearl inching her way across the floor, struggling to crawl with her ankles bound together and her hands tied behind her back.

"Come on, Pearl. I'm going to undo your hands and let you do something for me."

Pearl reached him and twisted her body around, but Jordon could now only see part of her legs, from the knees on down. Pennyrile still had said nothing, but he watched and shook his head slightly from side to side.

"Now, Pearl," Moody said, "get up on your knees and unbutton my fly."

"Don't make me do this here, Moody," Pearl said, beginning to sob.

"You like to do it, Pearl. You've told me that a hundred times. No, a thousand."

Pearl said, "Please?"

Jordon got enough breath in his lungs to say, "You've already told us how bad you are, McCain. You can't prove anything by abusing this girl anymore. That just makes you look weak, you slimy sonofabitch. Can't you see that?"

McCain laughed, a high, uncontrolled cackle. "Show yourself, Jordon. Stick your fucking head around the door and say that."

Jordon tried to speak again, but broke into another coughing fit that ended with more foamy blood to be spit out.

"You want some cough medicine?" McCain said. "Come in here and I'll give you some." He laughed. "I'm going to give Pearl some right now." His voice became harsh. "Get on with it, Pearl."

Everything in the suite was quiet, except for Jordon's shallow, rattling breathing. He put the shotgun down long enough to take out his watch and look at it. It had been nearly twenty minutes since he had left Young Harry down at the square. There couldn't be much more time left before the dynamite blew. Only seconds maybe. It could go anytime, he knew.

He heard Pearl gag and cough in the next room. And he could see Pennyrile had squinted his eyes shut and was gritting his teeth.

From out in the street came a wave of applause, and somebody was blowing a bugle. "It must be over," McCain said. "Yeah, here they come. Old John L. and his boys in that long fancy roadster, waving like FDR himself. By God, there's Happy Chandler with him, flashing his big smile and counting up all the votes he's gathering in today from the coal diggers."

Maybe he's watching the street the way it seems, thought Jordon. Or maybe it's bullshit. Maybe he's watching the doorway while he talks, waiting for me to show myself. What are the odds? Fifty-fifty? Probably. What are the odds we'll get out of here alive unless I make some kind of move? With each passing second, they're dropping toward zero.

He breathed as deeply as he could. It was showdown time.

Jordon took the shotgun in his good right hand, sat up as far as he could in spite of the pain, and got his feet planted on the floor, set to lunge.

He counted to three, though he couldn't imagine why, then, using his legs like a catapult, he threw his body toward the doorway and rolled. The searing pain that shot through his body and brain almost made him pass out. But he could see now into the bedroom, see that McCain had, indeed, been watching the parade outside.

Everything seemed to be moving in slow motion now. Pearl, while McCain had been distracted, had produced from somewhere a shiny little derringer pistol that she was aiming at McCain's chest. McCain turned back to her from the window with a look of astonishment. "What's that? A toy?"

McCain was raising his own pistol toward Pearl's head when she dropped her aim to his crotch and pulled the trigger, firing from a distance of less than a foot.

McCain's scream was an awful thing to hear. He twisted his head, and when he did he saw Jordon lying on the floor of the other room. McCain swung his pistol toward Jordon and was aiming it at his chest. Before he could fire, however, Jordon had squeezed off the last round in the sawed-off shotgun.

McCain's head disappeared, most of it flying out the window in little pieces. His last act on earth, the shot he'd meant for Jordon, went wide by at least a foot and a half. It would

not, Jordon thought, have pleased a sharpshooter like Mc-
Cain had he been there to see it.

"No time," Jordon said, struggling to breathe. "Pearl,
untie Pennyrile's hands. Get your feet loose. Let's try to get
out of here . . . before we're all blown to hell."

"There really is dynamite downstairs?" Pennyrile asked,
as Pearl tried to get his hands loose.

Jordon coughed. "My guess is the fuse is already lit."

"Good God a'mighty!" Pennyrile said, working frantically
at the rope on his ankles.

Jordon struggled to his feet and looked out the window.
Down below, Ike Sewell and the men who had helped him
set the dynamite charge were slinking away from the hotel
to take cover behind a row of parked cars. They glanced back
over their shoulders and up at the window.

In the hotel room, the three of them were on their feet,
starting for the door. Then Pennyrile turned back and
grabbed the briefcase filled with his money.

"You still haven't learned you can't take it with you?"
Jordon said.

Pennyrile clutched the bag. "Maybe not, but I aim to take
it as far as I go."

Jordon looked at the '03 Springfield with the telescopic
sight lying on the bed. "I think I'll take this," he said. "I
might want to do some hunting if we make it out of here."

At the door, Jordon glanced back. The last thing he saw
in the room was McCain's headless body sitting in the chair
by the window, his crotch soaked with blood. It was a picture
Jordon knew he would not forget for the rest of his days.

Holding on to one another, the three of them ran, stum-
bling down the hall, down the stairs, across the lobby and
out into the sunlight. They kept running, until they were
beyond the parking lot and under one of the big oaks. Then
they collapsed on the ground. Jordon wheezed and rasped,
trying to get his breath. He wondered if his effort to get out
had been worth it. He felt like he would certainly die. His
breathing was ragged and he had started to cough and spit

blood again. His upper body was a single mass of pain.

He looked at the hotel, sitting silent and empty in the morning sunlight.

"Maybe they didn't light the fuse," Pearl said. "It could have been a bluff."

"Maybe it went out," Pennyrile said. "I've seen 'em do that."

They watched and nothing happened.

Jordon tried a deep breath, but it was cut short by the knife of pain.

At that instant it happened. The entire corner of the Buxton Hotel that faced the square disintegrated into splinters and flew in every direction as the bone-rattling, marrow-jarring explosion reverberated through the town. Every window in the hotel, it seemed, and probably half of those within a thousand yards, had been shattered by the blast.

As the echoes of the explosion faded, the shower of bits and pieces of wood and glass and debris started to rain down on them.

Jordon listened to the ringing in his ears and watched the huge old oaks, their limbs still swaying and quivering from the blast. He saw the sun streaming down through the leaves, dancing in the dappled shade underneath. Maybe, he thought, maybe I will live a while more. I kind of hope I do.

Pearl was the first who spoke. "Wonder if they'll find enough of Moody to bury?"

"I doubt it," Pennyrile said, glancing at the sky. "I didn't see anything that looked like a body floating around up there."

"The question we ought to be asking ourselves," Jordon said, "is not whether they will or won't find a piece of Moody McCain big enough to have a funeral over."

"What is it then?" Pennyrile asked.

Jordon said, "This: Does anybody here really give a damn?"

Pearl and Pennyrile looked at each other. Then they both looked back at Jordon, grinned, and shook their heads.

"WE'RE GOING TO HAVE TO stop somewhere and buy you a shirt a few sizes bigger if it's going to fit over all this tape and cast," Cassie said. "Sometimes, I think you're more trouble than you're worth."

"Not possible," Jordon replied. He grimaced from the pain as he stood and walked over and looked out the window of the hospital in Danville.

"Did you know that Dr. Ephraim McDowell performed the first successful ovariotomy here in 1809?" he said.

"Not in this hospital," she said. "It's not that old."

"No, but in this town. Some say a crowd waited outside his office all night to see if the woman was going to live. If she had died, they were going to string him up."

"You are a fount of fascinating knowledge."

"Just another piece of useless information I picked up somewhere in my undisciplined reading. Are we ready to go?"

She took him by the good arm and steered him out into the hall. At the front desk, the woman said, "Mr. Jordon, a call for you. Long distance."

Jordon looked at Cassie with surprise, then took the receiver. "Jordon."

"I hear they're springing you today." It was HR Buxton.

"I'm on my way out. Where are you?"

"At home. Resting."

"How are you feeling?"

"Not bad. It wasn't quite a heart attack after all. Just a

real bad bout of angina pectoris. The doctors say I have to take it a little easier. How are you?"

"Aside from a cracked collarbone, a couple of broken ribs, and a collapsed lung which is now reinflated, I'm good as new. Or will be in due course, I hope."

"I wanted to catch you in case you might be thinking of going off someplace. I'd like to talk to you."

"Not again. I don't think my health can stand it."

HR laughed. "No, no. Nothing like that. I just wanted you to know that I've been having some talk with the leaders of the union local, Emerson Calhoun and the others. I expect there's going to be a strike before we can get together on a contract. But I hope for their sake as well as mine it won't be a long one. And I think most of them feel the same way. Maybe we can avoid it altogether. We're still talking, anyhow."

"That's good to hear."

"I think after what's happened, there's not going to be any massive violence here in Stanton County. If it does come to a strike, I'll do my damnedest to see that there'll be no gun thugs turned loose on our people."

"Like I said, that's good."

The line was silent for a moment. Then HR said, "Would you consider working for me now?"

"No."

"I didn't think so." HR paused. "Your hospital bill is being sent to me."

"Thanks."

"Well, I'll let you get on with it."

"Yeah."

They hung up.

In the car, as Cassie drove them back toward Stanton County, she said, "So he wanted you to work for him."

Jordon said, "Yeah."

"And you said no again."

"Right."

"Are you satisfied it was Asher Jennings and McCain who were behind Willis's murder?"

"It makes sense. The worse things get around here, the cheaper property gets. Jennings and the people behind him needed the turmoil. I guess they figured things would settle down and coal would boom again in a few years. And they'd reap a fortune."

"You're satisfied, then?"

"Who's ever satisfied? To get to the bottom of everything, I reckon a person would have to go all the way back to Adam and Eve and Satan and the Fall. But it's as much as I can do. I feel better about it."

She didn't pursue it, and after a while Jordon shook his head and grunted. "Old HR Buxton's like a damned hummingbird."

"How so?"

"You ever watch a hummingbird, darting around from one bloom to another, like in a bunch of hollyhocks? He flies up, down, forwards, backwards, sideways. You name it. He moves in whichever direction that suits him, without warning. Just goes for what he wants. Totally unpredictable. That's HR Buxton as far as I'm concerned. Personally, I'd much prefer to rely on a deck of cards."

"Even though his lust for power and money are a lot stronger than most folks', I thought maybe you'd started to think he had some kind of integrity."

"Maybe he does, but I could never be at ease around him. We come at life from two different directions, that's all."

They rode for a while more without talking.

"So it's back to Della's for you?" Cassie said.

He shook his head. "I'm figuring on moving my game down to Black Cory's place at Stateline. I think I might like it better there."

Cassie reached into her purse, which lay on the seat between them. "I almost forgot. Pennyrile came by the courthouse to see me. Somebody told him you and I are friends. He gave me this to give to you." She handed him a fat brown envelope, sealed and unmarked.

"What is it?"

"He didn't say. Just wanted to make certain you got it."
Jordon tore it open. It was full of money. A letter was
inside. Jordon unfolded it and read out loud.

> *Jordon. There's $5,000 here. A token of my appre-*
> *ciation for saving my life and Pearl's. I know you*
> *didn't do it for money. But all the same, I want you*
> *to have this. If you don't want it for yourself, I'm sure*
> *you know someone who can use it. Pearl and me are*
> *on our way to New Orleans for a vacation. My*
> *maiden voyage with the young lady, so to speak. Pearl*
> *sends her regards. We hope to see you when we*
> *return.*
>
> *Respectfully,*
> *Pennyrile Gruber*

Cassie smiled. "He'll never be the same after two weeks
in New Orleans with Pearl."

"Sounds like a pregnant idea to me," Jordon said.

"What? A trip to New Orleans with Pearl?"

"A trip, darlin'. Somewhere away from the mountains for
a little change of scenery."

She didn't say anything.

"With you," he said. "Would you like to go someplace?"
He tapped the envelope on his knee. "I thought I might give
four thousand dollars of this to Willis's wife. And maybe we
could take the rest and put it to good use while I recuperate."

She drove on without saying anything. Then, as they came
around a little curve, at the side of the road lay a fat king
snake about three feet long, deep in the throes of digesting
something. It had begun to ease its way onto the pavement,
then apparently found the effort too much.

"Stop the car for a minute," Jordon said.

She put on the brakes. Jordon got out, found a forked stick
beside the road, and lifted the snake into the air, then took
it to the other side of the road and dropped it down the bank.

Back in the car, he said, "Well, dog days are finally over.

Maybe the snakes can get back to seeing where they're crawling again."

"I drove by the millpond yesterday," she said. "Saw a bunch of kids in swimming."

After a while, he said, "So what about the trip?"

"I'd like that," she said. "Very much."

"Where would you like to go? How about New Orleans? Maybe we'll run into Pennyrile and Pearl."

After a moment she said, "I think I'd like to go someplace a little cooler."

"Like where?"

"What would you say about Niagara Falls?"

He thought about it and grinned. "Is there a message of some kind there for me?"

She smiled back at him. "Only if you're looking for one."

"Can you get away for a couple of weeks?" he said.

She slowed down and pulled the car to the side of the road.

"Why are we stopping again?" he asked.

"What was it you asked me just now?"

"Can you get away for a couple of weeks?"

She leaned over and wrapped her arms around him, taking care not to squeeze him too hard. She kissed him on the ear, then whispered, "Can a hummingbird fly sideways?"